WELCOME TO THE SHOW

17 HORROR STORIES ONE LEGENDARY VENUE

Compiled by Matt Hayward
Edited by Doug Murano

Let the world know: #IGotMyCLPBook!

Crystal Lake Publishing
www.CrystalLakePub.com

ISBN: 978-1-64370-471-5

Cover Art:
Ben Baldwin—www.benbaldwin.co.uk

Layout:
Lori Michelle—www.theauthorsalley.com

Proofread by:
Paula Limbaugh
Amanda Shore

WELCOME TO ANOTHER CRYSTAL LAKE PUBLISHING CREATION.

Thank you for supporting independent publishing and small presses. You rock, and hopefully you'll quickly realize why we've become one of the world's leading publishers of Dark and Speculative Fiction. We have some of the world's best fans for a reason, and hopefully we'll be able to add you to that list really soon. Be sure to sign up for our newsletter to receive two free eBooks, as well as info on new releases, special offers, and so much more.

Welcome to Crystal Lake Publishing—Tales from the Darkest Depths.

OTHER ANTHOLOGIES BY CRYSTAL LAKE PUBLISHING

C.H.U.D. Lives!—A Tribute Anthology

Tales from The Lake Vol.4: The Horror Anthology, edited by Ben Eads

Behold! Oddities, Curiosities and Undefinable Wonders, edited by Doug Murano

Twice Upon an Apocalypse: Lovecraftian Fairy Tales, edited by Rachel Kenley and Scott T. Goudsward

Tales from The Lake Vol.3, edited by Monique Snyman

Gutted: Beautiful Horror Stories, edited by Doug Murano and D. Alexander Ward

Tales from The Lake Vol.2, edited by Joe Mynhardt, Emma Audsley, and RJ Cavender

Children of the Grave

The Outsiders

Tales from The Lake Vol.1, edited by Joe Mynhardt

Fear the Reaper, edited by Joe Mynhardt

For the Night is Dark, edited by Ross Warren

Or check out other Crystal Lake Publishing books for more Tales from the Darkest Depths.

Readers will inherit the world.

TABLE OF CONTENTS

WHAT SORT OF RUBE

Alan M. Clark

I STEPPED OUT of the side entrance of The Shantyman into the alley on my way to find something to eat. The bright daylight dazzled me and I couldn't see right off. I heard a voice coming from the shadows, and took a fright—I knew enough about the dangers of San Francisco's Tenderloin to be on guard.

"A bit of kindness, sir?"

Seeing a beggar, perhaps forty years old, holding up a bent tin cup, I relaxed.

"Didn't mean to frighten, sir."

He sat in the shade in a wooden contraption, a low-slung sort of a cart with four metal-rimmed wheels. His lower legs were missing. Looking at him, my first thought, *Is he deserving?* was a disappointment to me. In a city with so many beggars, I had an inclination to turn away from them. Young and always in a hurry, I didn't want to listen to their pleas.

Of course he's deserving, I told myself, *he's a human being*.

Possibly, he saw the change in my manner as I approached across the alley.

"No need for pity sir," he said. "Been 'round the

world on sailing ships, I have, taken large pleasures in life. Now I take smaller ones, simple as that. Though I must depend on others' kindness, I get by as I can, and work hard at it."

He sounded English. His clothing, although threadbare, appeared clean, telling me that he still had his pride. His red-rimmed eyes had a determination about them.

A banjo player, I'd just that week joined the band that supported the Saturday and Sunday matinee performances at the music hall. Mostly, I worked in the city as a rough carpenter. Lots of work there. I also had a dream of becoming a journalist. Raised in humble circumstances in San Francisco during the gold rush, I'd seen a lot of suffering and lives destroyed in the boom years—the stuff of human drama. Despite my initial reaction to the beggar, I liked to think I cultivated a tolerable patch of compassion for the common man. Unwed and with no one to support but myself, I had some coin. I fished in my pocket, pulled out two bits and dropped it in his cup.

"Generous, sir," he said. "Thank you."

"Any man—" I began, intending to say something like, "—in your condition, deserves sympathy."

He cut me off, and I was glad, as I would have regretted the words. "You think me sad?" he said with a huff. "I could tell you a story about a man who lost everything on an island in the South Pacific, one that'll bring a tear to your eye and make your small hairs toe the line, standing at attention."

He'd caught my interest. *Perhaps he has a gift for that*, I thought, *and that's how he gets by*.

Inspired by a friend who sold stories to the

magazines that bought fiction, I kept a lookout for good tales to write. "If I bought you a meal," I said, "would you tell me the story?" I pointed past the entrance of the alley to Slim's Tavern across O'Farrell Street. A fellow band member had suggested it as a good place to get something to eat.

The beggar gave me a gap-toothed smile. "I don't mind if I do." He shoved off from the building. Pushing on the wooden spokes of his barrow's wheels with his hands, he moved quickly to cross O'Farrell Street during a short break in the traffic. Hurrying to keep up, I was nearly clipped by a carriage that rushed by.

"I'm Beverly Culbert," I said as I caught up.

"Unusual name," he said. "The other boys must've given you hell for it."

"As a matter of fact, they did."

"My own brought me no end of trouble," he said, easily negotiating a path around the horse apples in the road. "Guthrie."

In the tavern, a tall, thin fellow called out from behind the bar, "Mr. Leechgreen, good to see you."

"Slim," Guthrie said in greeting.

The proprietor, I presumed. Apparently my new friend was well-regarded in the establishment.

He turned to me again. "That's right, Guthrie Leechgreen. Ha! How's that for a name?"

I chuckled with him as he led us toward the rear of the dining room. A few of the patrons sitting at tables paused in their eating, drinking, and talking to stare at Guthrie. The noise in the place, loud at first, became quieter by the time we found a booth where we might have some privacy. Guthrie parked his barrow alongside the booth, and easily climbed up onto one of the two worn wooden benches. I sat across the table on the other.

A barmaid approached. My new friend ordered the ham and potato soup, and a glass of ale. I had the same.

"You give me a good enough story," I said to Guthrie, "I'll write it up and sell it to a magazine." The way he looked at me, I felt a bit foolish saying that, and hastily added, "If I earn anything, I'll give you a piece of it."

"I'll give you the unvarnished truth, Beverly," he said. "What you do with it is up to you."

Somehow, I'd gotten keyed up, my mind moving too fast, and my mouth running to catch up. Thinking that the magazines wanted certain types of stories, I said, "This tale of yours, I guess from what you've said that it has tragedy."

"In part, it's about how I lost my legs," he said.

"So, this is your story, Guthrie?"

"I said I'd tell you a tale about a man who lost everything. I haven't lost everything."

"Does it also have romance?" I asked hopefully.

Again, his gaze unsettled me. "This isn't some dime novel, Beverly. What I'll tell happened, in some ways is still happening."

Though his expression left me uneasy, that fed my eagerness to hear his tale.

The barmaid brought our food and drink. We ate in silence for a time. Overeager to hear his story, I worked to polish off my meal quickly with the hope that Guthrie would do the same. I became so intent on doing so, I didn't notice that he'd finished before me and set down his spoon.

"Me and Matthew Hedgeweird were shipmates ten years ago," he said. "Matt I called him. The man could sing—a shantyman, he were."

"He sang the songs that help labor onboard ships?" I asked.

Guthrie nodded. "Matt were particularly clever—funny and bawdy—with the call and response. In one of his, he'd call out, 'How many tits on bow-legged Jenny?' And the answer would come, 'Enough, enough for everyone.' Then, 'How did her legs get so bent, boys?' And the answer, 'a-riding, a-riding everyone.'"

I smiled, and he grinned. I'd begun to feel more at ease.

"Crews worked harder when he led the labor." Guthrie said. "But it weren't just his cleverness. His voice drew you in like no other. Beautiful! He were good with ballads too, could pull the tears from your eyes, make your heart sing like a bird in its cage.

"'I was my Gypsy grandmother's favorite,' Matt told me. 'Nana, she thought herself a sorceress, gave me a blessing, a charm for my voice. She told me it would give me a leg up in life. Not sure I ever believed. I had a *talent*. That's all. It's held me back, though. I've gained a reputation for my singing, and ship's masters want me for nothing but shantyman.'"

"Was he bitter about it?" I asked.

"Nah, not Matt," Guthrie said, "a happy, big-hearted fellow. He were my *pal*, even if he were an Irishman. I don't mind telling you I loved him like a brother.

"We'd both signed for a voyage with a company in Liverpool a year earlier and had become acquainted while on the sea. Our ship, The Moth Pearl, lost some of her rudder off the California coast and landed in San Francisco for repair. British companies sign sailors for the voyage, and pay only one month's wages until the ship reaches home port. We were beached here for a week and more with little funds."

"San Francisco is no place to be without money," I said, immediately regretting stating the obvious.

"Even if you have all your limbs," Guthrie said. "I had mine then. Young men who had been at sea for months, we wanted good food, liquor, and women, so I suggest to Matt that we set up on the street as buskers to make some money; Matt will sing, ballads mostly, and I'll take up a collection from the audience. We set up in Union Square, draw quite a crowd. Before approaching us, the copper what has the square as part of his beat waits 'til we've earned enough to pay him to look the other way. We have it to spare, though—indeed, enough to stay at a hotel, rather than a flophouse.

"Second day at the square, I say to Matt, 'I'm beginning to believe in your grandmother's blessing.'

"He scoffs, but has a mischievous smile that tells me he's always known the truth—his voice *is* charmed through sorcery. We eat and drink, yet find no clean women that'll have us. At night, we rest on a feather bed.

"Last day in San Francisco, a young woman—beautiful, dark Polynesian eyes, pale white skin, glossy, jet hair, done up with fine pins—appears in the crowd what gathers in the square. She has a sweet girlish smile to offset those mysterious eyes. Matt sees her, and something changes in his voice. He were singing 'The Cruel Sea Between Us.' Do you know it?"

"Yes, the one about a shipwrecked man separated from his lover," I said.

"Can't help but sing that with feeling," Guthrie said, "and Matt were doing its author proud. When he sees the young woman, his voice becomes better still. He gives each verse such a longing that tears spring to the eyes of men and women alike, there in Union Square."

From his description and the far-off look in Guthrie's eyes as he'd described the young woman, I knew that he'd been as smitten with her as his pal had been.

"For all I can see of Matt's feelings for her," Guthrie said, "her rapturous gaze as she looks upon him tells of even greater fascination and yearning. I'd never believed in love at first sight until that moment, certainly not something so sudden and certain.

"I see her moving toward Matt at the end of the song. Finished taking the collection, I approach him. I know he wants to talk to her, and I want to remind him that we have precious little time before our ship weighs anchor that evening."

More than that, I thought, *Guthrie feared losing his pal.*

"'Kalina Bryte,' she says in introduction, a bit breathless. She beams for him, and he basks in the glow of her beauty. 'You have a most extraordinary voice,' she says. 'My father, Stewart Bryte, owns The Great Western Music Hall. If you were to sing for him, I'm certain he'd give you a chance to win an audience on the stage. Would you come to the music hall tomorrow? I will be there to introduce you.'"

"Wasn't that the music hall that burned to the ground where the Shantyman now stands?" I asked.

"Yes," Guthrie says.

With a pained expression, he lowered his head and an almost palpable sadness rose from him to stand between us. For a moment, I feared that his tale would end suddenly and he'd excuse himself. Seemingly, with an effort, he shrugged it off and continued.

"Matt cannot gather himself to speak to Kalina. Though he's smiling, he has a fevered look.

"'Excuse us for a moment,' I say, and take Matt aside. 'You heard the bells for half past four o'clock. We have less than half an hour to get to the ship. You can visit the music hall when we return from Astoria. The ship puts in here for victuals before heading further south."

"'I don't want to go to Astoria,' he says, and he looks surprised to hear the words himself.

"'You would *abscond*, Matt?' I ask. 'The shipping office here would pass on your name. You'd have to sign a different name in the future, and if caught–'

"'Rarely is anyone caught' he says. 'The world is large.'

"'Think, man,' I say, gripping his shoulders. 'You don't even know this woman.'

"A change comes over him. The fevered look in his eyes vanishes. 'A few short weeks,' I say, 'and I will see you to the music hall myself.'

"He nods his approval, and we approach Miss Bryte. Matt still cannot speak to her. His face beams for her, as hers does for him. I explain to Miss Bryte that we are headed for Astoria and will return in a few weeks.

"She has a look of deep disappointment. Seeing a pain on Matt's face, I know he cannot bear her distress.

I take his arm in a grip meant to be painful. He looks at me, nods again, and I release him.

"'Come in any Saturday,' Kalina says, 'and I will be there to introduce you to my father.'

Guthrie paused to down the last of his ale.

I motioned for the barmaid to bring us more.

"Thank you, sir," Guthrie said. He quaffed half the new glass before continuing.

"Matt, he speaks of nothing but Kalina all the way to and from Astoria. If anything, his feelings for her deepen. Matt aches to return to San Francisco to be with a woman he's never even spoken to. He's worthless as a deck hand. His singing suffers as his heart isn't in it."

Listening to Guthrie, I got the idea he'd told the tale many times. Something about the delivery of his words was too smooth, too few "uhs" and "ers," those pauses we all make to give us a chance to think about what we're saying next and how to say it. I didn't know what to make of that. Was it all a lie, a yarn he'd spun to get a free meal from time to time?

Whatever the case, he had me hooked.

"We arrive back in the city on a Thursday," Guthrie said. "'I won't wait until Saturday to see her,' Matt says to me. I try to reason with him, to say that showing up unannounced, he risks the displeasure of her father. Matt won't have it, so we head over—" Guthrie gestured toward The Shantyman. "—to what was then The Great Western Music Hall. We enter the place and approach the barkeep in the tavern adjoining the theatre. You know the sort of place—it's noisy, stinks of drink, tobacco, and hard-working people, and has all manner of men and women, some of them bloody rough, a few dangerous.

"'I'm here to see Kalina Bryte,' Matt says to the barkeep, 'upon her invitation.'

"I can't believe my ears. Lovesick, he has no sense of propriety.

"The barkeep looks Matt and me up and down, then turns to the other fellow tending the bar and says, 'I'll be right back.' He passes through a door. Some minutes pass. All the while, Matt smiles, but I get this uneasy feeling. The barkeep appears on a balcony above the taps and knocks on a door. A nattily-dressed dark-haired fellow with a mean goatee answers the door, looks down at us when the barkeep points in our direction.

"I figure the man is Mr. Stewart Bryte, Kalina's father and owner of the establishment.

"I don't like the way he looks at us. Matt, he seems happy with what's happening. He beams, and elbows me lightly in the ribs.

"Mr. Bryte says something to the barkeep, who nods and walks away. He reappears behind the bar and says, 'Miss Kalina isn't here. Mr. Bryte says he's been expecting you. If you'll go through the alley to the rear of the building and knock on the door there, someone will take you to Mr. Bryte so you can sing for him.'

"Again, Matt pokes me and beams, and I figure my fears are ill-founded. We thank the fellow, walk around to the back of the building, and knock on the door.

"I don't remember much after that, don't truly remember knocking on the door, just assume we did."

Guthrie's face reddened. "Shanghaied," he said as if embarrassed to admit it. Slim, behind the bar, took notice of Guthrie's distress, but did nothing, as if he'd seen it before.

How many times had Guthrie sat at that table and told the tale, I asked myself.

"Clubbed over the head," he said. "We wake up far out to sea."

Considering what it said about Guthrie, I could understand. No man likes to admit he's gullible. I sat up straight, more intent on his words as the story had gotten a lot more exciting.

"We're in the hold of a ship, manacled to braces," Guthrie said. "Matt wakes before I do. He's fit to be tied, out of his head from a blow that left a big purple bruise on the right side of his skull. The color has spread across half his forehead and darkened the ear on that side. He's ranting about Kalina's betrayal, even in the midst of wailing about wanting to get back to her. It's madness.

"My head aches, and I figure I've got a similar bruise. I'm not acting like he is, though.

"I don't know what will become of us. All seamen have heard the harrowing tales of those who survive such slavery. Some that are shanghaied never return; others are lost for years before escaping and finding their way home. The master of the Moth Pearl will think we've absconded.

"Someone comes for us. He's a big fellow, Maori maybe, got big jagged tattoos on his face and arms. We're taken before what must be the ship's master and he looks us over. I think he's a Dutchman. I can't understand his language. I do understand his gestures.

"He wants Matt thrown overboard. I beg and plead, but the Dutchman won't hear me. When the Maori fellow speaks, though, he listens. Matt is taken below, and I'm put to work with the other deck hands, all the while, the threat of punishment pushing me to work hard. I'm set to various maintenance tasks, making repairs, and manning the bilge pump. That's near a full-time job. I've never seen such a leaky vessel.

"Looks like an old bilander. That makes sense with a Dutch Ship's Master. Two masts: the main rigged lateen, the foremast square-rigged. Not made for the open Pacific. I can't figure how it got so far. The condition it's in says something for the difficulties."

Guthrie had lost me with the seaman's jargon, yet I tried to hold my questions until the end. He must have seen I didn't understand, because he frowned and bit his lower lip for a moment.

"Matt," Guthrie said, "he's brought back on deck a day later and put to work. He's still not right. The Master has him whipped twice before realizing it doesn't improve Matt's performance. He's set to splicing, and when he can't manage that, he's put to work with a holystone."

I shook my head slowly so Guthrie would know I didn't follow him. Again, he frowned. "Landsman," he muttered with an air of disappointment.

"Seven men on that wretched vessel," he said, "the Master, the Maori fellow, three other white crewmen and us. We're the only slaves. They feed and shackle us at night when we sleep. No one will talk to us. Perhaps they have no English. They speak to the Master in his language. I still think it's Dutch.

"I'm worried about Matt. He doesn't get any better. At least he doesn't get worse.

"'I hate Kalina for what she did to us,' he tells me."

"'What did she do?' I ask.

"'She's a crimp,' he says.

I'm surprised. "Matt thought she crimped for her father?"

"Yes," Guthrie said, "but I don't think Mr. Bryte was even in the shanghai business, just used it to rid himself and his daughter of Matt and me. I didn't believe the sweet girl had anything to do with what happened to us. I had seen how she looked at Matt. Would that she'd looked at me that way. Her father was expecting us to come to the music hall. I think she told him of the young man with the golden voice, and, in doing so, allowed her feelings for Matt, those I saw all too clearly, to show. I've seen the look Mr. Bryte had when he saw us at the bar. Scorn for Matt's countrymen is widespread. I think he feared losing his daughter to an Irishman.

"'No,' I tell Matt, 'Kalina had nothing to do with it.' I think that he will not see, though possibly he cannot see.

"Weeks go by aboard the bilander. At night, the stars tell me we're headed southwest, maybe to Australia or New Zealand.

"My fearing what a storm will do to that wretched little ship must have brought one down on us. The storm comes up dark and brooding. We're lashed with wind and stinging rain. Quickly, we're in fifty-foot seas. Time loses meaning. We ride on our arses as one wave after another washes the deck. Rigging comes loose. Spars and blocks swing dangerously.

"The world cracks open with thunder, not from the sky, but beneath us—we've struck a reef. The ship flies apart in two pieces. Matt and me, the Maori fellow and one of the white crewmen, are in the bow. I see the captain and at least one other going down with the stern.

"The bow is turning, pitching over as the stern drags on us. Cables snap, whip through the air, and then we're free from the stern. It's gone down. We all scramble, helping one another to stay atop the bow as it turns. It does not go down. I can feel it banging against the reef below. We all five cling to the bowsprit, none willing to let another go down. The Maori fellow catches me twice and keeps me from falling. Matt, holding on with both arms and legs, is calm through it all, his look untroubled. He helps the white crewman maintain his grip. As the sky brightens and the storm abates, we see land not ten chains away."

"Chains?" I asked. "Oh, yes, about twenty yards each, right?"

"Twenty-two. We can swim it, and do so, when the sea has calmed.

"*They* are waiting for us."

"They?" I asked.

"Islanders," Guthrie said. "I don't know. They might have been shipwrecked there too. They look something like our Maori friend. He doesn't speak their language—none of us do. They're small—a head shorter than me—and near naked. One wears an ancient tricorn hat and leggings made from the scraps of a sailor's trousers. He has a musket what's at least fifty years old. It's nearly as long as he is tall. The firing mechanism is frozen with rust. I'm certain it won't fire. One of them has a rusted whaler's harpoon. Others among them have bone-tipped spears.

"The Maori fellow is afraid. He breaks away and runs. The harpoon finds his back and he falls.

"The islanders raise their weapons and shout at us. We cower on the beach as the one in the tricorn pulls a knife, approaches the Maori fellow, and cut his throat. He smells the knife, then smiles for his brethren.

"Cannibals!" I said. "You lost your legs to cannibals?"

"Look at your eyes," Guthrie said, "about to pop out of your face. Don't get ahead of me, young man."

I was already trying to think of how to write it all down in a manner that would be palatable to those who read magazine stories, soft men and women who had seen little of the world. I should include myself among them. Although I still had some doubt about the veracity of Guthrie's tale, I'd become certain he was indeed a man who had seen something of the wide world.

"Of course," he said, "we do as they command. They take us off the golden sand into the buggy green scrub. The other white fellow and me, we're glancing at each other, each of us hoping the other has an idea how to get away. Neither of us has a notion. Couldn't share them if we did since we don't speak the same language.

"Matt, he's not truly with us." Guthrie points a finger at his head and throws up his hands.

"We come to a place of tall cane and stunted trees. There's a pit, maybe fifteen feet deep, like an old stone well, half filled in with small shards of bone. They shove us in, post guards and leave us there for days. They lower a skin with water in it from time to time.

"Matt has a fever. He rants in his sleep and so we don't sleep well. The other fellow with us—we learn that Joop is his name—he tries to suffocate Matt while I'm asleep. I wake up and pound sense into him.

"Finally a woman—she looks like one of the islanders—comes to bring food, some sort of tasteless root mush. Upon seeing her, Matt goes wild.

"'Cruel, wicked!' he cries. 'Why, Kalina? I loved you, and you sent me to my death.'

"Ah," I said, "in his fevered state, he thought she was Kalina."

"Not nearly so pretty," Guthrie said, "but, yes, the woman has some of the Polynesian look about her that Kalina had. She's frightened away by Matt's shouting.

"Once she's gone, Matt begins to talk, and speaks more than he has for many days. 'Kalina used my Nana's charm to lure me here,' he says. 'Now, I'll use it to make her pay,' He explains that when his grandmother died, he felt the magic of her blessing become his own. 'She said that would happen,' he says. 'I've decided what to do with it. I turned it over in my heart. What was love for Kalina is now hatred. What was blessing will be curse and live long after me.'

"I pay little heed to his words."

Guthrie paused as if to gather his resolve. His features hardened, his lips formed a grim line, and I could tell that what would come next would be painful memories.

"Something is in the root mush the woman gave us," he said. "Though tasteless, so hungry were we, we'd eaten it all.

"I know nothing until the next day. I awaken to Joop's wails of pain. His arms are missing. The shoulders have been seared with fire to stop bleeding, the stumps angry-looking and blackened. The man is pure misery.

"After that I don't want to eat anything the woman

brings for fear that I'll be next. She hides from Matt, but I see her toss our food into the pit wrapped in broad leaves. As hungry as Matt is, I cannot stop him from eating, and he sleeps. Joop is too wretched to partake. I pretend to eat as the woman watches me, then I lie down and close my eyes."

"Joop, he screams and shouts when the islanders come for me. Matt doesn't awaken. I watch through the smallest slit in my eyelids. They drop a notched pole, sort of a crude ladder, into the pit. One of them climbs down and pokes me a few times. I remain limp so he'll become confident that I'm asleep. He ties some kind of cord around me, and his fellows up top haul me out of the pit. Luck is with me as the rope isn't too tight. They're wresting me up over the edge, and I get free, start running.

"Ha—the look in their eyes as I take flight! They don't have any weapons ready and their legs are shorter than mine, so I get away, head into the brush and lose sight of them. I wander for most of a day. The pit had been cool, but in the open with no water, the sun is merciless.

"I approach the water's edge as I consider swimming to the next bit of land—looks to be a mile or two away. If there's a strong current between the islands, I could be swept out to sea. I'm at war with myself, not wanting to die in the open ocean, not wanting to leave Matt behind, not wanting to be eaten."

Guthrie went pale. I tried to imagine being faced with such choices. He allowed some silence between us.

Slim, behind the bar, had been glancing over at us

from time to time with a look of concern. Somehow, I knew it wasn't because we were taking up space that arriving patrons might use. He and Guthrie had a rapport that wasn't clear to me.

"I'm easy to spot," Guthrie said, "standing there on the beach. I see them running toward me, five of them, the fellow in the tricorn following at a slight distance.

"I have to decide. I'd rather a watery grave than to be eaten, but on land, I'll still have a chance to help my pal. I run away along the beach. It's flat and firm. I can outrun them. The beach turns left ahead, just around a stony prominence. Beyond, I find myself in a small lagoon, walled in by high slabs of rock. With its palm trees growing from the short cliffs, and a small cascade of water emptying into the lagoon, it would be a beautiful place to relax if that were possible.

"There's no way out. I'm boxed in, and they'll be upon me within moments. As I make my way to the little waterfall, I think to myself, *At least I can get a cool drink before they catch me*. I'm strangely calm, so that when they arrive in the lagoon, I stand and gaze at them evenly. They don't make threatening moves as they approach. Oddly, they seem most interested in my legs. One looks me in the eyes and smiles, making movements with his right hand so it appears to be a little figure running. I understand that he is delighted with my speed. They all are, laughing and gesturing toward me and especially my legs.

"They circle me, and my gut clenches. I have a moment of panic that propels me between two of them in an effort to escape. They take me to the ground. The one in the tricorn hat has caught up. He lifts his musket and brings the butt of it down on my head."

During the ensuing pause, Slim brought us each another glass of ale. "On the house," he said to me. With the sympathetic look he gave Guthrie, I became certain they'd been friends for a long while.

Guthrie began again. "I wake up in the pit. As my mind swims back up to wakefulness, I can tell from the growing pain that I don't want to be there. I know my legs are gone, but I can't see them at first. Matt is near naked. He's wrapped his clothing around my stumps like bandages.

"Matt, bless him, tries to sing me lullabies, I suppose to help me sleep. What else can he do for me?

"Thankfully, I am *not* fully awake. That's how it feels. The pain is almost the entire world. Even so, I know the wounds should feel worse.

"I am aware enough to consider the islander's fascination with my legs. I'd heard that cannibals liked to take in what is most powerful in others. I'd shown them the strength of my legs, and they'd taken them as food. I remember that Joop's arms had been strong ones, heavily muscled. In the midst of this realization, I see the woman who brings us food looking down from the lip of the pit. She watches and listens to Matt sing to me. Like so many others I've seen over time, her open, wide-eyed expression tells me that she finds his voice spellbinding.

"'Shut your mouth, Matt,' I say. He ignores me. I grab and try to shake him. I have no power in my frame. 'They will eat your voice,' I try to shout, pointing up at the woman on the lip of the pit.

"She's gone. And Matt, he stops singing long enough to say, 'When I die, Mr. Bryte, and all he has will suffer, his beautiful daughter, and the generations that follow. Though the music hall will brighten the days of audiences, only darkness will grow in the hearts of those who desire to perform there.'

"The islanders are crouched at the lip of the pit as Matt begins singing again. I cannot hold myself awake. Shamefully, I fall back, and allow his song to lull me to sleep."

Guthrie is silent for a long while, his head bowed, eyes downcast.

I want to know what happened next! I cannot bear the wait. I am on the verge of reaching across the table to stir his shoulder several times. Out of respect, I restrain myself.

"They've taken Matt's tongue and returned him to the pit," Guthrie says quietly. "All is lost. We are a pit of misery, all three of us. The others are not here to say, but I believe I can speak for all three of us when I say that we just wanted life to end.

"It does for Matt first, and I am glad for him." A tear spilled down Guthrie's cheek. "At some point I awaken to find that Joop is gone. In my agony, I am envious of the two.

"Then, I'm being lifted out of the pit, and I am ready for the end. I dream that I am taken to the water and placed in a boat loaded with faggots. Like a Viking burial, the boat is set aflame and cast adrift. Instead of the pain of burning flesh, I feel a comforting warmth.

"The bow of the Moth Pearl, fetched up on the reef, had attracted a crew looking for salvage," Guthrie said, "They'd sent men onto the island looking to renew their ship's supply of water. I'd been found and rescued. I would not understand that for at least a month, so destructive was the corruption that took hold in what remained of my legs."

"Finally awake enough to understand something of my situation, I discovered that I was being nursed back to health by the Sisters of Mercy at San Francisco General Hospital—a bittersweet thing to hear the nuns' Irish brogue.

"I had just enough fear of Matt's curse that I wanted to find Kalina and make sure she stayed safe. I learned that The Great Western Music Hall had burned, that Stewart Bryte had perished in the fire, and that Kalina had been maimed. She was, in fact, recovering from severe burns at General Hospital while I was there.

"The moment I see what the fire has done to her, I understand that the curse—Matt's curse—is real."

His story done, Guthrie fixed me with a stern eye. "Beverly, I tell the story to you, young man, because you perform in the band at the Shantyman."

"How do you know that?" I asked. "I did not say."

"Doesn't matter how I know," Guthrie said, shaking his head. "What's important is for you to know that the place *is* cursed, just as Matt said it would be, and that you will suffer if you continue to play there."

"Well," I said, willing to play along, "it's not The Great American Music Hall."

"This is not a jest," he said. "The new music hall was opened by Stewart Bryte's brother, Eldon after he inherited the land. Its name is The Shantyman. Do you think Matt didn't have a hand in that somehow?"

"Mr. Eldon Bryte," I said, "a man with a wealth of timber holdings, gave it the name. Another name for lumberjack is shantyman. And just how would a curse have traveled across the Pacific to reach San Francisco?"

Guthrie huffed. "You know the rules, do you, what governs such things?"

I'd become angry. What, I wondered was he after? "I brought you here to buy you luncheon," I said, "out of the goodness of my heart."

"You still pity me?" Guthrie asked.

"If your story is at all true," I said, "and I have begun to have my doubts—"

Guthrie interrupted. "If you had not invited me, I'd have made the invitation so that I could sit with you, Beverly, and tell the tale. I tell it to all the new performers at the Shantyman. Surely you don't think that begging is best done in an alley."

I held my silence as I thought about that.

"In the last two years," Guthrie said, "The Shantyman has seen its best singer, Dorothy Hendricks commit suicide, its orchestra leader, Charles Lucern die in an opium den, and its top comedian, Lawrence Eddie killed in a hunting accident. And how many more?"

"What sort of rube do you take me for?" I asked. "They say mobsmen were after Mr. Eddie because of his gambling debts. And surely you know that the pressures of finding fame are many, that those who seek notoriety on the stage are often, though brilliant, fragile and must perhaps be a bit mad to begin with."

Slim approached. "Another hard case?" he asked.

Guthrie nodded. "I've done what I could," he said, shrugging.

"Come with me, young man," Slim said.

"You're not gonna—" Guthrie began.

Slim cut him off. "Yes, I am. She said she doesn't mind."

Guthrie hopped into his barrow and followed. Slim led me to the swinging doors I'd assumed led into the kitchen. He opened them, and I saw the kitchen staff going about their work. Against the far wall, a woman stood at a sink washing dishes.

"Darling," Guthrie called out.

She turned around. The burns had withered half her face. The other half had kept its perfection of beauty. "My wife, Kalina," Guthrie said.

I found myself speechless. I don't know why. Her presence did not lend veracity to his tale. Yet I knew that the Bryte family were well-to-do. What was she doing at Slim's washing dishes?

She seemed to anticipate my thoughts. "I will have nothing to do with my family," she said.

And what was Slim's part in it—just a friend?

All three looked at me without a hint of cunning. Even so, I couldn't help thinking they were involved in a conspiracy of some kind. To what end, I hadn't a guess.

I knew that no magazine would want that story. Who would believe it?

I remained angry as I turned to leave the tavern, having the foolish notion that Guthrie had somehow robbed me in that alley. Robbed me of what, though—innocence, a sense that I knew what the world was made of? Couldn't I just return to my soft life?

"Let him go," I heard Slim say behind me. "Like you said, you've done what you could. He'll chew on it."

That, I did.

I quit the Shantyman within the week.

Many years have passed since I heard Guthrie's tale. In that time, those working the music hall have seen a lot of tragedy. I don't go near The Shantyman. I've often wondered if Guthrie still begs in the alley that runs along beside it, and what will happen once he's gone.

NIGHT AND DAY AND IN BETWEEN

Jonathan Janz

July, 1926

. . . AND WHEN RAFT stepped out of the darkness and peered across the dew-glistened street, he felt a tug on the right side of his mouth, the involuntary half-grin that accompanied a breakthrough. Beyond the street, he spied the porch, the maroon canvas overhang, the cursive name, the nightspot to which his search had led him. The Penelope at the end of his *Odyssey*.

The other side of Raft's mouth twitched too.

THE SHANTYMAN, the moon-white script read.

Of course, her name wasn't Penelope—it was Clara—and Raft hadn't been searching for twenty years, but rather a day shy of three months.

Still. Three months was longer than it had ever taken him. He wasn't known as the top bloodhound on the West Coast because it took him a quarter-year to track down his marks. He'd earned his reputation because he was fast.

And he was merciless.

Raft took one last drag on his Murad—the cigarettes had started him coughing last year, but lately the cough was less persistent—chucked it at the brick alley wall, and started across the road. Christ, it was muggy. His buddies back in Hollywood claimed winter was the humid season in San Francisco, but clearly they were full of shit. Breathing the July air was like plastering a brine-soaked washcloth over his mouth and sucking.

He couldn't wait to get home.

A sleek black Mercedes bore down on him, its driver beeping the horn like a goddamned kid. Raft saluted him with a middle finger and kept walking. He was almost to the curb when the smartass laid on the horn again, and this time Raft did stop, stopped and swiveled his square jaw and angular cheekbones and harpooned the horn-happy bastard with his eyes.

The honking abruptly ceased. Raft continued to stare the idiot down, the man's curly blond hair coiffed like some chorus girl's, the guy's lips disappearing inside his troutlike mouth as he realized what a mistake he'd made.

Raft let him squirm, leveled his sharkish grin at the guy for a full fifteen seconds before he continued toward the curb, and when he stepped up, the cheerful sodium glow cast by the Shantyman's entryway illuminating Raft like he was the main attraction at tonight's show, he made sure to square up to the driver, to let him behold the breadth of Raft's shoulders, the width of his corded neck.

The driver looked absolutely ill now, and when he finally remembered to roll forward and rejoin the sporadic flow of traffic, he offered Raft what was no doubt intended to be a conciliatory smile.

Raft let his own grin slide off his face, let the predator's scowl settle in its place.

The driver's eyes widened, and the Mercedes leaped forward as if goosed by a lusty boozehound's fingers.

Raft climbed the porch steps and glowered down at the doorman. Little guy, but tough-looking. Pugnacious, like a bantamweight boxer moonlighting between fights.

"You got money?" the doorman asked.

Raft took in the burgundy suit, the matching tie with a weave so thick the ivory collar couldn't quite contain it. Christ. Might as well make the guy wear clown makeup.

"Somethin' funny?" the doorman asked.

"Only that suit," Raft answered. "Can't you afford a ticket booth?"

The doorman's eyes glittered. "It's inside. But I'm asking you if you got money."

"More than you make in a year," Raft said and tapped the pocket of his bomber jacket, the one he'd gotten after arriving home from the Great War. He was sweltering in it, but it concealed the bulge in his left side, and that made the discomfort worthwhile. If this little bulldog found out he was packing, he might make a fuss, and Raft didn't need that. He wanted to see Clara before she saw him.

More importantly, he wanted to catch Lonnie "Spider Fingers" Livingston unawares.

Raft was shouldering past the doorman when the little bulldog put his hands on Raft's arm.

Half-in, half-out of the doorway, Raft stared straight ahead. “You got one second to let go of me.”

“Don’t threaten—” was all the doorman got out before Raft swung the guy around and crashed him into the heavy steel door. The guy’s head thudded against steel, rebounded, and before Raft could judge whether the guy was conscious or unconscious, alive or dead, Raft leaned forward, grasped him by the collar and a leg, and somersaulted him over the railing. The doorman’s muscled body landed with a deep *whump* on the sidewalk below. Without pausing, Raft stepped inside.

And heard her voice.

Clara.

She was singing a song he didn’t know, something disposable, the melody unworthy of her. Overlaying her voice, grandstanding as always, he heard Lonnie Livingston working the piano.

The nightclub was sweltering; he could tell that right away, even before the heavy door wheezed shut behind him. Raft scanned the crowd as he descended the stairs—A hundred and fifty patrons? A hundred seventy-five?—but he made an effort not to glance to his right, toward the stage. He wanted his first glimpse of Clara, Clara in the flesh and not as he’d seen her in the photographs and on her audition reel, to be from straight ahead, and the only way to accomplish that view was to make for the rear of the nightclub, where the mahogany bar was centered.

Raft never knew where the manager came from, but by the time Raft was leaning an elbow onto the bar, the manager was there, rudely close, blocky shoulders and broken nose filling his vision like a derelict barge.

"Here on business?" the manager asked. Unlike the doorman, the manager was dressed to the nines, his purple cravat a garish compliment to the black tuxedo and two-toned shoes.

No point in denying it. "I need to see Clara," Raft said.

"Doesn't everyone?"

The bartender, an older man with pouches under his eyes and a few strands of alabaster hair Brilliantined onto a liver-spotted pate, was approaching.

Raft said, "I thought folks came to hear Spider Fingers."

"For a while they did," the manager allowed. "But now Clara's the real draw." The manager's look darkened. "Lonnie doesn't croon like he once did."

"Get you something?" the bartender asked.

Raft glowered at the gaunt bartender. "You can get your face away from me."

The bartender recoiled, but the manager brayed laughter. He patted Raft's triceps through the bomber jacket leather. "Please, my good man, there's no reason to be combative." A glance at the bartender. "Please pour a glass of our finest bourbon."

Raft pocketed his big hands, straightened, and stared at the manager. They were roughly the same size and build, Raft a decade younger. "That what you're drinking?"

"I don't drink while I'm working," the manager said. "May I have your name?"

Raft told him.

It earned him a smile from the manager. Or maybe it was a sneer. "Quite a handle," the manager said. "Is that your real name?"

Raft didn't answer. The name was an alias. He'd met a young actor named George Raft last year and had liked the name so much he'd used it on jobs ever since.

The manager smiled. "You're already in the spirit."

"I don't read you," Raft answered, accepting the bourbon from the bartender.

"Here at the Shantyman," the manager said, "we can be whatever we want to be. You prefer to don a name like Raft, that's your prerogative." He tapped himself on the purple handkerchief that jutted from his pocket. "I go by Summers. It's not my real name, of course, but since it *is* my favorite season . . . "

"The hell's so nice about it?" Raft demanded. "Down by the wharves, the air's like breathing lukewarm fish soup."

The manager's demeanor shifted, a stiffness coming into his shoulders, an alertness around the eyes. "You've visited the wharves?"

When Raft didn't answer, only took a swig of the bourbon, which had zero taste whatsoever, Summers went on, his voice prodding like some fussy doctor's speculum. "What were you doing down there?"

But rather than answering, Raft experienced a sensation he hadn't experienced before. It was more than déjà vu, more than familiarity. As the first few chords echoed from Lonnie Livingston's Steinway, swooping across the sweaty nightclub and whispering over Raft's flesh, he was overtaken by the notion that this was where life had led him. The ugliness, the deprivation, the struggle. The scuttling around in lightless places because the glow of humanity was too bright, too cruel. And as before, rather than Lonnie's jaunty tenor, it was Clara who carried the melody, the song like, yet unlike any he'd heard before:

"I had thought of telling you
They're the reason why I'm blue.
Not allowing you to be
Living in a part of me."

Raft's mouth pooled with saliva, but he couldn't swallow, couldn't breathe. Though Clara was peering at the ceiling, her profound blue eyes studying a night sky visible only to her, Raft couldn't escape the notion she was singing to him.

No. *About* him.

Clara's pale skin coruscated with twirling stars, her silver dress's sequins throwing the spotlight's glow in a million directions. On the Steinway, onto Lonnie Livingston. Onto the swaying, benighted crowd.

Most of all, onto Raft.

He hoped Summers was watching the performance too instead of watching Raft. Because at that moment Raft knew he cut a comical figure. Mouth agape, a tide pool of spit glinting at the corners of his mouth, eyes as naked and starey as those of the most smitten teenage boy ever to sneak onto a studio back lot in the hopes of catching a glimpse of his favorite actress, his own personal goddess.

Worshipfully, Raft listened to Clara's soulful and gloriously tragic chorus:

"Sun and moonlight start to fade
Dead along the promenade.

Night and day and in between
You're the one who haunts my dreams."

And Clara did look at him then, and Raft knew. Evidently, Summers felt the crackling of the invisible tether that spanned the room, because he interposed his bulk between Raft and Clara, her sweet, curving cheekbones replaced by Summers's hacksaw features. Raft scowled at him, but rather than looking alarmed, Summers said, "Before you make a mistake, you'll need to know what happened, why you're too late."

Raft's eyes narrowed.

"That's right," Summers went on. "You're too late by a couple months." A hesitation, the murky eyes strafing the vaulted ceiling, the stamped bronze and coffered walnut. "Time is funny here. You get lost. Forgetful. The energy is so strong you feel enveloped. Encased."

Raft fought the hot tide of impatience. "The fuck are you talking about?"

"She's gone, Mr. Raft," Summers said, still with that musing cast to his features. "This place is a magnet. Terrible things have happened in the Shantyman. Terrible things." Summers's eyes traced the antique ceiling; his face clouded, and he actually shivered. If it was a put-on, Raft decided, it was a convincing one. "The . . . energies that have been generated by the gruesomeness, those energies . . . they call to those who lust for shadows."

"'Blood will have blood,'" Raft muttered.

Summers's eyes fell on him, blinked, as if seeing him for the first time. "Why, yes, Mr. Raft. That's *exactly* what I mean. I never would have pegged you for a Shakespeare man."

Raft stepped closer, his nose mere inches from Summers's. "You have thirty seconds to tell me about Clara."

Summers actually smiled an apology. "It will take longer than that, Mr. Raft."

"Two minutes," Raft said. "By the time the song is done, I better know everything."

Summers pursed his lips. "I'll try, Mr. Raft. But I warn you—"

"No warnings," Raft snapped. "Talk."

Summers's grin was singularly unpleasant. "As you wish."

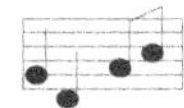

Summers said, "We first met Clara in late February."

"That long ago?" Raft asked quickly.

"She followed Lonnie here the night his final Hollywood show concluded."

Raft made a fist, almost did the same with the hand grasping the bourbon. He relaxed his grip a moment before the glass shattered.

"I was told she stayed in Hollywood longer than that," Raft said. "With a friend."

"Who told you that?" Summers asked. The unpleasant smile resurfaced. "The friend?"

"Traitorous little shit," Raft said and knocked back a slug of bourbon.

"You mustn't blame the young woman," Summers said. "Like so many aspiring starlets, Clara's friend is living hand-to-mouth. The studio heads, the directors, they take what they want but make no promises. Besides," Summers added, "we paid Clara's friend handsomely."

Raft's fingers twitched. "To exploit Clara," he said.

For the first time, Summers's insouciant façade disappeared, in its place something skulking and nasty. "You're such a saint," he spat. "Hired by her parents to haul her back to her wretched life. She's just a paycheck to you, so stop behaving as though you're the morality police."

The fine hairs on the back of Raft's neck stood on end. He yearned to peel that smirk off Summers's ugly features, to do it slowly, luxuriantly, to revel in the man's shrieks and to leer into his tomato bisque of a face and watch him gurgle his last breaths.

But he couldn't do that. He'd come too far.

Gradually, he began to calm.

If Summers noticed these changes, he made no sign. "We never advertise," Summers said. "Had Clara not followed Lonnie up the coast that night, she'd have never known he was playing the Shantyman next."

"Who runs a business that way?" Raft asked.

Summers flourished a hand. "Look around you, Mr. Raft. Do these folks look like your run-of-the-mill socialites? Teeming from night spot to night spot, always on the lookout for the newest, chicest trend?"

And Raft realized Summers was right. So transfixed by the sight of Clara had he been, and so mesmerized by her dulcet voice, that he hadn't noticed how self-possessed these patrons were, how unlike the pretty faces he was accustomed to. Oh, there was attractiveness here. And money. But it wasn't the brassy sort of clientele that frequented Hollywood's hot spots, or, he was sure, the swankest nightclubs in San Fran. No, here were self-made men and streetwise women, too schooled in the wiles of mankind to affect those wiles any longer.

Summers was going on. “We were delighted, of course, to host Spider Fingers Livingston. Though we have an impeccable reputation, we don’t often book acts as popular as Lonnie.”

“You pay him a lot?” Raft asked, interested in spite of himself.

“A fair bit,” Summers allowed. “But it was the magic of the Shantyman that attracted Lonnie. The mystique.”

“Your two minutes are up, Summers. Take me to Clara.”

Summers chuckled, his belly tremoring. “Oh, I can’t do that, Mr. Raft. Not yet. We’ll go to her in a little while, once her set is done and the crowd has dispersed.”

Raft seized Summers by the sport coat, jerked him closer. “You’re stalling.”

Summers returned his gaze serenely. “Control yourself, Mr. Raft. You’ll want to hear the rest of the tale.” A wink. “Then you can decide if you really want to trouble yourself with Clara.”

It took everything he had, but Raft decided it might be preferable to wait. What he had in mind would work better in an empty nightclub rather than one filled to capacity. Lonnie had begun to play another tune, this one lighter, less brooding. Clara’s lilting voice joined in, further mitigating Raft’s stormy mood.

He released Summers, nodded toward the bar. “You got water back there?”

“Of course,” Summers answered. As he motioned toward the emaciated old barkeep, Summers continued. "Lonnie acted exasperated by Clara's trailing him all the way to San Francisco, but it was clear to me he was flattered. You see, Lonnie's ego is the equal of his talent."

"I'd say it surpasses his talent," Raft said.

"A water for my friend, please," Summers told the barkeep. He turned to Raft. "You mustn't be so critical of Lonnie. He had the most soothing voice."

"I've heard him."

"On the radio," Summers said. "On phonographs." He shook his head. "Recorded voices sound so tinny, Mr. Raft, particularly voices like Lonnie's. No, he was undoubtedly talented."

"Why do you keep saying *was*?" Raft asked. The bartender placed a glass of water on the bar, and Raft took it wordlessly.

"When Clara introduced herself to Lonnie," Summers went on, "she made no pretense about her interest in him. She said she'd become an actress because she wanted to find truth in the world, but instead she'd only encountered . . . "

"Predators," Raft finished.

"Quite right," Summers said, sobering. "Clara said—this was shortly after Lonnie arrived, mind you . . . it must have been five in the morning—she said she'd sensed truth in Lonnie's singing, in his lyrics, and she wanted to become part of his act."

"Bet he liked that."

Summers's eyebrows rose. "Wouldn't you? A beautiful young woman like Clara driving through the small hours of the night just to declare her desire to work with you?"

Raft's gaze roved over the tops of the gleaming

heads and settled on Lonnie Livingston, his pale skin, his auburn hair, close-cropped on the back and sides, glossy and curly on top. He supposed he could see why women might swoon for the musician, but that didn't make Raft want to pulverize him any less.

Summers went on with the tale, though Raft could have guessed the gist of it. Lonnie had listened to Clara sing, judged her good enough, and told Clara he'd take her on, but only on a trial basis. Clara eagerly accepted. They played together, and the show was a hit.

"Then," Summers said, his fingers steepling at his waist, "Lonnie started gambling again."

Raft nodded, unsurprised. He knew Spider Fingers Livingston suffered from a gambling affliction—roulette or baccarat when he was in polite company, poker when he wasn't. That he'd relapsed was the most predictable twist of all.

Raft glanced across the nightclub at Lonnie, noticed how he never opened his mouth. "That what happened? He got into the wrong people for too much money and they fixed his jaw for him?"

The crowd had begun to thin out, but Summers still looked around to make sure no one was listening. He sidled closer. "Tell me, Mr. Raft. When you were at the wharves, did you notice anything unusual?"

He glared at Summers. "You got something to say to me, say it."

Summers chewed his lip, went on. "Lonnie's habit consumed him, like habits always do. First it was a friendly game with the dock foreman and his workers, low stakes and good company. Soon he was consorting with the less savory individuals who live by the sea."

Less savory, Raft thought. *You can say that again.*

"He allowed Clara to accompany him," Summers said, and before Raft could let loose with a string of expletives, Summers added, "I know. It was unforgivable."

Raft sipped his water, but it did nothing to assuage his burning throat.

"For weeks this went on," Summers said, "and Lonnie's debauchery grew progressively worse. His debts larger."

Raft's heart thumped like a giant tympani. He'd guessed the rest of the story, but he had to hear it. He had to be sure . . .

"I told you the Shantyman possesses a rare kind of energy," Summers said. "And so it does." More patrons were filing out, yet Summers's voice grew more hushed anyway. "But that energy, that thrum you feel within these walls, it's like a beacon. One that transmits darkness rather than light. And those who spend time here, the individuals who absorb that darkness . . . they carry it with them."

"Don't lecture me about evil," Raft said.

"You've seen them?" Summers guessed, his eyes widening.

Raft said nothing.

Summers reached up, massaged the skin around his Adam's apple. "Then you know what happened."

Raft's voice trembled a little, but he managed to get out, "Lonnie had a choice. Either be killed, or . . . " He cleared his throat wetly. " . . . or let them have Clara."

Summers had paled. "Nasty business."

But Raft said nothing. He was staring at Lonnie. At the gutless coward who, even now, was being broadcasted by every radio station in the country.

"As I told you," Summers said, his voice doleful, "there *is* no Clara anymore. She's gone."

"How much longer until everyone clears out?" Raft asked, his eyes never leaving Lonnie Livingston.

"Mr. Raft—"

"*How much longer?*" Raft barked.

Summers sighed, checked his watch. "It's midnight now. The rest of the patrons will be gone within the hour, I should think."

"I'll wait," Raft said.

"She's gone," Summers repeated. "You're wasting your time and needlessly courting danger."

Raft tilted back the rest of his water, handed the glass to Summers. "I'll wait."

And with that, he moved to the center of the room, where the sparse club-goers parted to grant him passage. He took a table not far from the stage, scooted out his chair to face Clara, and crossed his arms.

Clara's eyes found him before long, and unless he was mistaken, she sang the next song to him.

It took longer than an hour for the patrons to vacate the Shantyman, but not by much. Though Raft didn't check his watch—that would require tearing his eyes off Clara—he estimated it was one-thirty when the metallic clack sounded, the main door locked for the night.

Summers passed Raft's table, made his way up the steps to the stage, and then, the carbon arc light illuminating him, the manager spoke to Lonnie and Clara in undertones. To Raft it looked like a poorly-rehearsed stage play, the actors fumbling for their lines while the audience shifted restlessly. At length, Lonnie nodded, unconcerned.

But Clara appeared frightened.

Summers motioned toward Raft. "Our stars will see you now, Mr. Raft."

Raft downed the rest of his water, wiped his lips with a shaking hand, but his eyes remained on Clara. For her part, Clara appeared to be studying a spot between the baby grand piano and where she stood, as though the stage itself might possess the answers she sought.

Raft mounted the steps, his eyes flicking to Lonnie Livingston. The musician wore an amused smile now, the same condescending expression he'd no doubt directed at Clara the night she'd followed Lonnie here. He likely believed Raft was here for an autograph.

Raft forced his fists to unclench.

"Lonnie, Clara," Summers said, "please say hello to tonight's guest. He calls himself George Raft."

Clara kept her eyes averted. Lonnie only watched him in that aloof way.

"'Tonight's guest,'" Raft muttered. "You say that like it's a frequent thing, bringing someone up here to meet the performers."

"Our *stars*," Summers corrected.

Lonnie grunted, gave a dismissive shake of his curly head, and lit a cigarette. A Murad, Raft noticed. Lonnie blew smoke in his direction, the scent of the Turkish cigarette wafting over him.

"You're right, Lonnie," Summers said, as though Lonnie had spoken. "We mustn't keep Clara waiting."

Raft glanced at Clara, saw how she'd placed a hand on the corner of the black Steinway as if to steady herself. Her chest was heaving, the sequins of her silver dress catching the arc light and spangling the stage around her.

Look at me, Clara, he thought. *Look at me, please.*

But she wouldn't. Not yet.

He sensed Summers creeping nearer. When Raft turned and regarded the manager he discovered the big man's hands were occupied, one with a small but wicked-looking sickle, the other with a snub-nosed Smith & Wesson revolver. A .357, from the looks of it.

Raft smiled. "You think you're gonna stop me with that cap gun?"

Summers laughed. "Not kill you, Mr. Raft. I only need to incapacitate you. Besides," he added with a one-shouldered shrug, "I'd rather not taint your bloodstream."

Raft glanced at Clara, saw her chest was heaving.

"No," Summers went on, "rather than forcing me to shoot you, it would be better to lean forward and offer up your throat. You see, Clara hasn't fed for several nights. She . . . " An icy grin. "She *resists*. But when I saw what Clara had become . . . when I realized what price Lonnie had paid for giving his beloved to the beings that dwell beneath the docks . . . I knew Clara and Lonnie would become permanent fixtures at the Shantyman."

Clara's shoulders spasmed.

Summers nodded. "I told you that the Shantyman thrives on the darkness, Mr. Raft. I learned it soon after I acquired the business several years ago." Something haunted permeated Summers's features. "I learned that the power that resides here must be satiated. You see, I have to slake that energy's thirst. Just as you must slake Clara's."

Raft looked at Clara, who stared back at him with tears shimmering in her eyes.

"Say it," Summers said.

Raft only gazed at Clara, imagined how horrified she must have been when Lonnie offered her up.

"Say the word," Summers demanded, raising the revolver.

Raft's mouth had gone dry, but he managed to say, his voice little more than a croak, "She's a vampire."

A single teardrop crawled down Clara's cheek. It was answer enough.

From his periphery, Raft saw Lonnie make to rise, but Summers's harsh voice rang out. "Sit, Lonnie. I may need your assistance."

His complexion the hue of spoiled ham, Lonnie sat and faced the keyboard like a scolded child.

"Now open up," Summers instructed.

Lonnie drew in shuddering breaths, even rocked on the bench a little, but didn't comply.

"I said open your *mouth*," Summers commanded.

Looking nothing like the cocksure entertainer with whom the public was familiar, Lonnie writhed on the bench, his eyes brimming with tears. From between his closed lips came a weird mewling sound.

Summers leveled the gun at Lonnie. "If you wish, Lonnie, you may take Mr. Raft's place tonight. Your blood is as potable as his."

Lonnie glanced at Summers, his expression difficult to behold. Then, he turned to Raft and opened his mouth.

Where Lonnie's tongue had been was now only a crimson mass of scar tissue.

"*Yes*," Summers said, nodding. "Do what you do

best, Lonnie. Save your own skin. Your tongue was a small price to pay the vampires, wasn't it? After all, you're not a slave to the thirst the way Clara is. You don't have to commit murder."

Clara gasped and turned away, her hands clamped over her ears. Raft stared at Summers and thought, *You unfeeling son of a bitch.*

Clara now stood at the edge of the spotlight, half-illuminated, half-enshadowed. Abandoned by the man she'd trusted, damned by the fate he'd thrust upon her.

It took all he had, but Raft forced himself not to go to her.

Summers's grin grew predatory. "Sorry, friend. It's all part of the chain. Clara needs sustenance, and you're the lucky winner tonight." He waved the revolver carelessly. "So what will it be? The bullet or the blade? The gun might be quicker, but the sickle is more intimate." Brandishing the sickle, he studied Raft. "I know you want to be close to Clara. It was obvious the first time you laid eyes on her."

Raft put a vise on his emotions. He chuckled, regarded his shoes, which he'd appropriated from the affluent businessman he'd murdered the night before. "It's funny, Mr. Summers. I've never much liked the idea of someone draining my blood. I don't think I'll let that happen."

Summers drew closer. "You're acting like you have a *choice*, Mr. Raft. This is your end. This is—"

Raft swatted the revolver away. It skimmed off the tilted piano lid and tumbled off the stage. Bug-eyed, Summers tore down at him with the sickle, but Raft easily sidestepped the whooshing blade. His hand closed over Summers's and squeezed. There was a dull cracking sound. Summers emitted a high-pitched groan and dropped the sickle.

Raft spun Summers around and seized him by the throat. Though she stood several feet away, he heard Clara's sharp inhalation.

Summers's face was going red, now indigo, his feet scissoring like a slumbering beagle chasing rabbits. Two feet off the ground Raft lifted him, and when Raft opened his mouth and revealed his daggerlike canines, Summers's eyes shot wide, a frightened moan escaping from his diminishing airway.

"Play it," Raft ordered.

Like a red-haired statue, Lonnie only gawped at him. Raft jerked his head around, pierced the musician with an orange-eyed glare. "Play the goddamned song. *Now.*"

Lonnie jolted, looking paler than usual, and cleared his throat. Moments later, the first few notes of "Night and Day and in Between" began to sound.

Summers was slapping at Raft's squeezing hand, frantic now, but Raft paid the dying manager no mind. He craned his neck farther—God, his range of motion was extraordinary, just one of the innumerable improvements born of the Change—and regarded Clara. Her eyes were rapturous.

"Miss Russell," Raft said, "I'd be honored if you'd drink with me."

She started forward, but he brought up his free hand, then blushed when he realized how brusque the gesture had been. "I'm . . . forgive me, Miss Russell. But I'm like a kid right now . . . all aflutter." He ventured a feeble smile. "I'm wondering though . . . could you maybe sing for me?" A sideways nod at

Summers, whose fingernails were digging moist troughs in the back of Raft's hand, wounds that would soon heal, just like his lung cancer. "I can make him last awhile longer." Raft swallowed. "I promise he'll be fresh when you're done."

Clara spared Summers only a quick glance before her eyes latched onto Raft's. He was pleased to note the way her smooth chest heaved, the keen interest reflected in her blue eyes, which had begun to glint orange when they caught the arc light.

Lonnie, who'd been repeating the opening preamble as they'd spoken, nodded like it was none of his business, provided Clara with a preparatory flourish, and began to accompany her.

"Sun and moonlight start to fade," she sang, her voice smokier, sultrier than it had been. "Dead along the promenade."

Raft's body untensed, a sigh drizzling over him like a soothing July rain. Distantly, he felt Summers tear through the tendon of Raft's index finger, but that didn't matter. It would heal within the hour. Right after he guzzled Summers's blood.

Clara was smiling at him.

"Night and day and in between," she sang. "You're the one who haunts my dreams."

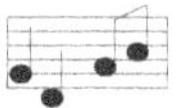

. . . and when it ended, and Lonnie's fingers tinkled out those final silvery notes, Summers was dead, limp and purple in Raft's grasp. He had no idea when he'd killed the nightclub manager. Maybe during the second verse, perhaps nearer the song's end. At any rate, he and Clara fed together, spreading Summers's body on the Steinway's now-closed lid and starting, out of mutual courtesy, on separate wrists. Their drinking was polite at first, almost shy. As Raft had instructed, Lonnie was playing another tune, Cole Porter's "Let's Misbehave," and though the pianist's fingering was stiffer than usual, Raft thought he acquitted himself well, all things considered.

Clara requested Gershwin's "Primrose," and as Lonnie, her erstwhile boyfriend, started on the melody, Clara turned her lambent orange eyes on Raft. She didn't need to ask the question. He merely nodded, indicating the dead man's throat, and, her blood-moist chest heaving, Clara sank her teeth into Summers's jugular.

When she'd fed, she peered up at Raft guiltily, but he made sure he wore his broadest grin to show her it was all right.

And it was. For the first time in months, everything was as it should be.

"I looked for you at the wharves," Raft said.

Her orange eyes widened, some blue permeating the irises. "I hope they weren't too rough with you."

He let the hardness seep into his grin. "No harder than they were on you."

Her eyes lowered, and for a moment she seemed little more than a child. A frightened child with blood smeared all over her face and torso.

"Sometimes," she started, but her voice was scarcely audible above Lonnie's plinking. Raft shot the pianist a look, and Lonnie cringed, continued on pianissimo.

"Sometimes," Clara continued, "I imagine them coming through those doors. Coming for me and dragging me away from here. Dragging me under those docks . . . that terrible fish smell . . . their hideous chortling . . . ”

Raft stepped around the Steinway. “They won’t bother you again.”

She peered up at him. “You’re only one—”

“He’s dead,” Raft said. “The creature who turned you.”

Her lips parted, her eyes almost full blue. “But how . . . ”

Raft knelt before her, took one willowy hand, and kissed the back of it. “Three months, Clara. It took me three months to get to you. The folks at Universal told me you’d gone to ‘Frisco, and when I arrived it didn’t take long before someone said he’d seen you. A cab driver, he said he’d taken you to the wharves.”

“Following Lonnie,” she said. “He’d been playing poker down there, squandering his gifts.”

“No, my dear.” Raft kissed the hand again, more fervently this time. “You’re the one who’s being squandered.”

A harsh laugh, and when he looked up at her he saw her wipe her eyes with the back of a bloody hand. It left an auburn streak on her temple, like Egyptian mascara. “There’s no talent to waste,” she said. Eyes shimmering at the stamped bronze ceiling. “They told me so at Universal, Sid Keller said—”

“—that if you went to bed with him, he’d give you a lead role.”

She looked startled. “How did you . . . ”

“Sid Keller will be dead by the end of the week,” Raft said. “There’s a young director there, William Wyler. He’s obsessed with you.”

Clara bit her lip. “I don’t think I know him.”

"He knows you. He heard the recording you made. He saw your screen test. Said he'd never seen someone so natural on camera."

Clara started to smile, but then it faded. "They won't let me leave. The vampires by the wharf . . . "

"They're dead too. All of them."

Clara touched her throat.

Raft went on grimly. "They turned me the first night." A mirthless chuckle. "I couldn't believe it. That fucking cabbie, he was a familiar for them. Served me up like filet mignon. I spent a few days puking my guts out under the docks, shivering, sure I was on death's doorstep."

Clara gazed down at him, her eyes profound. She knew exactly how he'd felt. Of course she did.

"But the thing about me, Miss Russell, is I never know when to quit."

"You wanted revenge."

"Sure," he allowed. "But even more, I wanted to find you. I'd told your parents I would, and I wasn't gonna let a job go unfinished."

Something troubled touched Clara's eyes, and Raft's suspicions were confirmed. He stoppered the rage before it showed in his face.

"Anyway, I picked them off one by one. Every couple nights, I'd take another down." He grunted, smiled his lopsided smile. "Funniest thing about vampires. No matter how many have been staked, no matter how many have been beheaded, they always think it won't happen to them. The bloodlust is so governing, all they can see is the victim in front of them." Raft's smile disappeared. "Not the monster behind them."

Her eyes were gentle. "You're not a monster."

"I am," he said. "I was even before they turned me. In the war, I killed so many. And this face . . . "

"It's a handsome face," Clara said. She touched his cheek, the soft fingerpads threading through the hair above his ear. It was all Raft could do not to moan aloud.

He closed his eyes and thought, *Handsome. Christ, she even seems to believe it.*

"You're sure they're all dead?" Clara asked, her voice soft.

All Raft could do was give her a torpid nod. Her caresses were like harp vibrations, light and golden, yet penetrating so deep they warmed his soul.

And though her fingertips continued to blaze rows of pleasure through his scalp, her next words came out in a toneless rush. "What about my parents? Will you tell them you found me?"

The soul-deep hurt in her voice brought Raft to his feet, made him grasp her bare shoulders. "Your dad. He . . . did stuff to you?"

Clara was stiff as marble in his grip.

"Your mother let him," Raft went on. "She goes along with whatever he says."

Clara didn't speak.

"You went to Universal to get away from your father."

Her eyes fixed on his.

"And all you found was another version of him."

Her chest trembled, but she didn't look away. Goddammit, the woman was a fighter.

Raft let a thumb stroke the warm knob of her shoulder. "Why don't we pay your dad a visit?"

She was quiet so long he thought she wouldn't answer. Then, "Can we pay them both a visit?"

He was going to answer in the affirmative, but she was rocking onto her tiptoes and covering his mouth with a kiss. My God, he could have died there and then, so sublime were her lips. Waves of arousal undulated through him, but more than that, there was love. Yes, Raft thought. Love. For maybe the first time in his wretched life.

She pulled away, eyes shining up at him. "Let's get out of here," she said.

He nodded. "This place has too many ghosts."

Clara bit her bottom lip.

"What is it?" he asked, making sure to keep his voice gentle. He'd have to get into the habit. Clara had experienced enough mistreatment for ten lifetimes.

"Won't they suspect me?" she asked. "After we're done with my parents? After you . . . pay a visit to Sid Keller?"

"You'll have a different name," he said. "Folks in pictures always do. And I was thinking . . . "

She peered up at him with a hope that hadn't been there before. "Yeah?"

"They're saying there will be films with sound soon. A couple people I've spoken to, they call 'em 'talkies.'"

Her eyes widened. She'd already gotten it, but he said it anyway. "A woman like you, who can sing as well as act . . . that's a hell of a combination."

The good humor returned to her face. Her fingers twined with his, and with a last look, they started for the doors.

They were nearly there when Lonnie hailed them with a weird, anguished moan. The pianist couldn't speak, of course, but the plea in his eyes was plain: *What about me?*

"You get to live," Raft said.

Lonnie's shoulders drew inward, his head down.

The pianist's abjectness enraged Raft. He took a step toward the stage, but then he remembered: This was Clara's problem. This was the *world's* problem. Men always telling women what to do. Guys like Raft deciding matters for women like Clara. When she had twice the brains he had.

He drew in a deep breath, faced her with his chin lowered. "Your call."

Clara was watching Lonnie, her lips pursed slightly, a calculating gleam in her eyes. "Let's keep him around," she said. "His songs amuse me. Plus, if we need errands run, Lonnie can do them."

Raft nodded, eyed the pianist. "You got a car?"

"A Bentley," Clara answered. "Last year's model."

Lonnie nodded eagerly.

"We'll let him drive," Raft said.

"Only if you stay in the backseat with me," Clara said.

Raft glanced down at her, surprised.

Unabashed, Clara smiled back.

And with Clara humming "Night and Day and in Between," Raft walked hand-in-hand with her out of the Shantyman.

IN THE WINTER OF NO LOVE

John Skipp

THE STREET WAS a neon nightmare, a low-rent Disneyland of sleaze down which Marcie tromped in army boots. It was cold—at least for California, with the chill November wind blowing in off the ocean—and in her ankle-length coat of ratty fur, she felt like the least-naked woman on the strip.

All around her, the strip clubs, sex shoppes and movie theaters splayed posters of beautiful brazen women in their undergarments or less, the most revealing of them covering their nipples with their own hands, or somebody else's. Only three of the women in the posters were her.

It let her know where she stood in the pantheon of fuckability, if nothing else. And she rated pretty high, if you trusted the hungry hungry hippies sharing the sidewalk with her.

"Hey, baby. Hey, baby. You're bee-*yooooo*-teefull," crooned the scrawny black junkie at the corner, by the liquor store. He wasn't a pimp, but he sure dreamed of being one. She could see the glazed dollar signs in his eyes.

"Yeah," she said. "So what else is new?"

He laughed like that was the funniest thing he'd heard all night, though she bet he laughed like that all the time. She tried to imagine him before his idealism peeled off, if he ever had any at all. Then again, her own wasn't doing so hot these days, either.

Compassion, baby, she reminded herself. *Everybody's hurting out here.* Tonight, if nothing else, was all about the compassion.

In another world, things would have played out differently. In her dreams, they most certainly had. In her dreams, she kept her heart intact, and let her mind flow free.

But tonight, the red light was against her, so Marcie lit a smoke while she waited to cross, the cold wind blowing out three matches before she finally got it fired. She only had two packs of matches and five cigarettes left to get her through the night, until some moneyed gentleman or lady ponied up and bought her another day in paradise.

This was not the groovy San Francisco she'd dreamed of.

But it sure as shit was the one she got.

The sexual revolution was already decaying by the time Marcie made it to the free love capital of the world, in the summer of 1969. She had traveled a thousand miles times two, all the way from Milwaukee, Wisconsin, escaping the crew-cut legions of clueless men and finger-waggling helmet-haired Christian women who all wanted to call her a whore just because she loved to fuck, and was not ashamed of it.

She was only 16 in '67, when the actual Summer of

Love went down. Two more years of high school before she could possibly break free. But she followed the news of the emerging rebellious youth culture mounting there, and more importantly, listened to the far-out sounds emanating from that mecca: The Grateful Dead, Quicksilver Messenger Service, Country Joe and the Fish's "Feel Like I'm Fixin' To Die."

She was particularly intrigued by Janis Joplin of Big Brother and the Holding Company, and Grace Slick of Jefferson Airplane: one flagrantly screaming out her naked love and need, in the most powerful terms possible; the other a mysterious witchy woman who spoke in code, but expressed her power not a speck less clearly.

Marcie wasn't sure which one she wanted to be—a moot point, since she couldn't sing a note to save her life—but she knew *where* she wanted to be. She wanted to be where the action was. She wanted to be part of changing the world. So the Monday after graduation, she packed her paisley rucksack with a couple changes of her hippest clothes, stole $137 from her dad, wrote a goodbye note, and hit the highway thumb-first on her way to the West.

The first guy to pull over had a brand new VW van with a GAS, GRASS, OR ASS—NOBODY RIDES FOR FREE bumper sticker slapped across its glove compartment. His name was Dewey, which pretty much described his eyes the second she got in the passenger seat. Even his long, scraggly ponytail popped a boner.

"Oh, wow," he said. "You look like Jane Asher. Or that movie star, Sharon Tate. Anyone ever tell you that?"

"Not since breakfast, baby." Cracking herself up with how easily those saucy words sprang to her lips. "So how far are you going?"

"How far are *you* going?" with a cuddly apelike leer.

"All the way to San Francisco, lover," she said. "It's gonna be groovy. You wanna come?"

And come he did, all the way across the country. She was low on gas and grass, but she had plenty of the third; and when he'd start to nod out at the wheel, sticking her hand in his pants always seemed to perk him up. In this way, they made it all 2,173 miles in just five days, with plenty of time in Dewey's optimistic little back-of-the-van love nest to make it worth everyone's while.

Dewey thought he was going to college in New Mexico, maybe joining a band, but she quickly changed his mind. His parents, of course, went out of their gourds. But if this was free love, he wanted waaaay more of that particular slice of the Age of Aquarius.

When they landed in the Haight, second week of June, they thought they were in paradise. There was the Fillmore West, the Avalon Ballroom. All their favorite bands, performing nightly. And the streets were overflowing with colorful characters, psychedelic art, posters for protests and rallies and Be-Ins every which way they turned.

To see it all laid out before you like that, you'd think the war in Vietnam was really *going* to end. That equal rights for women and minorities was really *going* to happen. That you *could* reject Madison Avenue and the military/industrial complex, live a life that was simpler, more spiritual and free, less crawling with ancient dogma and narrow-minded dogshit.

But it didn't take long to figure out that they weren't the only people who came here without a plan. Because there was no plan. There was only a dream. And for every dreamer who landed even the smallest of happening gigs, there were six hundred others just wandering around, desperately hoping they could bum a next meal, talk someone into letting them crash at their pad, survive long enough to not give up and go back to their parents' basement in Ohio, or Vermont, or wherever the hell they came from.

Marcie and Dewey were able to keep finding overnight parking spaces while they sussed out the scene. But those spots were in increasingly scary neighborhoods. Pretty soon, they were spending more time in the Tenderloin than the Haight, watching middle-class creeps cruise for hookers in drag or otherwise, on their way in or out of pornographic clip shows and tittie bars.

Marcie being Marcie, it didn't take long for her to make friends, or something like them. The appetite for beautiful women was bottomless in *every* social circle, and she definitely ranked. They found themselves invited to lots of parties, including orgies where she passed herself around first with gleeful abandon, then increasing discernment: learning who to screw just how and when, in order to get her foot in the door. And it wasn't like Dewey wasn't getting laid. Just not half as much as she was.

She landed a part-time job at a hip record store—not enough to live on, but definitely enough to help—and met tons of musicians breaking in from the margins. This was ostensibly good for Dewey, too, as he was pretty good on bass. And she was totally rooting for him.

The problem was he wasn't *that* good. Not enough to stand out in this incredibly competitive crowd, where originality was key.

Worse, he still thought he was her boyfriend.

That's when shit started to get weird between them.

"Which part of 'free love' don't you understand, Dewey?" she ranted, in one of their increasingly frequent arguments. "I came here to discover, and experience, and grow. Not to be dragged down."

"And I came here to be with you, Marcie!" he threw back. "That's what *you* don't understand!"

"Oh, baby," she said, pulling him close. "I'm with you right now, aren't I?" Then she put her tongue in his ear, which always made him weak-kneed, and they settled back down on his filthy mattress for a quick one that was far more sad than joyous.

Afterward, as she held him while the tears wore streambeds down his cheeks, he muttered, "I thought we came here to change the world. But the world's just changing us. And I don't like it."

She nodded and turned, lit a stick of incense, helplessly thinking there wasn't enough sandalwood and patchouli oil in the world to get the stink out of this van. And though it pained her deeply to admit it, that's when she knew they were coming to the end.

Better luck next life, she thought. And found herself wishing that next life would come a little sooner than later. Because this one was really starting to suck.

As the weeks dragged on, he had nothing but the

money he increasingly begged from his parents, slowing to a trickle as their patience wore thin. Meanwhile, she found that stripping was a great, easy way to make quick cash. And when the opportunity to shoot a couple of scenes with some of the ladies came up, she was not about to ixnay $100 for fifteen minutes of going down on Mitzi or Darla. She was already doing that action for free.

The day after she found her own apartment, and did a cosmic three-way on acid with the drummer from Ultimate Spinach and a psychic healer named Wowza Majeur—to which he was not invited—Dewey found the needle in a parking lot with a passel of other smackhead losers. And that was that. Now he was needy on every level. And she just couldn't do it.

The day they broke up—August 9th, one week before Woodstock staged the last great gasp of the flower power generation—was the day Sharon Tate was found murdered. Marcie came home to the sight of the front page story, taped to her door, with Tate's name crossed out and her own in its place. Beneath it, he had scrawled YOU'RE DEAD TO ME. And that was the last time they spoke.

It had been five months now since they landed, almost three since they'd seen each other. But when she heard he got a gig with the house band at some dive called The Shantyman, she figured she owed him at least this much.

Which brought her, at last, to The Shantyman's door. With the little sign out front that said:

TONITE!

BLACK SUNSHINE

There was a $3 cover, collected by the balding troll at the ticket kiosk. He licked his lips as he gave her change, let his gaze linger uncomfortably long. Pretty standard skeevy male chauvinist behavior. She rolled her eyes and strolled inside.

At first, she wasn't sure this could be the right place. The bartender looked to be at least 60, with a longshoreman's sense of pure rough trade style; and the three cackling cadavers holding court at the bar before him were equally antique. It looked more like her dad's VFW post in Milwaukee than anything she'd seen since she got to the Bay area.

But then the room opened up, and she saw the black light posters adorning the dark wood walls: Mr. Natural, Keep On Truckin', the obligatory dayglo peace symbol. It was pretty clear the owners of this dump had figured out no one wanted to hear Benny Goodman any more, made a few cheap concessions for the hippie demographic they needed if they wanted to keep the doors open.

But it didn't cover up the fact that, as hole-in-the-wall joints went, this one was pretty creepy. She could almost taste the history, and it didn't taste good. A quick peek at her watch said it was quarter to eleven. She figured she'd catch ten minutes of their set, then get the hell out of Dodge and back to the land of the slightly-more-living.

And that was when the band came on, with four

drum stick clicks in the dark followed by a sonic boom: one-half power-chord, one-half pre-recorded atomic blast, the Hiroshima mushroom cloud suddenly projected on the wall behind the stage.

Suddenly, she could see the members of Black Sunshine in stroboscopic silhouette. The gaunt, towering lead singer, swaying around the mic stand he clutched in one hand. Not exactly handsome, but snakily compelling nonetheless.

The guitarist and organist to either side weren't great lookers either. But the notes they hit were haunting on top of the hypnotic tom-tom trance state being laid down by the drummer, whose face remained hidden under a curtain of greasy bangs.

And, no fooling, there was Dewey on bass. He was staring at the floor, thudding out a sinuous pattern to the primal beat that didn't sound San Franciscan at all. More L.A. More like the fucking Doors, all dark and doomy. But pretty good. It suited the mood she was in, peace and love not having quite lived up to her expectations.

"Right on, Dewey," she muttered softly. "You sound good, baby. Good for you."

There were maybe forty people on the open dance floor, floating around like undersea creatures, getting their lethargic freak on under the strobing lights. People didn't dance together. They danced around each other. Sometimes eye-to-eye, but more often than not off in their own world.

Marcie wasn't judgmental. She liked to get super-high, too. Get into her own space. Let the spirit guide her. But there was something about the hollow-eyed emptiness in the faces of the people spinning around her that only reinforced The Shantyman's sketchy-ass vibe.

These were the people who had fallen off the fringes of the fringe. The castoffs of the countercultural revolution, far more narcotic than psychedelic. Bottom-feeders, with no bottom left to feed on. The lostest of the lost.

For the second time, she felt the urge to leave. But the music was powerful, growing more so by the second. And like a train wreck in the making, she wanted to see what happened next. It was definitely not the weirdest scene she'd stumbled into, or ever would, if she was lucky.

She wondered who had some pot, at least. Started scoping out likely suspects as she steered her way to the front.

The farther in she went, the toastier the room got with unwashed body heat, so she opened her jacket, revealed her coochie-high skintight pink velvet micro-mini dress. It was one of Dewey's favorites, and she wasn't sure whether it was to torture him or reward him. But it glowed in the black light, and strobed in between. One fact was for certain: It was made to be seen.

The lead singer spotted her first, raised a hungry eyebrow before suddenly remembering it was time to croon. He cast a gaze back at Dewey, with a knowing grin. And then, at last, began to sing:

It's dark tonight
In the winter of no love
All the stars you came to shine with
Are not glittering above

And, oh, your disappointment
It just fits you like a glove
What's so easy
Makes you queasy
In the winter of no love

In the time it took for that verse to flow through, she felt the gentle push of the crowd from behind. They were moving slowly toward the stage, mesmerized by the throbbing groove and his rich, deep baritone voice. She, too, was starting to move with the rhythm, the intoxicatingly persuasive syncopation.

And when a pasty-faced scarecrow in a Nehru jacket passed a doobie her way, she gratefully accepted, took a long toke, passed it back. He nodded, unsmiling, returned his gaze to the band.

By the time she exhaled, it was already too late.

Suddenly, the room seemed to skew sideways in all directions at once, as her vision went fisheye.

Her brain and the floor turned to mud, the strobing lights like pulsars flaring numbly within.

Ooooooh noooo *went a voice she barely recognized as her own, as the angel dust took effect. She didn't know what PCP was, but she knew what it was doing, elephant-tranquilizing her as surely as a dart to the neck.*

She stumbled back as if to fall, but the press of bodies kept her upright, rubberband limbs all but useless as her gaze bleared toward the stage.

And Dewey was looking at her now, face mutating as the world went wrong, his eyes black holes that glittered redmeat red at on/off intervals. His sharkmouth crawled up either cheek in a grin too huge for comprehension, his fishbelly creme bass bending and writhing in crotchulous undulation.

And as his fuzzed-out bass notes hammered through her bones, she felt the call of the walls, the floor and ceiling, as sure as the words now being chanted by the band.

All you who are lost
Belong to us
All you who are lost
Belong to us

Something tore inside her bowels, like a menstrual cramp only higher, and seemingly farther away. She vaguely felt wetness run down her legs, wasn't sure if she was peeing or bleeding. There was a hand holding her up by the right shoulder. Its fingers runnelled down the front of her coat like fatty wax.

And her vagina filled with something thick as cock, with none of the pleasure.

From within.

All you who are lost
Belong with us
In the winter of no love

Marcie screamed as her lower intestines crawled out of her holiest of holes and out into the room, waggling blindly wormlike, curling toward the sound. She felt herself emptying, screamed again, reeling back against the wall of bodies.

But they were already melting, too. Bodies sagging, as faces dripped. A bouillabaisse of rotten squalor, giving themselves up at last to the only place that would have them.

Being claimed by this hellhole, and Black Sunshine.

Now she knew why they were the house band.

Marcie toppled on top of a sloe-eyed blonde whose eyes oozed out to either side. Her slick hand grazed Marcie's cheek before its arm dissolved into the floor.

*Then came the onslaught of lead guitar, every raw treble note a rivet driving itself into her flesh. It tried to pin her, but she crawled with all her might, finding strength through fury. Going*I will not die like this.

The next body she met was already liquefied but for the skull, which crumbled like a candy shell. She clawed past it, felt her fingernails snap as she grabbed the wooden floorboards, felt the floorboards grab back. Ancient mouths with thick splinter teeth, opening up to sample, bite, and suck her in.

She screamed again: a wail somehow strangely in tune with the music that assailed her. The most in-tune her voice had ever been. And that scared her most of all.

There is no other
Place for you
Will be no other
Trace of you
Come wallow in
The waste of you
Come on
Come on

COME ON!
COME ON!

She could not look back over her shoulder. She could not look back over her shoulder. She did not want to see her guts slide across the floor behind her, moving inexorably toward the stage. She did not want to see the triumph in Dewey's eyeless eyes as his own dark umbilicus crawled out his ass and down his stupid bell-bottomed pants leg in an attempt to fuse with hers.

And she was emptying. Yes, she was. Belly concaving to the ribcage, the spine, as more and more of her squeezed then squirted out her pussy and into the room. There was no question that she was dying now. The only question was where.

The door was a trillion more than 2,173 miles away, but she knew it when she saw it, crawling past the bar, where the Shantyman regulars cawed like vultures, having seen this all before. Placing bets on how far she'd get. Eyes black as Satan's coal.

But she was not going back. She was going forward, one desperate lunge at a time. The music still huge, but receding as an angry honking cabbie drove by, honk like the voice of God saying you know who you are, you know who you are.

There was no troll at the door. No cover charge on life. She saw headlights, heard voices through the floating rectangular slab as the miles turned to inches turned to nothing turned to there . . .

. . . and her lungs pulled her still-beating heart down and down, toward the blackness beyond . . .

And then there was light. Amazing light.

The color of which she had only dreamed.

Her face was at rest upon green green grass. Every filament bright, in the warm starlight. An infinite plane of glowing.

With a pair of hooves, stopping just an inch from her face.

"Hey," said a voice. "It's okay now. It's okay."

She blinked, looked up, fisheyed no longer as the black numbness shuddered out of her in a wave.

"What?" she said to the satyr who loomed above her: shirtless, hairy, not remotely scary, with a goatlike psychedelic glimmer in his eye that liked and loved and knew her in a flash, beneath his wild hair and great flowing horns.

"You don't ever wanna go in there," he said. "That's not why you came."

Marcie shook her head to clear it, not to disagree. Somewhere in the enormous distance, the last whimper of Black Sunshine echoed off to nothingness. Like they were never there. Like they never mattered at all.

"Where am I?" she said.

"Where you always wanted to be," he said. "And all you have to do is let go."

"Right." As she helplessly started to cry.

"Release your attachments."

"Oh, God . . . "

"Forgive yourself."

Choking. "I am so sorry I hurt him . . . "

"Aw, sugar. It happens. Just don't do it again, if you

can help it" he said. "You'll get better with practice, okay? That's what we get whole lives for. Lives upon lives upon lives."

"OH, GOD!" As her cord to the world, the dimension she once knew gut-snapped at last. But her heart still with her. Her spirit intact.

"The world you want may take decades or centuries to happen, back there," he said. "But it's already happening here, forever. This is where you're going. This is where the best of you, the soul of you, has always been. We all know how cool you are, and how well you mean, and how beautiful you will always be, even if you come back ugly in disguise. Because that's how the game is played."

It was the most perfect thing he could possibly have said, all infinity flowing before and beyond them.

"So where's the party?" she asked, grinning, as he helped her to her feet.

"Up here," he said. "And I think you're gonna like it. Rumor has it you're a fucking firecracker."

"You better believe it, lover," she purred into his ear. Stuck her tongue in. Made him weak in the knees.

As winter turned to summer once again.

WOLF WITH DIAMOND EYES

Patrick Lacey

VINCENZO LUCILLE IS living a nightmare.

According to photos, his eyes are bloodshot. The surrounding dark circles have aged him. And that's saying something. At seventy-two, he is the oldest and last remaining survivor of the most infamous Italian progressive rock band. Much has been said of Harpie's last show at San Francisco's Shantyman club, but most of it is speculation. We can confirm a body count of nearly thirty, four of which belong to the group itself, but what *caused* the massacre is still up for debate.

As I knock on the door of Vincenzo's Soho apartment, I'm prepared for bookshelves housing ancient occult volumes, things you won't find in your local Barnes and Noble. The lights will be dim, the curtains drawn. I imagine a cauldron in the kitchen, boiling some concoction I'd rather not know about. These are stereotypes of course but it's hard to deny Harpie's long history of black magic rumors. Depending on whom you ask, Vincenzo and his fellow band mates, Giuseppe (vocalist), Antonio (keyboardist), Simone (lead guitarist), and Lorenzo (bassist and other instrumentation) were up to some shady business in the seventies. The rumors range from ritualistic sacrifice to conjuring spirits. It's probably all conjecture, I tell myself, as the door opens.

I'm greeted with freshly brewed coffee instead of incense. Large, picturesque windows instead of a dark tomb. The man standing before me is nowhere near as haunted as his photos would have you believe. He simply looks as though he hasn't slept for ages.

Vincenzo nods. "Come in, come in."

I step inside. There *are* several large bookshelves but nothing screams *witchcraft* or *demonology*. Instead there are rows and rows of pulp mysteries and an alarming number of Clive Cussler novels.

He leads me to a small alcove that passes for a dining room, tells me to sit. Moments later, he returns with two cups of espresso. The glasses and saucers clink together as he sets them down, hands shaking badly. Nervous, perhaps. And with good reason. This is his first interview since the late seventies. He has all but sworn off the public. A journalist's wet dream. But he grew tired of answering the same questions. Questions I myself am about to ask. I squirm in my seat. Vincenzo isn't the only nervous one around here.

The espresso is dark and strong and I politely tell him it's . . . *different* than the Dunkin Donut's coconut mocha iced coffee I'm used to.

"Terrible," he says, sipping his own. "Coffee is not meant to be sweet. It should be strong, bitter, black." His accent is a strange mix of his homeland and New York City.

"How long have you lived here?" I look out the window of his third floor apartment. Across the street is, ironically, a Dunkin Donuts. Next door is an antiques shop that's seen better days. The display window is cracked and yellowed, obscuring whatever might lay inside.

Vincenzo sets his cup down and clicks his tongue. I'll learn this is his way of recalling information. He needs a long time to think. Harpie was known for their drug use, specifically that of the psychotropic variety. "Twenty years, about." There's that accent coming out, switching the order of words.

I nod and ask if he understands why I'm here.

He nods back and his eyes turn to slits. He clicks his tongue, though I haven't asked another question yet.

It's coming up on the fortieth anniversary of Harpie's last show, which ended his tenure as a musician. He enjoyed a mildly successful solo career in the early eighties before fizzling out of the public spotlight for good. The man sitting across from me does not want to discuss memories he's avoided for half his life. But, I remind myself, he agreed to the interview. He must have *something* to reveal.

"You want to know what happened," he says after an uncomfortable silence.

"Yes. I realize you've discussed Harpie's final show countless times but you've never come out and said exactly what transpired. I'm looking for the truth."

He laughs at that. "I will give the truth but I can't promise a good story."

I beg to differ. The fact he's talking at all will make for a good story. A good paycheck too.

Vincenzo rubs his eyes. He looks more like his photo now. A man with a terrible secret. When his story is through, I'll learn it's hard to blame him for keeping quiet all these years. Some tragedies are better left unsolved.

For a moment, I think I've lost him. I say something to steer him along. "Who were the killers, Vincenzo?"

He shakes his head. "Not killers."'

"Someone had to have murdered those people."

"Yes. *One* killer. Not killers."

"Only one?" Combing through old interviews and conspiracy theories in preparation, it had always been plural. Kill*ers*. Murder*ers*. And the occasional creat*ures*.

"Only one."

"Was the man one of your fans?"

"Not a man. Not entirely."

I nearly knock over the handheld recorder I set up upon arriving. My hands fidget at his last words.

"Are you aware of our last album?"

"Of course. It was the soundtrack to *Wolf with Diamond Eyes*." I watched the film for research. It's a well-executed if somewhat by-the-numbers Giallo, a sub-genre of Italian cinema that saw its height of popularity around the time of Harpie's last show. The word Giallo translates to "yellow," a reference to pulp novels (similar to those on Vincenzo's bookshelf) that were available on drug store book-racks. The covers and spines were often yellow, hence the name. Later, these trashy novels would translate to the big screen. Giallos enjoyed a stint of success due to such directors as Dario Argento and Lucio Fulci. *Wolf with Diamond Eyes*, though, was written and directed by a lesser-known filmmaker, one Lawrence Sanfillipo. Some speculate this is a stage name, for there isn't a whole lot of information available on him. He made several low budget Giallos before disappearing from the film business for good. Not unlike Vincenzo.

"Yes," he says. "Our best seller. We were able to watch it before it was released to write the score. That movie—it may seem, how you say, hokey, but back then, it was terrifying."

I'm not sure "terrifying" is the word I'd choose. The plot is thin at best, a black-masked killer in a trench coat stalks college co-eds who, for some reason, don't seem to wear bras or underwear. "What, exactly, did you find terrifying?"

"It was the man in the mask. The one who killed all those people."

"The man in the mask scared you?"

"Yes, he scared me. Because it was *him* that night. That night at the Shantyman."

My mouth hangs open but I can't summon the strength to close it. "That's quite the implication. Are you saying a man who played a costumed killer in a movie took to killing in real life?"

"No, not the actor. *His* name was Harold and he died of overdose before the film was released. I am talking about the killer himself. You see, he stepped *out* of the screen, so to speak, and into our world."

It's a long time before either of us speaks. The apartment is no longer charming. While there aren't any pentagrams etched into the floor, the man before me has gone from eccentric to unstable in seconds. "Where's your bathroom?"

"You think I'm crazy."

I shake my head. "Of course not. I'd like to continue the interview if you don't mind. I'll only need a few moments."

"It's down the hall and to the right."

I stand too quickly and follow his directions. The hallway is littered with Harpie posters, all of them placed in expensive-looking frames. For someone who wants to forget the past, he's doing a poor job. I locate the bathroom, across from what appears to be the bedroom. The door is partially open and I see a bedside table. The journalist in me wants to investigate but fight-or-flight wins out. I close the bathroom door and throw cold water onto my face. This is the biggest story of my career. The money could be life changing. I make a promise to my reflection. Finish the interview and get the hell out of Soho.

I flush the toilet, try to compose myself, step back into the hallway.

Vincenzo is still sitting at the table. "You think I'm crazy," he repeats without turning around. "I don't care if you believe me or not. It isn't my concern."

I sit back down and ask him to go on.

"I am sure during your research you heard about . . . certain activities Harpie was involved in."

"You mean *occult* activities."

"Yes. Those."

"I assumed they were just rumors."

"They for the most part were. But all rumors are a bit true, aren't they?"

"I suppose so."

"The Shantyman has a long history of strange happenings. You are aware of this, I'm sure."

"Yes, I'm aware." If given more time for this assignment, I would go into detail about San Francisco's Shantyman. Harpie's last show (and only North American appearance) is far from the only unexplained phenomenon within the club's walls. There has been a slew of unsolved murders throughout the years but I'm drawn to Vincenzo's story. To my knowledge, his case boasts the highest body count. That's no easy feat considering the venue's history.

Vincenzo pulls out a silver case of cigarettes. "Do you mind?"

"It's your home."

He lights one, breathes for an eternity, exhales. "I've been clean for many years. No drugs or drink. Just these. They will end up killing me." He points to his chest. "The doctor begs me to stop. My lungs sound tired. Much like me." He looks out the window, perhaps at the Dunkin Donuts or antiques shop, perhaps at something I can't see. For the rest of the interview, I remain quiet. You'll understand why.

"I was the outsider of the band. I had a wife and a child—before they left me—and I did not wish to fall into bad habits. Drugs were one thing. Black magic another. Lorenzo was the first to dabble. Between our third and fourth albums, he went on holiday for three months. I do not know where. He changed his story all the time. One day Transylvania, the next Norway. All that I know is he came back a changed man. He had lost weight and looked like the skeletons on our album covers.

"Our music was different from then on. Darker. Being the rhythm guitarist and the family man of the band, my involvement was less as time went on. The guys wrote the songs and I played them. When we got the *Wolf* gig, I didn't like what they were writing. It didn't sound like music at all. It sounded . . . like pain. Like the soundtrack to not a movie but hell itself."

He stubs his cigarette and immediately lights another.

"The guys had a hard time writing the score. Nothing fit. There were plenty of bloody pictures in Italy but *Wolf*—it got under your skin. One night during recording, I left the studio early but I forget my house keys. When I went back, the lights were off and there were candles lit. I saw too many people in the control room. The producer and engineer had stepped out. There should've been only four. But I saw five. The fifth was not *in* the band. He was the man in the mask, you see. The man who killed at our last show.

"I don't know what they said or did. All I know is that I saw the killer with the black mask next to them while they hummed something under their breath. It would become the melody to the title track.

"After that, I started coming around less. When it came time to tour for *Wolf*, I was not a happy man. My daughter, Violet, was just learning to walk and I missed a lot of moments. When I returned, I was different. Not like Lorenzo but different just the same. What I saw that night at the Shantyman—it took a toll on me. Anger and drinking took over and my family took off. They were smart to do so. But I digress.

"Despite everything, I was still excited to play the Shantyman. It is the dream of every musician. Think of a band that is important—*timeless*—and they have played there. Like I said before, about the club's history—it adds a certain, shall we say, morbid charm. The night of our last show, I tried to stay away from the dressing room. Had a bad feeling. Call it a hunch. I stood outside the door before show time, waiting, as they guys hummed that same melody. They whispered too. I heard a voice that I did not recognize above the others. When the door opened, I pretended to pace, blamed it on nerves. They said nothing as we went to the stage. Nothing else that night or ever.

"We played three older songs before *Wolf* came up on the set list. The house lights dimmed. The audience cheered. I waited for the guys to count me in.

"And when the lights came back on, I saw him."

Saw who? I want to ask but I already know the answer.

"He was different from the movies. Trench coat more ragged and ripped. His mask wasn't how I remembered. It seemed too dark, like it was not a mask at all but flesh. He held something in his hands and I knew what it was by the time he raised the knife and cut the girl standing next to him. She screamed but the music was too loud.

"I screamed too—and tried to stop playing. Except I couldn't. My fingers—they worked against my wishes. I turned toward Lorenzo and he winked at me. I knew then. Whatever he learned in whatever place he visited—it was worse than I thought. He smiled as my hands played on their own.

"The crowd did the same. They stood still, watching instead of fleeing, many of them dying while frozen. The man with the mask took his time, cherishing each swing of the blade. The blood covered the floor like a flooded basement. He made his way to the stage and I watched him kill my band mates. My *friends*, no matter how far apart we'd grown. He took Harpie out one by one. Until he got to me."

I finally speak up. "Why didn't he kill you?"

"Because he told me something. A secret."

"What secret?"

He opens his mouth and for a moment, I think *This is it, the big reveal, what I've been waiting for*. But he shuts it quickly and reconsiders his next words.

"I am afraid I cannot say. For that would mean passing it on to you."

"Passing *what* on?"

"The curse—if that's what it is. Whatever Lorenzo brought back. Some knowledge we are not meant to know. As long as I do not speak it aloud, we will both live. At least I think that's how it works. I am no expert."

It sounds like a veiled threat or perhaps I'm just paranoid. Either way, I decide to end the interview. When you're a journalist, you follow your gut. Sometimes it tells you to charge forward. Other times, like this, it tells you to run away as fast as you can. I heed my gut's advice and thank Vincenzo for his time.

He sees me out and asks one last question.

"The interview. Please do not make me sound crazy. I have been holding on to this for very long. I do not have my band or my family. I have nothing but my name."

"Of course." I wonder how to write this story while maintaining his credibility, decide to worry about it later, and jog down the stairs.

At home I take a long shower until the water runs frigid. It doesn't wash away the fear like I'd hoped. Every few moments, I'm certain I hear my back door creak open. Just nerves, I tell myself.

After, I open my laptop, write some notes, drink a glass of wine, watch a romantic comedy on Netflix, eat leftover Chinese, and complete countless other arbitrary tasks that will delay the inevitable process of writing the article.

Finally, I sit back at my desk, another full glass of wine in hand. The drink has gone to my head. It calms me some, creates the illusion that everything is as it should be.

I write three or four paragraphs before my mind wanders. It's too hard to concentrate, so I decide to listen to our interview. The sound quality isn't great. I've been promising myself a new recorder, something that comes across as halfway professional, but journalism isn't the world's highest paying profession.

I sip the wine and file my nails while listening, about to shut it off when we arrive at the moment where I excused myself to the bathroom. My face grows cold but not because I recall the faucet water.

Vincenzo goes on speaking; to whom, I'm not sure.

His apartment seemed empty. I heard no one else. From my research, he appears to live alone. As he mentioned, his family left long ago. I think back to the bedroom, how the door wasn't quite closed, wonder if anyone was in there. Waiting. But for what?

His words aren't in any language I've ever heard. You'd think it was just gibberish except there's a certain cadence to the syllables, order within the chaos.

The cold spreads from my face to my body as a theory creeps into my mind.

What was it Vincenzo had said?

As long as I do not speak it aloud, we will both live.

But he *had* spoken it aloud while I was out of the room. And now, whatever curse he mentioned—it's here with me. I'm sure of it. As sure as I am of the shadow that appears on my desk before me. The computer screen fades to black, going to sleep, and I'm in the club—in the Shantyman, where the house lights have dimmed and everyone is waiting for their favorite Italian prog rock band to play their favorite horror movie theme.

Except unlike the house lights, the screen stays black. Black enough so that I can see the reflection of the figure standing directly behind me. As unnatural at it seems, and as scared as I am, I'm not the least bit surprised at the trench coat and the fedora and the mask. All of them black, of course. Blacker than anything I've ever known.

I clutch the nail filer like a knife and spin around, ready to stab the thing, the man, whatever it is, with my makeshift weapon.

But there's nothing there.

I'm alone again, though it feels like the opposite is true.

I grab my jacket and hail a cab to Soho, stop on the sidewalk between the Dunkin Donuts and abandoned antiques store. It's a long time before I can convince myself there's no one staring from inside the shop. Or maybe there is. The windows seem dingier now.

Across the street, the apartment building is mostly dark. The city may never sleep but it does rest every once in a while. Aside from the distant sound of traffic and chatter, New York is preternaturally quiet.

There is a sole light on across the way. And in that bright square, an old Italian man watches me. He is statue still, as if he's been waiting. I suppose he has.

He nods to me as if we've entered some secret agreement.

It's my curse now, mine to pass on to the next unfortunate owner.

Assuming I find someone in time.

From behind, I hear the antiques store's front door unlock, hear it open, hear footsteps draw near.

I break into a sprint.

The night isn't over just yet. The bars are still open and there must be someone starved for a good story. I'm a journalist, after all. It's what I do.

I'd love to tell them about a man named Vincenzo.

PILGRIMAGE

Bryan Smith

A TOUR BUS pulled into an almost empty parking lot early in the afternoon on the sixth day of August in the year 2019. Adjacent to the lot was a single one-story building. The only other vehicle in the lot was an unoccupied 1970s-era Chevelle. The old muscle car was in pristine condition, with new paint, new tires, and a set of fancy new rims that gleamed in the brilliant glare of the San Francisco sunshine. Of the eye-catching ride's owner, there was no sign, but Jason Dobbs knew one thing for sure—whoever the owner was, he or she was rolling in cash. That or in hock up to their eyeballs, because a top-notch restoration job on a car of that vintage couldn't be done cheaply.

He nudged the person in the seat next to him, then pointed out the window. "Hey, George. Check out the sweet wheels."

George Sanderson took a break from making out with Karla Donahue, his girlfriend, and craned his head around to look in the indicated direction. "Oh, wow. Nice old school transpo."

Jason nodded. "Hell, yeah. Can't you just see

yourself rolling down the strip back home in that thing in, like, 1976 or whatever?"

George grinned, warming to the idea. "Sure can. Bunch of hot girls in the back. Bell-bottom jeans and tube tops. Awesome tunes cranking on the 8-track player while a fat blunt gets passed around."

Karla leaned over the guys for a look at the subject of conversation. She did so at an angle that allowed Jason to see straight down the front of her top. The view was pretty breathtaking. She had incredible breasts. His face flushed hot as he stared down the valley between them. He was pretty sure she'd done this on purpose. It was not the first time she'd blatantly taunted him with her sexuality. As always, he felt a mixture of titillation and shame. This was his best friend's girl. He felt he should do something to discourage the behavior, but how he might go about doing that without making things awkward or even hostile between the three of them, he did not know.

She had choppy dyed-black hair that wasn't quite shoulder length and was dressed in the manner of rock and rollers from a bygone era. The outfit included a studded black leather biker jacket, a studded dog collar around her throat, a tight, low-cut red top that left very little to the imagination, black-and-white striped pants, and Doc Martens. Rings adorned nearly every finger. Some were plain bands of various colors, but the selection included multiple skull rings. Dramatic black eye makeup rounded out a look Jason figured was best summarized as "rock and roll wet dream."

She pulled back from the window, returning to her seat on the other side of George. "I don't think they had that term back in the 70s. Blunts. That came out of hip hop. I think."

Jason turned his face toward the window, hoping the others wouldn't see the bright red tinge to his cheeks.

George, at least, seemed oblivious to his embarrassment, regarding his girlfriend with a frown as he said, "Okay, enlighten me. What was the preferred vernacular of the time?"

She grunted. "Doobies, I think."

George snorted. "Doobies? Like the fucking Doobie Brothers or some shit?"

"Yeah. Where do you think those guys got their name? They were a bunch of pot-smoking hippies."

George laughed. "You sound pretty knowledgeable on the subject. Name one song by the fucking Doobie Brothers."

"Shut up. That's not the point."

George laughed again and nudged Jason. "You listening to this shit, man?"

"Yeah, Jason," Karla said, her tone playful but with a subtle undercurrent of mockery. "We need your opinion on this all-important matter. You're the authority on all things retro."

Enough of the heat had faded from Jason's cheeks that he felt comfortable turning away from the window. "Actually, I don't—"

An abrasive burst of loud static from the overhead speakers made him grimace and fall silent. The abrupt sound elicited startled gasps of displeasure from several other people on the bus. All heads turned to the front, where a tall, abundantly bearded fat man stood with a radio handset gripped in one of his massive paws. He coughed and thumbed a button on the side of the handset. "Sorry, folks. Was having some technical issues. Anyway, I'm sure at least a few of you recognize the very famous building off to our right. It's been featured in several documentaries and a great number of the most iconic photos in the history of rock and roll were taken inside this storied edifice."

Some drunken-sounding individual from the back of the bus let out an obnoxiously loud whoop. "David Bowie! Woo!"

The fat tour guide smiled in an indulgent way. "You are correct, sir. Woo, indeed. David Bowie was one of the many legends to play a show on these hallowed grounds. Others you might have heard of include Led Zeppelin in their infancy, the Doors, Humble Pie, Jefferson Airplane, the Grateful Dead, Van Halen when they were starting out, and many more. Lot of the biggest and most influential punk bands of the 70s played here, too."

The same drunk from the back let out another whoop. "Sid Vicious! Sex Pistols! Woo!"

Karla snorted laughter and raised her voice in a whoop of her own. "Woo! Rock and roll! Woo!"

The drunk in the back laughed so hard Jason worried the force of it might result in a seizure. On the bright side, at least it would shut him up.

The tour guide's smile looked strained now. He cleared his throat and again thumbed the button on the side of the handset. "The Shantyman has always been more than just a legendary place to see live music performed. It is a destination. It is living history. The venue has played host to a dizzyingly diverse range of artists, including some who later became figures of myth in their own right. And it is a place where the ghosts of the past never seem far away, where guitar chords struck at the end of legendary performances decades earlier seem to linger in the air still, at least for those attuned to the right mental frequencies. For those with a deep love for music, there is something almost sacred about the Shantyman. Little wonder, then, that so many are willing to travel from so far away to experience the special vibe of the place firsthand."

Like us, Jason thought.

The guide sounded like he was reading from a memorized script and probably was.

Karla raised a hand. "I have a question."

George smirked. "Oh, look at the proper schoolgirl. Being all courteous and shit. Not bad for a high school dropout."

Karla glared at him. "Shut up."

The tour guide sighed heavily into the live handset, a sound replicated in distorted fashion through the overhead speakers. "What would you like to know, miss?"

The angry look on Karla's face was immediately displaced by a mischievous smile. "Is it true Johnny Kilgore of the Sick Motherfuckers blew his brains out right over there?" She twisted in her seat to point in the general direction of the venue's entrance. "Right about where that penis on wheels is parked?"

A few of the other passengers giggled at this remark. Predictably, the drunk in the back honked more obnoxious laughter. Jason wished he had a hatchet to bury in the guy's head. In a way, it was more than a bit hypocritical. He had, after all, indulged in his fair share of public drunken buffoonery in the past. It occurred to him that what was really bugging him here was the way the guy seemed so locked in on Karla with his over-the-top reactions to her every remark. He was jealous of the spontaneous camaraderie that had developed between her and this stranger. Which was ridiculous. She wasn't his girlfriend. The only one entitled to any feelings of jealousy here was George, who either was oblivious to their rapport or simply didn't care. In his friend's place, Jason would have a hard time being blasé about it.

The tour guide again cleared his throat and spoke into the handset. "That is the unfortunate truth, yes. The year was 1979. The band to which you referred had just played their first headlining gig at the Shantyman, which was a big deal for them. Back then, it wasn't easy for a band with a name like that to market themselves effectively. The sign on the marquee billed them as the Sick M.F.'s, which caused some drama between the band and venue management. This apparently offended the late Mr. Kilgore's sense of punk rock purity, and near the end of his band's set that night, he announced he would be killing himself as soon as the show was over. Unfortunately, it seems no one took this threat seriously. Not until it was too late."

Some on the bus made clucking sounds of disapproval while others with grim expressions shook their heads at this tale of rock and roll tragedy. Jason wasn't one of them, having been familiar with the details for years. The same was true for Karla, of course, who was being a tad disingenuous by inquiring as to the veracity of something she already knew all about.

The tour guide paused for a moment while some of the passengers aimed their phones at the venue to snap pictures. When he sensed the majority of his customers had finished recording this moment for something resembling posterity, he again thumbed the button on the side of the handset. “Okay, then. If there are no other questions, it’s time to move along to the next stop on the tour. We’ve got a ways to go before we’re done and a schedule to adhere to.”

Karla abruptly stood up and moved into the center aisle between the rows of seats. “We’ll be getting off here.”

George did a double-take at this unanticipated declaration before glancing at Jason with raised eyebrows. “Uh, you heard her. Guess we’re debarking. Any objections?”

Jason sighed. “Would it matter if I had any?”

George chuckled. “Not really, man. It’s cool. We’ll just get an Uber back to the hotel later.”

“Fuck it, then. Let’s go.”

They both began to rise from their seats.

As the three of them began to move down the aisle toward the front, the tour guide moved aside to allow them room to pass. When they were within range, he addressed them without speaking into the handset. “It’s early in the tour, guys. Sure you want to get off now?”

By that point, Karla had already descended the short set of steps at the front of the bus and was standing in the parking lot, where she was lighting up a cigarette. George glanced back at the tour guide, grinning in a sheepish way as he shrugged. “Already a done deal, looks like.”

The tour guide nodded. "No skin off my back. Just remember there aren't any refunds. Doesn't matter where you get off."

George cackled and said, "That's what she said, bro."

He descended the steps to the parking lot without another word.

Jason directed a cringing look of silent apology at the tour guide, shrugged, and followed his friends out the door. He held a hand to his brow to shield his eyes against the glare of the sun as he approached them. His friends had donned sunglasses as soon as they'd stepped out into the sunlight, but he'd left his own pair behind at the hotel. George had one of Karla's cigarettes wedged into a corner of his mouth, and she was holding the flame of her Zippo to its tip to light it for him. Jason had known George for a long time, going back to middle school. He'd never smoked at all until hooking up with Karla about a year ago, but now he indulged on a regular basis. She had a habit of taking two cigarettes from her pack and passing one to him without asking if he wanted one. Jason had a feeling George just went along with it because he thought his girlfriend would disapprove if he didn't. And George kind of idolized Karla. In private conversation with Jason, he often called her "the coolest chick I've ever fucking met."

Jason didn't much care for the smoking, but he could understand.

He kind of idolized Karla, too.

And now he felt a bit awestruck at the sight of her. Dressed like she was while standing outside one of the most storied music venues in the world, she looked like a rock star who had arrived early for a gig. With his shaggy dark hair, black clothes, and lanky good looks, George could pass as one of her bandmates. Unlike his girlfriend, however, the guy couldn't play a lick of music. His singing voice wasn't such hot shit, either. He did have that same effortlessly cool 70s rocker look, though. This sometimes made Jason feel a little lacking by comparison. He was just an ordinary, kind of nerdy-looking guy. The kind of guy a wild child like Karla would never go for, or so one would think. A tiny hint of a smirk dimpled one side of her mouth when she glanced his way and caught him staring at her.

He glanced away from her just as the door to the tour bus hissed open again, allowing one more passenger to disembark. A skinny young guy in a tie-dyed shirt and raggedy jeans grinned and waved when he saw them. He had fair skin and what Jason thought of as lazy, heavy-lidded eyes. They were the eyes of a dedicated weed-smoker. He also had long blond dreads.

The tour bus pulled away from them, turned about in a wide circle, and drove out of the Shantyman's parking lot, leaving the four of them alone there. Aside from the unoccupied car parked by the entrance, there was no indication of any other human presence in the area. Though he would have had difficulty articulating why in that moment, this made Jason feel uneasy.

"Hey, yo," the hippie kid said, calling out to them with a big, goofy grin on his face. "There room for one more at this party?"

Jason winced at the sound of the guy's voice. He always found that lethargic stoner drawl irritating. So many of those guys sounded just like that. But that wasn't the real reason for his instinctive dislike of the interloper. He'd heard this particular obnoxious stoner voice several times already. This was the annoying guy who'd spoken up several times from the back of the bus.

He looked at his friends and mouthed the word "no" as emphatically as he could manage. They were both looking right at him as he did this. There was no doubt they understood what he was trying to silently communicate. George gave a slight nod of understanding, and Jason knew his old buddy was on board with his desire to send the guy on his way.

Karla, however, had other ideas.

"Sure, pal. So long as we can have some of whatever you've been smoking."

The stoner's grin got bigger and goofier. He hooked his thumbs under the green straps of a backpack and tugged at them. "Absolutely. Got plenty to go around. Got some magic mushrooms, too, if you're interested. Really potent shit, yo."

Karla laughed. "We'll keep that in mind for later, maybe. Meanwhile, break out the fucking weed."

The guy removed the backpack, unzipped a side pocket, and took out a baggie filled with an ample supply of the green stuff. Also stuffed inside the baggie was a glass pipe. He took out the pipe, tamped some weed into the bowl, and fired it up, after which he took a big hit and held the smoke in as he held the pipe out for whoever wanted to hit it next.

Karla flipped her half-smoked cigarette away and snagged it from him, held the flame of her Zippo to the bowl, and took a big hit of her own. She then passed the pipe to George, who took a more modest hit before offering it to Jason.

Jason declined with a wave of his hand. "Not interested."

George shrugged. "Suit yourself."

He and Karla took turns taking additional hits before passing the pipe back to the hippie kid at his request. The kid pinched another nug out of the baggie and refilled the bowl. He sparked it up again with the plastic gas station lighter he'd used before, put the pipe to his lips, and inhaled deeply.

Karla coughed a couple times and made a face. "I feel a little weird. Not high exactly. Just weird. Like my head's inside a glass box or something, disconnected from my body and the rest of the world. There's something not right about your weed, man. I've got this chemical taste in my mouth." Her features shifted, conveying anger as she grabbed hold of Jason to keep from toppling over. "Jesus. It's laced with something fucked-up, isn't it? Industrial solvents or some shit. Pesticide, maybe."

The hippie kid laughed as he took the pipe away from his mouth. "Nothing so mundane as that. This is my own special blend, though. Designed to induce a certain pliable state of mind. Open to suggestion. Some of the ingredients are what you might consider . . . exotic."

Karla took a lurching step sideways, dragging George along with her. They took another awkward step together before simultaneously dropping to their knees. Karla looked at Jason. Her mouth moved, but no words emerged. There was a look of pleading in her eyes. She wanted help with something, but he had no clue what manner of assistance she needed. In another moment, she and George fell over and lay motionless on the ground.

Jason gasped in shock. "Fuck!"

The hippie kid laughed again and took another long drag from the pipe, his puffed-out cheeks turning red as held the smoke in for an extended period. In the grip of a mounting panic, Jason grabbed hold of the guy by an arm and roughly spun him about so they were facing each other.

"What have you done to them, asshole!?" He snatched the pipe from the kid's hands and squinted at the bowl. At a glance, the partially charred substance inside it looked no different from regular weed, but that didn't necessarily mean anything. He held the bowl to his face and sniffed. The odor did seem off in a way that was hard to pinpoint. "You better not have poisoned them, motherfucker."

The kid opened his mouth and expelled a pungent cloud of smoke directly into Jason's face. Some of the smoke went up his nostrils while more of it went straight into his open mouth. He relinquished his grip on the kid's arm as he gagged and took a staggering step backward. At once he detected that chemical taste Karla had described. It made the inside of his mouth feel like it was coated in a fine layer of liquid metal. The sensation was horrifying and he felt an instinctive, all-consuming need to rid his body of it as soon as possible. He gagged again and bent over at the waist as he repeatedly spat phlegm at the parking lot asphalt. No amount of this relieved the strange sensations plaguing him.

He dropped to his knees and in another moment toppled over and rolled onto his back with a groan. The hippie kid came closer and knelt next to him with the same blissed-out smile as before, but there was something in the set of his features that hadn't been there originally. Something sinister. There was also something not quite right in the texture of his skin. The longer he stared at the kid, the more that skin didn't look real at all. It looked kind of fake, like stretchable plastic. He had the feeling that if he could lift his hand and reach out to the guy, he would be able to peel back that phony outer layer of pseudo-flesh and reveal the true horror beneath.

But he didn't have the strength for that.

He was still conscious, though. Unlike his friends, he was still able to groan and squirm around minutely on the ground. He supposed he'd gotten a weaker dose of whatever had crippled them because he hadn't drawn the smoke directly into his lungs via the pipe. The hippie kid with the fake-looking skin blew another cloud of smoke into his face, causing him to cough and gag yet again.

The kid shook blond dreadlocks out of his face and grinned. "You're right, you know. About the diluted effect of the second-hand smoke. No worries, though. You'll get the necessary dose soon enough."

That this creature could read minds didn't even rank among the top five most scary things about it, as far as Jason was concerned. This thing masquerading as a hippie kid wasn't even human. It was some kind of monster or demon. And it had targeted him and his friends for reasons he couldn't even begin to fathom.

He coughed so hard it made his lungs hurt. "Wh-what . . . are you?"

The creature smiled. "I am The Traveler. Time is an illusion. Did you know that? I could explain it to you, but there's no time. Hah-hah. Anyway, she wanted you, you know. That girl. It's true. I looked into her mind and saw it. She wanted you to fuck her, but you didn't have the guts to go for it." He glanced at the girl's unconscious form. "Such a shame, really. To let down a girl that pretty." He grinned as his gaze returned to Jason. "Your problem, Jason, is that you're too much of a good guy. You'd never betray a friend's trust. What you don't know is George killed that kitten of yours that went missing a few years back. Such a cruel and petty act. There was no real reason for it. Other than pure malice, that is. Dear, sweet George has a hidden inner darkness. Guess he was never really worthy of your blind loyalty, huh?"

Tears misted Jason's eyes. "Why . . . are you doing this?"

The creature chuckled, a sound that made Jason think of the tour guide's distorted voice crackling through the speakers in the bus. "Because I can. Because it amuses me. Your friends are not dead, by the way. Quite the contrary. I'm sending each of you on separate journeys through the timestream, all in some way connected to that building over there. The girl asked about the night Johnny Kilgore killed himself. Well, she's about to witness the event firsthand."

Jason sniffled as his vision began to blur. "This is . . . crazy. Can't be real."

"Oh, but it is." The creature inhaled deeply from the glass pipe, held the smoke in for a moment, and then expelled it into Jason's face. "Did you know that the Stooges played a show here fifty years ago tonight? It's true. It was the day after their first album was released. Little known historical fact, several members of the Manson family were in attendance that night. This was three days before the infamous Tate-LaBianca murders. The raw violence and energy in the protopunk music they heard that night had a galvanizing effect on some of them. It's too bad ol' Charlie wasn't there. The experience might have elevated his game, made him an even more effective sower of chaos and dread."

Jason coughed. "I have no idea what you're talking about. And none of that sounds true."

The creature laughed. "The timestream consists of an inestimable number of interweaving strands. Along some of those strands, what I've told you is demonstrably false. Along others, it is the absolute truth. As you're about to find out."

The plastic baggie full of that toxic weed was in the thing's hands again. Now he scooped out a handful of it and forced it into Jason's mouth. Jason gagged and spat some of it back out, but the creature clamped a strong hand tightly around his jaw, closing his mouth and forcing him to swallow the weed. A short time later, he experienced something similar to the sensation Karla had described. His head felt separate from his body, somehow heavy and weightless at the same time.

The brilliant blue hue drained out of the sky above within seconds.

Darkness engulfed him.

An indeterminate period of incognizance ensued, during which he drifted in a formless black void. It was as if he barely even existed anymore.

As if nothing existed.

Then, abruptly, awareness returned in the form of

the driving backbeat of a distantly familiar tune. That rhythm was one he knew well, but an overwhelming sense of disorientation prevented him from identifying it right away. He heard other sounds, as well. Raised voices struggling to be heard over the amplified music. The hoots and hollers of a cheering audience.

He opened his eyes and saw that he was right up front inside the Shantyman, watching a primal rock band barrel its way through a song he now recognized as “1969”, a track from the self-titled debut album by the Stooges. Leading the band was the young Iggy Pop, a frenetic whirlwind of manic energy.

I’m not really seeing this, Jason thought. I’m not really here. This is power of suggestion bullshit. A drug-induced hallucination. That’s all.

He stood there swaying mindlessly to the beat a moment longer, feeling the heavy thrum of the rhythm section in his body. The floor seemed to vibrate beneath his feet. The bodies of others in the audience jostled against him. He detected the acrid scent of pot permeating the smoke-filled air.

Sure feels real, though.

The apparent reality of it all was suddenly too much. He spun away from the stage and began to push his way through the tight press of bodies. The closeness of those bodies and thickness of the smoke was oppressive, made him feel like he was suffocating. He needed to get out of the club, out into the clean night air. The press of bodies became less oppressive, less dense, as he neared the bar at the back of the club. This allowed him to take a longer look at the people around him. They looked strange, not right for the audience at a punk show. There was a lot of long, greasy hair. A lot of hippie garb and regalia. Headbands, peace symbol buttons, and so forth. Then it hit him. The audience didn't look right to him because this was the time before punk, when the Stooges were just the newest stage in the ongoing evolution of rock.

There were a lot of people at the bar. And a lot of drinks on its crowded surface. At one end sat an unguarded beer that looked like it had just been opened, its contents untouched. He snagged it while no one was watching and hurried out of the club, heaving a breath as he emerged into the warm California evening. The parking lot that had been empty before was full now. Surveying the sea of vehicles, he felt like he'd stumbled upon a vintage car show. He saw Mustangs and VW vans, as well as numerous sedans and sports cars of various makes. There was nary a sign of a Prius or any other modern vehicle.

All real, he thought. I'm really stuck in 1969.

Laughing with tears in his eyes, he took a swig of beer and sat his ass down on the curb. He didn't know what to do with himself. Accepting the reality of the situation presented a whole new host of problems. He had no connection to anyone in this time. His parents were out there somewhere on the other side of the country, but they were kids. There would be no point in seeking them out. He drank more of the beer as he sat there and thought about it. It all seemed so hopeless. He had no idea how to go about starting a new life in what essentially amounted to a foreign land, a place where he did not officially exist. Not on paper, anyway.

Then he thought about what the thing that called itself The Traveler had said. He was sending Karla back to 1979, to the night Johnny Kilgore of the Sick Motherfuckers killed himself not far from where he now sat. A tiny spark of hope flared to life inside Jason.

All he had to do was somehow survive the next ten years and return to this spot on that infamous date. He knew the details well. He could be right here at the appointed time when Karla arrived. He'd be a decade older than her at that point, but that wasn't such an insurmountable age difference, was it? He didn't think so, especially now that he knew about her private feelings for him. She would be thrilled to see him. He was sure of it.

And who knew what might happen then?

A voice spoke from somewhere right behind him spoke: "Hey, cutie."

He shifted about on the curb and craned his head around, frowning at the familiar face staring down at him. It was a girl. A not unattractive one. She was no Karla, but she wasn't half bad, either. But he knew that face, was sure he'd seen it somewhere before.

He frowned. "Do I know you?"

She smiled. "I don't think so. We're just now meeting. My name's Suzie."

Then it came to him. Where he'd seen her before. Mostly from black and white photos in the pages of a dogeared old paperback book that had belonged to his father. This was Susan Atkins.

One of the Manson girls.

Before he could say anything else to her, he felt another presence rushing at him from somewhere off to the side. He turned his head around just in time to see another familiar face. This time the name came to him faster. Charles "Tex" Watson, another member of Charlie's family. He had something in his hands. A burlap sack.

Jason dropped the beer and tried getting to his feet, but a kick from behind sent him tumbling back to the ground. Then Tex and Leslie were on him. The bag was pulled over his head and cinched tight. Others crowded around him then, and he felt multiple sets of hands lifting him off the ground. He tried thrashing his way out of their grip as they carried him across the parking lot, but to no avail. An attempt to cry out for help earned him a hard thump over the head. A short time later, his abductors came to a stop and dumped him inside the spacious trunk of a car.

"Sit tight, cutie," he heard the one called Suzie say. "We're just going on a little adventure and wanted some company."

Jason squirmed around inside the trunk. "Where are you taking me?"

"To the desert. We've got this big thing we're doing soon. Some real Helter Skelter shit. We're sending out a message to the piggies of the world. One they won't be able to ignore."

A man chuckled. Tex, probably. "That's right, darlin'. But before the main event, we're gonna practice on this poor son of a bitch."

The trunk lid slammed shut.

Jason screamed with every bit of lung power he had as the Manson family members piled into the car. He screamed some more as the car's engine started and kept screaming as the car was steered out of the parking lot and into the city streets.

No one heard his screams or pleas for mercy.

No one except Charlie's chosen few, that is.

And no one else ever would.

Because all that remained of Jason Dobbs's future—aside from his pending agonizing death—was a rendezvous with a lonely hole in the dusty desert soil. A forgotten, unmarked grave that would forever go undiscovered.

A TONGUE LIKE FIRE

Rachel Autumn Deering

HARVEY MATTHEWS LISTENED to the girl crying from the other side of the door for some time. He tightened the grip on his Bible, clenched his jaw, offered up a silent prayer, and placed his palm flat against the heavy black door. It was smooth and cold. The muscles in his neck and shoulders ached and he realized in that moment how tense he was. He shifted his weight forward but the weathered hinges resisted, as if to ask, *are you sure you want to go in there?* He was more than sure he didn't, but he put his shoulder to the door and shoved inside, past the shadowy threshold, and into the gloom.

He saw her there, at the far end of the room, on the floor, hugging her knees in the weird yellow light. She looked odd and twisted, bent into an uncomfortable configuration, and her clothes draped like Spanish moss on southern oaks, tattered to the point of barely concealing the more private parts of her thin frame. Her ashen skin was streaked in places with blood, though the heavy shadows falling over her made it difficult for Harvey to determine if she was wounded, or if the blood was even her own. He took a few reluctant steps into the room. The girl wasn't a girl at all, but a woman, and she was chanting a strange, raspy, rhythmic sort of something into her closed fists.

The muted scratching of her voice grew louder and began to form words, and the words adopted a kind of tortured melody, like a chorus of gargled glass.

"Her hair was black as night
her skin was white as bone
Those blood-red lips were stained by sins
for which she could not atone
And the poison in her veins saw an end to a love
that was real, and sapphic, and tragic
She was borne to the grave by six blind shadows
with two left hands full of magic"

Her head snapped back and a raw scream rose up out of her throat. A flood of red light washed over the room, revealing a crowd of black-clad bodies amassed before the woman. They might have filled half the room, if they had allowed much space between them, but they pushed in close together and swayed to the rhythm of whatever spell was being cast over them. They were cult-like in their movements, a throbbing sea of leather and lace and white-painted faces. Harvey was hypnotized by it all. His mind was infected by visions of too-young people doing unspeakable things. Little misguided boys and girls—sons and daughters—degrading themselves in the booze-soaked back rooms of morally-bankrupt places like this. He felt things he did not want to feel.

Harvey Matthews hated rock and roll.

"Oh, hey! Hey, man!" A young guy in a button-up

shirt moved toward Harvey from the bar, shouting to be heard above the music. He was clean-cut and his clothes were remarkably ordinary. He looked nearly as out of place as Harvey. "Are you the religious guy?"

"Hmm?" Harvey's brow furrowed. He looked down at the oversized tome in his hand.

"You sorta stick out like a sore thumb on a hand full of polished pinkies." He shifted a cocktail to his left hand and extended the right toward Harvey. "I'm Ben, Hexx's manager. We talked on the phone last week."

"Good to meet you, Ben." Harvey wiped a sweaty palm across his slacks before reaching out to take the offered hand. "Thanks for setting this whole thing up. I appreciate you."

"Hey, no problem. You wanna wait in the green room? It won't be a whole lot quieter than out here, but at least you can have a seat while you wait for her to finish."

"I'd like that, thanks," Harvey said.

His eyes swept over the crowd again and he felt a sting in his heart. Any one of them could have been his daughter.

The air in the green room was thick with the smell of stale smoke—cigarette and otherwise—and the coffee table situated in the middle of the room, sandwiched between two sofas, was littered with beer cans and liquor bottles. Lines of white powder were scratched out across the surface of a mirror, punctuated by a razorblade and a bright green straw. The sound on the television in the corner of the room was muted, but the screen flashed with colorful images of an animated dog and a hippie kid in bellbottoms as they ran from a green-faced ghoul with red hair.

"You can have a seat over there. Anywhere you like, really," Ben said. "Sorry about the mess."

"I'm a father, Ben. My eyes have gone blind to messes." Harvey took a seat at the end of one of the sofas. He pushed a few beer cans aside and set his Bible on the table in front of him.

"You got kids, huh? Be fruitful and multiply, right? Isn't that what it says?"

"Yeah, I suppose it does. I got one kid. Singular. Daughter." Harvey fished a wallet from his back pocket and flipped it open to a set of pictures. A family photo and a senior portrait of a young girl. He offered it to Ben.

"Handsome family, my man. You've done well for yourself," Ben said. He smiled at the static faces. The young girl was terribly pale with dark features and no sign of a smile. Ben handed the wallet back.

"Thanks. They're my whole world," Harvey said.

The door swung into the room and Hexx stepped through after it, dabbing at her forehead with a towel. Blood mixed with thick white makeup and smeared around her face as she mopped at the streaks of sweat that threatened to run into her eyes. She exhaled heavily and smiled at Harvey, a genuine smile. Ben closed the door behind her and leaned against it. Harvey tucked the wallet back into his pocket and stood to his feet.

"Hi. Harvey Matthews," he said, waving. "You can call me Harv, though. Please."

"Harv it is. I'm Hexx. Jessica, if we're keeping things casual," she said. She sat on the sofa opposite the Bible, taking note of it, and draped the soiled towel across her left leg. She mimed like she was taking a drink at Ben and gave him a wink. “Something to drink, Harv?”

Harvey was terrified and his mouth was dry. He sat.

“I’ll pass, thanks. I’m fine. I don’t want to be in your hair any longer than I have to.”

“I can’t say I’ve ever been interviewed by a preacher before.” She laughed.

“Oh, I don’t intend to give the impression that I’m a preacher. I’m not.”

“Sorry to assume. You’re a Christian, though, right? That’s why you brought a Bible?” She eyed the weighty thing with its white leather cover and golden embossed cross.

Holy Bible. She focused on the words, unblinking.

Holy.

“Ben, clean up your shit, please.” She motioned toward the empty cans and cocaine. Ben handed her a bottle of water and snatched up the mirror and a few of the cans. He tried to hide his annoyance, but it showed.

“I do my best to be Christ-like, sure, but I fail as often as the next guy.” Harvey’s hands trembled. He laced his fingers together and cracked his knuckles to stop the shakes. “I’m not here to judge y’all.” He looked to Ben and managed a half-smile. Ben faked a polite smirk and left the room, letting the door close a little too hard behind him.

“That’s okay, judgment or not, Ben needs to learn to keep the stuff away from me. I’m working on three years being clean and I want to keep it that way.”

“Three years? Wow. That’s . . . something. That’s great.” Harvey’s heart sank into his stomach. He felt the sudden urge to follow Ben out of the room. To get away from the venue, far and fast. He breathed deep. "Congratulations."

"I just couldn't take it anymore, you know? It's an occupational hazard when you're in my line of work, I guess. Staying keyed up and crashed out lost its shine when the live show started to suffer and the crowds got smaller. I'm lucky I came around when I did and still had any fans left."

"Yeah. Gotta keep those . . . fans . . . " Harvey pulled a small notepad and a pen from his jacket pocket. He flipped through a few pages until he found a blank sheet, then started to scratch out a few quick words. He finished writing and tore the page from the pad. He folded it into quarters and set it on top of the Bible.

Jessica eyed the note, but she didn't ask after it. She looked back to Harvey. He sat with the pen on a new sheet of paper, ready to write.

"Hey, what's this interview for, anyway? Church bulletin, local rag, or . . . ?"

"It's actually for a psychology class. I'm writing a paper on the effects of art on adolescent behavioral disorders."

"Huh. I didn't take you for a college kid, Harv. No offense, but you're a little older than the average student."

"It's true. I never saw myself going back to school, especially at my age, but the wife left me earlier this year and I thought to myself, *why the heck not?* So here I am. Trying something new."

"Aw, shit, man. I'm sorry"

"Hey, don't mention it. Let's move on, huh?" Harvey scrawled a few words into the notepad then looked up at Jessica. "First question: Where did the Hexx character come from? How did she come to you?"

"I guess Hexx is just a product of everything I had to go through in my young life. All the family problems and the broken hearts and the self-doubt." Jessica shifted uncomfortably. She moved the towel to the arm of the sofa and crossed her legs under her. She nodded her head and continued. "Hexx is like the wall I put up to protect Jessica from all that pain, right? She's the guardian. The scary one. My stage persona really just grew out of that."

"So she's your way of getting rid of the things that bring you down. Getting that all out of your system so it can't eat at you."

"Yeah. Exactly, man. Exactly."

"And what do you think the kids who listen to your music do with all the pain you put off onto them?"

"Shit. I don't know. Relate to it, I guess? Maybe it helps them?"

"Huh. Maybe." Harvey's pen zipped across the paper, marking down line after line of notes. He pressed with such force that Jessica thought he might tear through the paper. His hands were shaking again.

"Why, Harv? What do you think?" Jessica watched with sad curiosity as Harvey wrote.

"I think," Harvey started, "that you should read . . . this." He finished jotting down a line and tore the page from the notepad. He handed it over the table, toward Jessica.

Jessica stared at the paper but didn't reach for it. "What's it say?"

"Take it. Read it." A tear slipped from the corner of his eye and slid down his cheek.

"Jesus, are you okay, man? Do you need a tissue or something?"

"Please. Just read it." Harvey sniffed and shook the slip of paper.

> *I listened to my little girl crying from the other side of the door for some time. I held my Bible tight and did what I could to prepare myself. I told myself I could do it. I had to. I put my hand to the door and it felt cold. The muscles in my neck and shoulders ached and I realized how tense I was. I tried to open the door, but I couldn't. It was like something was warning me. Like it was asking me if I really wanted to see what was behind that door. I didn't, but I opened it anyway.*
>
> *I saw her there, at the far end of the room, laying on the floor. My baby girl. She looked odd and twisted, bent into an uncomfortable configuration, and she wasn't wearing any clothes. Her perfect skin was covered in blood. I couldn't tell where it was coming from right off, but I knew it was hers. I heard the rasp in her throat when she took her last breath. Then she was gone.*

"She was one of those fans who never doubted you, Jessica," Harvey said. "Even at your lowest, she loved you."

"Why are you telling me this, man? Why are you laying this shit on me?" Jessica stood up from the sofa and looked down at Harvey. "I'm just some dumb girl who cries about her bullshit and puts it on a record."

"Sit back down, please."

"Why, man? So you can shit on me some more? Listen, I didn't make your daughter do what she did, okay? I don't make anyone do anything." She was crying now.

Harvey reached for his Bible. He took the folded note and placed it on the table. He sat the Bible on his lap and opened the cover. The pages inside had been cut away in the middle, creating a hollowed out core. He reached into the book and removed a handgun. "Please, honey. Could you sit down for me? And let's keep it quiet."

Jessica fell into a heap on the sofa. She couldn't take her eyes off the gun. She couldn't speak.

"Do you know how many of your songs end with some kind of suicide, Hexx?"

"I—"

"It's a rhetorical question. We both know the answer. Most of them. Most of your songs end with you killing yourself over some boy. Or some girl. Or something your parents said that made you cry." Harvey closed his eyes. "Do you know what kind of message that sends? Any idea how people like my daughter process that sort of thing?"

Jessica began a hushed prayer, speaking rapidly.

"You think God hears you? Hmm? Do you think a tongue that spits hellfire can raise a voice to be heard in Heaven?"

Jessica's prayer broke and dissolved into sobs and gasps for air.

"The book of James is fairly compact. It only contains five chapters and covers roughly three pages. The author didn't even consider himself important enough to claim an identity beyond 'James, a servant of God and of the Lord Jesus Christ.' Still, written in those few pages is one of the greatest lessons I ever learned, Jessica. Would you like to hear it?"

She looked up at Harvey, her lip quivering. She nodded her head.

"James says in chapter three: *The tongue is a small member, yet it boasts of great things. How great a forest is set ablaze by such a small fire! And the tongue is a fire, a world of unrighteousness. The tongue is set among our members, staining the whole body, setting on fire the entire course of life, and set on fire by hell. For every kind of beast and bird, of reptile and sea creature can be tamed and has been tamed by mankind, but no human being can tame the tongue. It is a restless evil, full of deadly poison.*"

"Okay . . . " Jessica managed.

"Your tongue sets lives on fire. Every word you put out into the world is loaded with consequences. Can you see that?"

"Yes?"

"No. I don't think you can. Not yet. But I'll show you." Harvey's thumb brushed over the textured grip of the pistol.

"Please don't hurt me," Jessica said.

"I'm not here to hurt you, darlin'." Harvey pulled back the hammer until he heard it click. The sound was amplified by the tension that hung between them.

Tears broke and streamed down Harvey's face. It pained Jessica to see, and she wanted to take up her towel and wipe away that sadness, but she couldn't move. She could only watch. Harvey rested his chin on the barrel. He swallowed hard.

"Your words have power. I need you to know that. Your words took my daughter away from me. Our family home became a crime scene and my wife couldn't see it as anything else after that, no matter how hard I worked to erase what had happened. She eventually left, and I couldn't blame her. My words weren't powerful enough to make her stay."

The door opened. Ben sniffed as he walked into the room, slapping a small stack of bills against the palm of his hand. "Payout from the door tonight was—"

"Ben. I need you to do me a favor, son." Harvey pointed the gun at him but kept his eye on Jessica. "I need you to go to the bar and I need you to call the police. Tell them to come right away. Tell them there's a man with a gun and nothing left to lose. Can you do that?"

Ben didn't speak a word. He backed out of the room and pulled the door closed.

"I don't want you to hurt anybody, Harv. Please. We'll get rid of the gun and I'll tell the cops Ben was being crazy. He's so fucked up on coke right now, they won't believe anything he says. Please, Harv."

"Shhh. Watch." Harvey pointed the gun toward the ceiling and took a deep breath.

"Harvey, no!" Jessica closed her eyes.

"Open your eyes, sweetheart. Please. I need you to watch this. I need you to understand what words can do. What fire can do. Please don't let this all be for nothing, huh?" Harvey let his mouth hang open with the last word. He slid the barrel into his mouth, scraping his teeth. Jessica watched.

The note was still folded on the table, but the smooth white paper was now dotted in red. Jessica reached across the table and picked it up. She unfolded it carefully and read what Harvey had written.

Ben shook as he approached the green room. His breathing was heavy and his vision was fading white and he thought he might pass out soon. He rested his head on the door and closed his eyes. He could hear Jessica inside.

He listened to the girl crying from the other side of the door for some time.

MASTER OF BEYOND

Glenn Rolfe

THURSDAY 2:55 AM

THE SIGHT OF the Ouija board spilled a trail of spiders down Jillian's spine. She wanted to tell Sean to put it back, to forget about this, but Cindy and Coop looked so damned excited, she kept her thoughts to herself.

"Yes," Coop said. "Let's talk to Satan!"

"Our luck we'll just get Jeff," Sean replied as he pulled out the board and planchette.

"Who?" Cindy asked.

"Our first maintenance guy. He was a grouchy old bastard," Coop told her.

"Cindy," Jillian said. "How could you forget? Remember, he used to tell you to call him Thunderlips?"

Cindy and Sean cracked up. Jillian used the light moment to scooch closer to Coop. He smelled amazing.

Don't get any ideas, she reminded herself. Cooper Murray was pure, unadulterated trouble. She'd already made the mistake of making out with him on New Year's Eve. Still, she hated messing with occult crap.

Even if it was supposed to be a toy. It felt blasphemous, not fun.

Sean set four black candles around the room: one on top of his record player to the right, one on the filing cabinet on the left side of the room, and two on the front corners of his desk. He shut off the lights and rejoined them around the board.

"Jill," Sean said. "I know how hot you are for Coop, but we need to stay in our places. Move back to your corner."

Her face flooded with warmth as she did as Sean said.

"It's okay, Jill," Coop said. "I'll be right here." He reached over and gave her hand a squeeze.

Sean designated himself the medium. No one argued.

Things were going fine until Jillian, her fingers fluttering above the planchette, felt something cold wrap around her fingers and flutter up her arms.

"Oh," she whimpered, pulling her hand back.

"What is it?" Cindy asked.

"Come on, Jill," Sean whined. "Would you put your hands back on. We were just getting it going."

"No, no I don't want to do this anymore."

She climbed to her feet and hurried out the door. As she stepped into the hall outside Sean and Coop's office, the lighting fixture above her head began to flicker and sway, casting amorphous shadows across the walls. Looking up, she nearly tripped at the top of the stairs. Her hand landed on the red fire alarm. She worried she'd set it off, but then, looking at its rough edges and chipped paint, she wondered if it even worked.

She hurried downstairs. The closed-up bar was lit only by the exit sign near the front door. Her nerves on edge, Jillian grabbed a bottle of vodka from behind the bar, took two big swigs, and pulled her keys from her purse. She paused at the door, listening for their laughter upstairs, but it was silent. Somehow that seemed worse.

She headed out into the night and went straight home.

"Jill," Coop said. "have you seen Sean this morning?"

"No, but I think I heard him moving around in his office. I figured he had some two-bit floozy in there. I've had enough of opening doors to half-naked women who have no class and even less self-respect."

Coop leaned on her desk. "God, I love you. When are we gonna go to bed together?"

"Probably already did in your dreams last night." She winked at him and went back to her Rolodex. "Listen, get up there and see if he's okay. I have a few more calls to make this morning to secure Bad Obsession—"

"Whoa, secure? I thought we already had them?"

"Don't freak on me. Jesus, they'll be here. The Sheraton on Bellevue had to close down due to that accident. I'm sure you heard about it, right?" She waited, but Coop seemed oblivious. "Well, there was a city bus. Driver had a stroke, crashed the bus into the lobby of the hotel and set the damn place on fire."

"Oh shit," he said.

"Yeah, oh shit. I've been hustling to find new accommodations pretty much since I got word of the closure, thank you very much. There's just some last minute minutiae that I need to nail down before they arrive tomorrow."

Coop stood and sighed. "Well, shit. Don't scare me like that, huh?"

He walked around the desk and leaned toward her cheek.

"Don't even think about it, Coop. Not after last time."

He straightened up and smirked. "Look, I thought we were past that?

"Hmm . . . "

He raised his hands in surrender. "Okay, okay, peace, all right? By the way, you missed out last night."

She didn't want to hear about that damned Ouija board. The creepiness stuck to her last night and followed her into her dreams.

"That's okay, Coop. I don't need a recap. I'm sure you guys had a good laugh at me running off like that."

"We made contact."

The words froze her veins.

Coop got a kick out of Jillian's nervousness over the board. Hell, he'd been a little creeped out himself when Eiddam said, "Hello." At first, he was certain it was Sean, but when the candle flames wavered and then suddenly blew out, they all shrieked before cracking up in the dark.

It was black at the top of the stairs. When the light bulb crunched under his boots, he laughed. Maybe it was old Jeff's spirit in here last night. Breaking shit, so they'd still need him.

When Coop opened the door to find his partner sitting in his chair, hands folded on the desk, staring straight ahead with glowing white eyes, he nearly stumbled back into the hall. Unfortunately, his body moved into the room involuntarily, and the door slammed shut behind him.

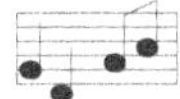

Jillian hated that she still wanted to be with Cooper, but she'd be damned if she'd make the same mistake twice. It's why she was so good at her job—she needed to focus on work to *not* think about Coop. His dastardly good looks and charm made him the quintessential "heartbreaker." Pat Benatar had definitely made his acquaintance at some point.

After locking down the Bad Obsession contracts, getting the hotel arrangements set for the band, crew, and that of the MTV crew, Jillian called the office to tell the boys the good news.

"Just thought I'd let you guys know we're all good for tomorrow." She waited. "What? No applause? No, 'Hell yes?'"

They remained silent. She hated when they put her on speaker.

"Hello?'

"That's perfect," Sean said. "Could you come up here for a minute? We have something we'd like to discuss with you."

He sounded strange. His voice . . . like he was trying on an accent she couldn't place.

"Ah, actually I'm on lunch now. I'll check in when I get back. Are you okay, Sean?"

"Yes, that will be fine."

"Um, okay," she said. "See you boys in an hour."

She didn't wait for a response.

At the bar, she couldn't shake the feeling that something was wrong with Sean. When Cindy arrived, she decided to get her thoughts on the matter.

"Am I crazy?"

Cindy tossed back her margarita, put her glass down, and said, "Well, sounds like Sean's hungover. What's new? Maybe he's nervous about tomorrow. I know I would be."

"Yeah, you're probably right, but he . . . he just sounded like someone else."

"What about Coop?"

"He didn't say anything."

"Coop? Silent? That's a first."

"I know," she said. She thanked the tall red headed waitress for her beer and took a sip.

Twisted Sister played from the speakers as Jillian fell silent.

"Coop mentioned that you guys met Egor or something last night," Jillian said.

Cindy bit her lip, her gaze cast down at the cross pendant on her necklace.

"What? Was it really that freaky?"

"I . . . " Cindy started. "No . . . it was just Sean and Coop fucking around. You're lucky you left. They had a blast at my expense, dumb shits."

"Assholes," Jillian said.

"Well, hey, if you still feel weird about Sean and Coop just head home. You said you secured everything for tomorrow's show, right?"

"Yeah."

"Well, then fuck it. They fuck off all day and night, screwing whoever they want, snorting whatever they want. You're clean as a whistle and do most of the damn work here. The Shantyman is packed again because of you. You do your job and do it fucking well. See what's up, and call it an early day, so we can have a late night." Cindy smiled.

"I think I will." Jillian held her drink up. "Cheers!"

"That's the fucking spirit."

They clanged their glasses.

"To tomorrow," Jillian said.

"To rock n' roll and the future success of The Shantyman . . . thanks to you!"

"Sorry, friend, but some of us just aren't cut out for this kind of power," the demon in possession of Sean Reilly spoke.

"Sean, what's wrong with you? Your eyes . . . "

Coop's spine stiffened as his feet left the ground. His broad shoulders drew back, pulled by an unseen force, stretching his skin, muscle, and tendons to the point of breaking. He screamed.

"What is this?"

"You are not necessary," the demon known as Eiddam said.

The white light from his eyes blazed within the office causing the blind and pathetic fool before him to cry out.

Eiddam watched with pleasure. The human's arms ripped free of his body and thumped to the floor. Obscene and intoxicating, Eiddam sucked in the blood, pain, and torment—an airborne pathogen. Perfection.

The human's wails reached their crescendo and then ceased; the sound of ruined flesh hitting the floor in a torrent of wet thuds was a symphonic masterpiece.

When the woman, this . . . Jillian, returned, she would accept his gift or suffer the same consequence.

In the rooms below, they gathered, ingesting spirits and carrying on, quenching appetites that would make Dionysus proud, but Eiddam would not reveal himself tonight.

The show was to be the Master's *coup de grâce.*

Earth would meet its future. Blood would fill the streets, and the Master's army would relish humanity's defeat.

When the girl never bothered to come back, Eiddam sealed the door and slumbered. He would need the rest for tomorrow's grand event.

FRIDAY

Jillian arrived at The Shantyman just before eleven in the morning. Luckily, she'd stuck to the beer last night. Her hangover was minimal. As expected, Sean and Coop were nowhere to be found, but she was too preoccupied directing various lighting guys and managers to worry about either of them. Cindy was right. She was the reason the club functioned at a level of professionalism not matched by any of its local competition. And as much as Sean and Coop liked to screw around, they always came through when it mattered most. They'd be here. Until then, she would be in charge.

Bad Obsession arrived promptly at five. The MTV crew, shortly after.

Jillian had everyone set up and ready to roll by 6:30 pm. Headbanger's Ball would shoot the band's act and cut and clip the performance for tomorrows broadcast as they saw fit.

The line of people waiting to get in wrapped around the block. This was the biggest night in The Shantyman's history.

Where the fuck are they?

"There you are," Cindy said, pushing past a group of big-haired blonde dudes that eye-fucked her as she stepped past. "Excuse me, fellas." She smiled and ignored their come-ons.

"Got a place we can have a smoke and actually fucking hear each other?" Cindy asked.

"My office, come on," Jillian said. "Mark?" She yelled to Mark Remme, one of their assistant managers and lead light engineer.

"Yeah?"

"I'm taking five before we get this party started. I'll be in my office if you need me, 'kay?"

"Sure thing, Jill. Have you seen or heard from Sean or Coop yet?"

"No, but they'll be here. Did you try upstairs?"

"Yeah, the door's been locked all day. I tried my key and it didn't work. They must have changed out the lock." A hot little brunette in a leather mini skirt and leopard-print halter top handed Mark a beer. He smirked, accepting the pint, looked back to Jill and shrugged.

Jillian winked and waved as she grabbed Cindy's hand and led her through the growing throng to her back office, "Dancing on Glass" followed them down. "Oh my God!" Cindy squealed. "New Crüe!"

She was the biggest slut for the boys in Mötley. She claimed to have fucked bassist Nikki Sixx while doing lines with the band last Christmas at some recording studio in Canoga Park.

"This is my record!" Cindy said, shaking her ass all way down the hall and into Jillian's office. "Care if I do a couple lines?" she asked, reaching for her purse.

Jillian pulled out a pack of Camel Lights and handed one to her. Cindy took the cigarette, set it on the desk and went for the blow again.

"Cindy, come on," Jillian said, lighting her smoke and then Cindy's. "I need you for a few minutes."

"Oh, all right," she said. "The night is young." She smiled and took a puff. "So, where the fuck are Sean and Coop?"

"I told you, they've been M.I.A. all day. I've been too busy making all this happen to chase them down." Jillian sat behind her desk, and put her Minnie Mouse ashtray where they could both use it. Flicking the ash, she continued. "I called upstairs twice, called them each at home at least five times apiece. Nothing."

"Odd. Where do you think they are?"

She was about to answer when the phone rang, startling them both.

"Hello?"

"I missed you last night."

She set her cigarette in the ashtray and covered the phone with her hand. "It's Sean," she whispered.

"I was tired. I had an early start today, so I went home."

"Come to my office."

She hated the sound of his voice. What the hell was up with that accent?

"Sean, is Coop up there with you?"

"In a manner of speaking," he said.

"The show starts in—" she looked at her watch. "Thirty minutes. You guys might want to come down—"

"I'm afraid I cannot. I'm not feeling quite myself. You'll be in charge tonight, but I'll need to see you first."

"Ah, yeah, okay. I'll . . . be right up."

"Splendid."

He hung up.

"What?" Cindy said.

"I don't fucking know." She lit another cigarette. "He's being really fucking weird. He said he doesn't feel well or some shit. Told me I'm in charge tonight. And Coop is up there, too, I guess."

"Whoa, you think it's like a test?"

"I kind of thought so, for a minute, but something feels off." She stood. "He wants to see me before the show starts. You're coming with me."

"Now, you're weirding me out," Cindy said.

Jillian led the way up the stairs. It was dark as hell. She tried flicking the switch, but it did nothing. As they got closer to the top step, she noticed the broken light fixture.

"What is it?" Cindy said.

"The light fixture. It's busted out. That's why it's so fucking dark up here."

"I don't like this," Cindy said, now clasping Jillian's hand.

Something crunched beneath her sneakers as she crossed beneath the broken light. "Found it," she said, kicking the broken bulb and pieces of the old fixture to the side.

She stopped outside Sean's office and knocked.

There was no answer.

"Come on," she said.

"He told you to come up. Just open it," Cindy said.

She turned the knob, and gently shoved the door. When it opened, Sean was sitting behind his desk, surrounded by candles. She flicked the light switch on the wall just inside the door, but the darkness remained.

"I've been waiting for you," Sean said.

Again, with that fucked-up accent.

"*You've* been waiting for *me*?" Now, she was pissed. She walked straight to his desk. "Sean, do you realize what the fuck is about to happen downstairs?"

"And you brought a friend," he said.

"It's just Cindy."

"I can wait outside, really, it's no problem," Cindy said.

He folded his hands over his stomach and leaned back. "Just what I was thinking," he said.

"I'll be right here if you need me," she said before ducking outside.

"Sean, MTV is down there. We—The Shantyman—are about to be broadcast across the fucking country. I don't even know what to say?" Jillian stepped to the desk, trying to hold her tongue as she wondered what the hell he was thinking?

"Have you been up here this whole time?" she asked.

"I've been here much longer than that," he said, rising to his feet so quick it startled her.

"Wh-where is Coop?" she said, taking a step back.

The door behind her slammed shut.

She turned at the sound.

"Coop?" Sean said. "He was torn from limb to limb until there was nothing left but pulp and human waste."

Before Jillian could move, her feet were off the ground. She shrieked as her body went prone, suspended in mid-air.

"You humans make the most delicious sounds."

Hearing Jillian's keening wail through the wall of sound from the club downstairs raised every fine hair on Cindy's body. She stood outside the door, the broken bulb above left her dressed in darkness.

She knocked before placing her ear to the door. "Jill? Is everything all right?" She couldn't hear anything else over the music. She pounded on the door with the underside of her hand. "Jill? Jillian. Can you hear me?"

She tried the knob and cried out as she pulled her hand away. It was red hot and now burning brightly, illuminating the gloomy space around her in a crimson glow.

Oh shit.

She thought of the damned Ouija board. That thing that spoke to them. *Eiddam.* What had they done?

Cindy turned and ran for the stairs, taking them two at a time, nearly falling twice as she made her way to the hall and toward the stage area. She needed to find Mark.

Jillian heard the pounding on the door. She knew it was Cindy trying to get back in, but she couldn't move. Her body floated over the wide desk. The candles below slid to the four corners, the flames flared around her as Sean's papers and magazines scattered to the floor.

"What are you? What do you want?" she whimpered, her back landing upon the desk.

The thing drank her in as the dancing fire flickered in Sean's eyes. His clothes split down the center of his body, as if sliced by some unseen force, and slipped to the floor. His exposed flesh bubbled, oozing mucus. Jillian's stomach turned like curdled milk.

"I am the one called Eiddam. I serve my Master, and he has waited more than a century to return to this place."

"This place?"

"There are many points around this wretched world, places of complete evil, where the veil has been thinned by the wickedness of mankind and the monsters on the other side."

He stepped toward her, blackened nails split forth from the ends of his fingers. Swiping a tear from her cheek, he brought the salty discharge to the snake-like tongue darting from his lips.

"How wonderful," he said, sucking at the wetness. His body shuddered. "Now, I'm going to give you an opportunity your companions were not extended."

"No . . . " she whispered as he reached for her. "Please . . . no . . . I'll do whatever you want."

"Yes. You will, won't you?" Eiddam said.

He reached down, touching a nail to her flesh, applying just enough pressure to penetrate the soft tissue. She trembled at his touch, too shocked to scream.

"It is okay," he said. "You can start screaming anytime you like."

As he pressed his dagger-like nail deeper and began to carve a line from her exposed navel to the middle of her chest, Jillian did just that.

Mark stood talking with a pissed-off-looking weasel in a Dodgers ball cap.

"Mark, Mark," Cindy shouted, falling into him.

"Jesus, Cindy," he said, holding her up. "What the hell's the matter with you?"

"Excuse me, Miss," the weasel said.

"Mark, it's Jill," she said

"Mr. Remme," the weasel pleaded. "We must get this start—"

"Jillian? Where is she?"

"Up in Sean's office, but the door's locked, they won't open it, and when I grabbed the door knob . . . ." She raised her scalded hand up to him.

"Come on," he shoved past the weasel, leaving the douchebag yelling in the background.

Finished, Eiddam freed her. Jillian slid from the desk to the floor. Her thoughts swirled, her vision distorted as a fog of oblivion fell over her.

The dreadful voice lanced her fading consciousness.

"*You* will open the doorway for the Master," Eiddam said.

Jillian fought to keep from passing out. The flames from the candles on the desk burned higher and higher. So high they should be licking the ceiling. A ceiling she could no longer see. She craned her neck toward the door. It, too, was gone. A smoky, fluttering blackness stretched from wall to wall.

Oh God, how am I supposed to get out?

"This building is older than you know. It has been the gateway for many monstrosities from many realms." He brought a hand to his chest, dug his talons in, and scraped off a large patch of dissolving skin, dropping it to the floor. The tiled floor below sizzling with each plop. "This place has always attracted the vulgar, the downtrodden, those with no place else to fit in, a place for all to give into their darker cravings. You shouldn't be all that surprised. It was you and your friends that invited us."

Invited? Us? Jillian couldn't think straight. She felt inebriated.

"You don't even realize the power the flesh has over you."

Jillian shook her head from side to side, the feeling of violation rising again like bile.

"But you see how weak it is? Yes? This—" he peeled off an area of tissue from his throat and threw it at her feet.

She scurried back, whimpering as he continued his grotesque exhibition and his vile sermon.

"This is *nothing*. This—" he pulled one of Sean's ears free "—is disposable."

She ducked as he flung it past her head, droplets of

blood splashing across her left eye and the bridge of her nose.

"What do you want from me," she screamed.

"You are an innocent among the sinners. You will be the Master's sacrifice."

His eyes began to shine a hypnotic white light. Jillian felt his magnetic pull.

"God, please."

"Oh, my love. *He* has no place here, but you, you will be adored forever."

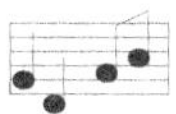

Beneath them, Cindy heard the weasel announcing Bad Obsession to the stage. The gathering throng of rockers exploded. It was the loudest crowd she'd ever heard at The Shantyman. She stood in the black hallway with Mark as they approached the office door. The knob no longer shined red, but Cindy couldn't bring herself to touch it. She found it hard to breathe up here. Like the air was a thick fog, heavy and wet.

"The door knob is ice cold," Mark said.

The thick air swirled around her. Cindy tilted, dizzy and nauseous. She stumbled off to the left.

"Cindy, are you all right?"

Mark sounded miles away rather than next to her. The room teetered. "M-Mark?"

"Cindy? Where are you? I can't see a goddamn thing."

The urge to get everyone out of the club suddenly seemed essential. "P-pull . . . " she coughed. Something thick and oily wrapped around her throat and slithered up to her lip. "Pull the fire . . . "

"What?"

"Pull the fire alarm!" she said, the thing around her throat began closing tight.

"But there's no fire?" The words slurred as they came from his mouth.

"Just do it," She managed to squeak out.

"Where the hell is it?" he asked.

"On the wall . . . "

"Got it!" Mark said. "You sure you want me to do this?"

"Arrrgghhh . . . y-y-yessss . . . "

Jillian watched in horror as the gash down her front—courtesy of the demon—began to pulse, but it did not bleed. How or why didn't matter. The entire night was beyond reason. Satisfied that her insides wouldn't spill out, she gritted her teeth and rose to her feet. Blood-spattered and shamed, she let the rage surge through her.

"Listen to them. How they worship. He will be here . . . " Eiddam, horns protruding from his skull, green, viscous sludge moving over the bones and muscle of what remained of Sean's body. He stretched his arms out in a Jesus Christ pose.

Jillian clutched at her faith and prayed to God that he would empower her just this once.

Guitars exploded below them. Rhythmic drums brought forth the primal and aggressive intuition within the many, the weak, the supplicant . . .

"Yes," Eiddam moaned. "The Master is coming . . . "

A deafening sound bleated out from overhead. The loud blast stunned Jillian into submission. Someone had pulled the fire alarm, but why weren't the sprinklers working?

The band below fell silent. The crowd went from screams of ecstasy to cries of panic.

It was Eiddam who now bellowed in rage.

Jillian stood, fists clenched at her side and ready to unleash her own brand of hell.

She bent before the desk, clutching the cheap metal and flimsy wood in her grasp, and flipped it over. The torch-like flames shot out and set everything ablaze, invoices, magazines, the small shag rug in front of the desk. All of it caught fire. Eiddam raised his arms over his head and wailed as the flames engulfed him.

All around them, the blackness that had started to devour the room dissipated, returning the four walls and ceiling of The Shantyman as Jillian knew them.

Eiddam fell to the floor, crawling, mewling, and reaching out toward her.

The office door flew open. Mark and Cindy stood, hands before their faces, as a viscous black cloud swirled around them before bursting in a blinding light that knocked them all to the floor.

Jillian heard Eiddam roar one final time as she was swallowed by the pain.

Eiddam felt his Master's rage as he continued to burn.

"No . . . please."

BROTHER, YOU HAVE FAILED ME FOR THE LAST TIME.

Eiddam's bubbling flesh and charred body spilled ichor as it was stretched by the invisible beings. He groveled, but to no avail. As the overhead sprinklers finally began to discharge, Eiddam, or what remained of him, dissolved into smoke.

Jillian awoke in the back of an ambulance. Mark and Cindy next to each other on one side, a paramedic on the other. She tried to smile but couldn't. She lay wounded, broken, confused . . . but alive.

MONDAY

Three days later, Jillian met Mark and Cindy at the club's front door. Mark had phoned her earlier to let her know the damage to The Shantyman was minimal, most of it confined to the upstairs office. She stepped from her car and took Cindy's hand.

"You look good," Cindy said.

"I'm feeling better, considering."

"It's cool that Sean and Coop left the club to you," Mark said. "When do we—"

"Never," she said. "I want nothing to do with this place."

"Woo," Mark said. "Thank God. I was hoping you'd say that. Frankly, even being this close again makes my skin crawl."

She felt it, too. Cindy nodded along. Jillian walked to the door. The posters for the momentous MTV Headbanger's Ball gig with Bad Obsession still plastered the entry way and the inside of the door. She pulled the keys out, gave them a once over, and then slipped them back in her purse.

"Fuck this place," she said. "Let someone else have it."

"Come on," Cindy said. "Let's go grab a drink or two or three."

"Nah, I think I'm gonna drive out to my mom's. Why don't you two go ahead."

She noticed the sparkle in Mark's eyes as the two looked at one another.

"Are you sure?" Cindy said.

"I'm sure. Go."

Cindy and Mark each gave her a hug.

"Call me, tonight, tomorrow, whenever," Cindy said. "I'm here if you need me for anything."

"Thanks. I will."

She watched them walk side-by-side. After a few seconds, Cindy grabbed Mark's hand. Maybe something decent came out of this after all.

She climbed into her car and headed for the freeway.

She thought of the horrible dream she'd had last night—the demons, the black fog, a throne made of human bones, and that vulgar imitation of Sean's voice whispering in her ear.

She took the onramp and fought her way into traffic. She was done with the Bay Area. She'd talked to a cousin in Riverside and had agreed to move into her recently vacated room. It was a nice complex with a fitness center, pool, and a hot tub. Hell could follow her, but it would have to catch her.

DARK STAGE

Matt Hayward

LEATHER-CLAD ROCKERS MILLED about the open floor of the Shantyman with their voices raised to be heard above the juke. Sweat, smoke and aftershave collected in an invisible cloud, hot-boxing the venue for another night of sex and sin. In the morning, recollection of those smells would send a hot jet of puke into the bowl of many unfortunate drinkers, but for now, tomorrow stayed at arm's length. The night had just begun.

At the bar, Fred involuntarily spat beer as his bones burned like hot coals. He slammed his glass to the countertop and clutched his fist with a wince. Only Tuesday night, and already he'd experienced several flairs. Arthritis at forty-three. Man, sometimes life dealt a stinker.

Paul paused with a handful of empty glasses behind the bar and arched a bushy brow. "Another one?"

"Make it a whiskey."

"I meant your hands, man. Bad?"

Fred flexed his fists and lay them out on the countertop, ignoring the layer of sticky film. His digits visibly shook. Goddamn it.

Paul sighed and grabbed a bottle of Jack, untwisted

the top. "Look, I'll make it a double and I'll make it free. Ain't gonna lie, this place won't be the same without you, man. You were the best sound guy I ever knew."

Fred gave a tight-lipped smile and watched the bartender pour, jealous of the smooth motion. He envied the majority of the population and their pain-free joints. "Much obliged, buddy."

Paul grunted and returned the bottle beside the others, most half empty even though they'd only restocked Sunday. Then he shouted for Justine to handle the clamor of drinkers who'd swarmed like the walking dead and stepped out from behind the bar. He pulled up a stool next to Fred, snorted. "Bossman due down soon?"

Fred eyed his whiskey, hands folded together while waiting for the tremors to pass. Pain thumped beneath his skin in rhythm to the music of the room's speakers. "He gets in at ten. Just enough time for me to catch the show tonight. Then I do what I got to do."

"He's not going to be happy about losing you, Fred. There's a reason he bought you out from the Fillmore. You know how to work a sound desk better than any man in all of San Fran."

"Don't I know it, babe." Fred reached for his whiskey and quickly scooped it to his lips before spilling too much. He gulped, returning the glass to the table with a hiss. The chore hurt more than he cared to admit. Hot liquor burned his chest and he relished the waxy air in his throat.

Paul shook his head. "Man, it's gotten bad, huh? Jesus."

"Looks like benefits for me until I find a job that

doesn't involve my hands."

For a moment the thought twisted Fred's guts and he eyed the wall of signed memorabilia behind the bar to avoid overthinking. His future looked as grim as most the Shantyman's pint glasses—but he had the choice to drink from one or not. A stupid thought. As teeth grinding as his hands could be, pain wasn't going to stop him living. Or so he told himself.

A framed and signed Bile Lords t-shirt he'd received from the band caught his eye and the memory of the show lifted his lips into a grin. That had been a night of true rock n' roll.

Paul noticed his line of sight. "That'd been a *real* one, eh? True music, man. Heals the heart."

"If only it could heal my damn body."

Paul snorted a laugh. Then Justine's yelling made him cringe. "Shit, man. I gotta get back. Look, enjoy the show tonight, all right? I'll give you a ride home after you talk with the Bossman. Drinks on me. Shame your last show is an open mic, but what can you do."

"What?" Fred squinted to the chalked sign above the bar. *Tuesday Night: Open Mic*. "Oh, goddamn it."

Open mics at the Shantyman carried about the same merit as a fart joke. Half-baked acts—typically formed just weeks before—came onstage and tried their damnedest to rouse a laugh in what'd become Shantyman tradition. Occasionally a try-hard band attempted an acoustic set in the hopes of appearing "high class," but lately the San Francisco music scene plopped out nothing but overweight Bon Jovi wannabes bashing out ballads to their front-row girlfriends. To Fred, a lobotomy held more appeal.

With a swivel of his stool, he caught a glimpse of

the sound console through the sea of drunks. The equipment had become an extension of his very being over the past five years, each fader and knob as familiar as a curve or limb of a lover. The idea of a new sound man getting his grubby fucking fingers all over the controls boiled his blood. Past the sound desk, the stage sat in darkness. The reputation of the open mic dictated no PA and no lighting. The less the patrons heard the blasted cat-wailing of bedroom rehearsed and tone-deaf Twisted Sisters, the better. 1992 had so far promised a bright future from the glitzy MTV butt-rock era, but Fred only hoped the direction maintained course and didn't nose-dive into dry cement.

Someone tapped his shoulder. He turned and came face to face with a ghoul.

The man stood over six feet tall, a long black coat cloaking his anemic frame. Greasy, grey-peppered hair strung across his face alongside a thick beard. The scent of tobacco smoke drifted from his body, but his eyes, nestled into dark pockets, burned with intent.

"Can I help you?"

The man nodded once, slowly. "Open mic?"

Fred now noticed the battered case alongside the stranger's leg. Worn leather like that spoke of many traveled highways and cities. Perhaps even continents.

"I used to run the desk," Fred said, "But tonight's a free-for-all. Go up now, if you like."

Shit, he wanted to add, *by the looks of things, you're the only one who showed, anyway.*

The stranger didn't blink, and his eyes burned a hole through Fred. "A man who throws caution to rules."

Fred expected a question but the statement hung

in the air and an awkward silence descended.

"You're not a glam act, clearly," Fred observed, breaking the tension. He eyed the stranger up and down. "And I'm interested in what you've got. Come on, I'll listen to you play."

The stranger nodded with eyes closed, his jaw clasped. His alabaster skin hinted at an illness, and by his slow, calculated movements, Fred needed to ask, "Are you okay?"

"I will be," the stranger said. "Come and listen to me play."

With a wince, Fred hopped from the stool as a lick of pain ignited in his knees and ankles. He rubbed his legs before reaching for his drink and swigging the last of it. He saluted Paul before leading the stranger through the boozy maze of the Shantyman's open floor. The half-drunk crowd remained stationary and Fred elbowed his way through, each stumble and collision setting his teeth on edge with agony. The stranger followed his path like Moses through the parted sea.

Fred peeled from the audience and made his way to the dim stage, catching his breath by the coolers. Cold air breathed down from an overhead vent, installed to keep musical acts comfortable. Fred usually complained about the waste of energy that the constantly running coolers consumed but right now he was grateful. A second later, the stranger exited the crowd and crossed to his side.

"There's another act," the stranger said. He cocked his head to the right, where by the sound desk, a Lycra-wearing duo basked in the attention of a gaggle of awe-struck rockers. The chicks were undeniably beautiful, their hair-sprayed styles sexy yet dangerous, with leather jackets leaving a sliver of toned stomach visible above hip-cinched pants. Stiletto heels put them both at an inch or two taller than the lust numbed gatherers. None of them paid Fred or the stranger any attention.

Fred nodded. “You know, even if they didn’t play music, if they simply went venue to a venue with guitar cases, they’d gather a better following than most starving bands these days. And fuck it, more power to ‘em, they know how to catch attention.”

The stranger didn’t respond and instead lay his guitar case on the floor. He popped the locks to reveal a time beaten Gibson. Grabbing its neck, he lifted the instrument to his side and kicked the empty case to the stage. “Pay them no mind. I want you to hear me play.”

That was all. A shiver crawled along Fred’s skin. Something about the stranger—his demeanor, his words, his look—just felt . . . odd. Yet, like before, Fred *did* want to hear him play. A musician who attracted attention with presence alone, no frills, glitz or peacocking, was a musician Fred itched to hear. He’d grown weary of the recycled synth-fused 80’s soundtrack and craved something raw. Something new. Something the stranger might offer.

Another wave of pain bloomed in his wrists and Fred fought the urge to groan. He motioned to the stage with a shaking finger as the agony bit, then hobbled to a nearby stool. His bones felt like brittle glass and he silently cursed an impartial god before gathering his nerves. “Stage is all yours, man. Knock ‘em dead.”

The stranger climbed aboard the plywood floor,

clenched his jaw, and sat. Two chest-high stools sat to the side of the stage for acoustic acts, but the stranger paid them no notice, opting instead for his own rump. In the darkness and the coolers, his hair blew around his shadowed face. With one creeping hand, he formed a chord, waited a beat, and then closed his eyes. From where Fred sat, he saw the stranger's lids flutter like a man hitting REM sleep, and for a moment, he pondered the stranger's age. The man could be forty or sixty, and both seemed likely. But before Fred could come to a conclusion, the stranger began to play.

The atmospheric white noise of the Shantyman faded as if sucked through a vacuum, the silence settling like a teacher shushing a giddy classroom. Surroundings melted, the low light dimming, and within seconds, only Fred and the stranger remained. Fred craned his neck this way and that, but beyond a foot in each direction and the stage ahead, only darkness lay. A thick curtain of black concealed the world beyond the music and attention the stranger did demanded.

The man stroked his first chord, a jangling D, and Fred's skin sizzled in response. The light hair on his forearm tickled and rose. The next chord came, followed by a quick diminished lick, and brought with it the numbness of a dentist's anesthetic. Fred's breathing hitched.

The stranger swayed in place, legs folded beneath him, and then parted his lips. His head fell back. A voice like aged whiskey and boiling nails spilled forth—the voice of a road worn warrior. The sound injected the air with a tangible, soothing warmth not unlike a hot bath, and Fred gasped.

As the stranger formed words, their sound lost to the offline thump of his brain, Fred understood their message all the same. Spoken in a language only known to music, the feeling promised the kiss of a lover on a lonely night and warmth in a storm. More than that, it promised no pain, and hot tears blurred Fred's vision as, suddenly, his agony dissolved. His fingers tingled and trembled, followed by his legs, and then it all faded to nothingness like a hit of H. A sound caught Fred's ear, other than the music, and he realized he was moaning, all along. He shivered involuntarily, and the stranger looked up, caught his eye—and the music fell silent.

The sounds of the Shantyman swelled from another dimension, people populated the darkness, forming all around, and the light increased until it reached its former state. The steady *thump-thump* of the juke slipped into being, giving life to the scene. A youthful heartbeat. All around, the chaotic noise and scent of cigarettes and hops returned.

Fred breathed heavily, sweat tickling his forehead. He ran a palm past his face before blinking his vision clear. The song—*could it even be called a song?*—still worked through his system like an opiate, but fainter now, and fizzling.

Only one thought occupied his brain. Just one.

Fred Williams was pain-free. And he cried.

One of the long-legged ladies crossed the room with a case in her hand and stood before him, her hip slanted in a conscious pose. She teased a cocktail stick between her cherry lips before giving him a once over.

"You runnin' this show?"

Fred looked up, sniffled. "Lady, I don't know who's

running this show anymore."

She cocked an eyebrow. "So, we can play now?"

A cheer erupted from behind her, followed by stomping feet, clapping hands and wolf whistles. Fred watched it all through the lens of a dream, a dream which was still fading as he struggled to keep a hold. He never wanted to lose the aura of the stranger's song. With a pain-free hand, he motioned to the dark stage. "It's all yours."

Then his stomach sank. The stage stood empty. The battered guitar case on the floor had vanished. And so, too, had the stranger.

Fred pushed himself from the stool and frantically scanned the room, spotting the tail of a long black cloak slip into the audience. The woman went to ask another question, but Fred shook his head and jogged after the stranger, barging into the wall of people whose eyes were glued to the glitzy duo about to perform. A large man elbowed him aside and Fred, surprisingly, laughed. No pain. He continued to squeeze his way through the organic sea and popped free near the bar. Looking to the left, he spotted the black-coated man stalk toward the exit. Fred ran.

"Hey!"

He placed a hand on the stranger's shoulder and spun him. He gasped.

A fresh-faced young man grinned at him, his skin plump and youthful. Jet black hair reached to his shoulders, which he flicked out of his face. Those eyes, brilliant blue and full of life, were all too familiar.

"How?" He asked.

The stranger only nodded. "Places to be, my friend. People to meet. I hope you enjoyed the show."

Then he turned and left. Fred stood in shock as the exit doors swung on their hinges, his heart thumping and his mind reeling. The faint sound of the glamorous duo drifting from the stage—a bad Guns N' Roses knock-off—hardly registered. Someone tapped his shoulder.

Thomas Whitman, the Shantyman manager, smiled. Then his eyebrows came together in a sharp V. "Everything all right, Fred?"

Fred shivered, struggling to keep his brain on track. The walls of the building suddenly felt too close, too confining. He needed space.

"Come, Fred. Come." Thomas led him to a free stool by the bar and Fred sat like an obedient dog. Nothing seemed possible, solid or real. Once more, he couldn't get over the rosy-cheeked man before him, who'd, up until recently, looked as gaunt as the stranger after a long battle with cancer.

Thomas Whitman looked him in the eye. "Can I get you water? You look like you've seen a ghost."

Fred licked his lips, dry and cracked. "Yes, please. Water."

Thomas motioned to Paul and an ice-choked glass slid across the counter. Fred drank greedily.

Thomas's narrowed eyes followed the glass as Fred placed it back to the bar.

"Now, then. Better?"

Fred nodded. "Better."

A banshee scream erupted from the audience as the duo onstage finished their first number, something about sex and sports cars. Then their next song began, sounding the very same, and Thomas clicked his fingers. "Earth to Fred, you there?"

"Huh? Yeah, sorry, Tom. I'm just . . . "

Just what? Still processing a song that cured your pain? Getting over the fact you just came into contact with someone who was most definitely not *human?*

Thomas grinned, his chubby cheeks lifting. "We're not here to talk about your retirement from the world of music, are we, Fred?"

A ball of ice hit Fred's stomach. "You know?"

"Of course, I know. I only hoped he'd come. Strange fellow, huh? Curious . . . " Thomas laced his fingers together. "Caught him in Seattle two months back at another open mic. Again in Portland a week later. Always traveling, always alone. Always with a song to sing. No one paid him any attention apart from those who knew . . . Knew he had that certain *something*. The open mic here was a . . . a bowl of milk for the cat. Get me? I gave him my card and told him about our venue. Prayed he'd show for you. This place has a long history of odd happenings, you know." He looked about the room, royalty surveying his kingdom. "These walls have seen more cures and curses than any place. And I wouldn't miss a day for the world. Your hands, pain free?"

"As good as in my twenties, Tom. I can't . . . I can't believe it. I can't believe any of this."

Thomas chuckled, his beach ball stomach jiggling. He gave Fred's shoulder a squeeze. "You're here for the long haul, boy. As are most of us. Like it or not."

Fred decided he did like it, even if he didn't understand it. He flexed his fingers and felt no pain whatsoever. The absurdity still failed to register. With a nervous chuckle, he reached for his water and took the glass to his lips. Then he paused.

The ice, half-melted, misted on the glass and trickled across his fingers. And Fred felt . . . *nothing*.

"Tom, I can't feel the cold . . . "

Thomas gave a knowing nod. "It's wonderful isn't it? The stranger took away my pain, too. No chemo for me, no needles or heartache. It's wonderful."

"It's not wonderful." Fred squeezed his thigh, digging his fingers deep into the flesh past his jeans. "Nothing. *I feel nothing*."

"No pain, kid. No more."

"No pain?" Fred laughed without humor. "No pain, no heat, no cold, no nothing, Tom! I feel *nothing*!"

"And you owe it all to this place." Thomas stood and looked to his audience, his people, his building. Then he nodded to the door by the stage where stairs led to his second-floor office. "I've got much to do," he said. "But I'm glad you're not going anywhere. Happy to have this all ironed out. If I could feel happy . . . " He laughed then, the action never touching his eyes. "Sit a spell and then get some sleep. I'll see you back in work tomorrow. And the day after that, and the day after that. Hell, have a drink on me. Relax . . . Enjoy the show."

OPEN MIC NIGHT

Kelli Owen

"THE FIRST TIME I saw Marla, she had just gotten off the bus from Missouri—the empty bottle of whiskey in her hand still coated in strychnine." Harry's eyes glazed over. He was remembering as he spoke, the details clear in his otherwise cataract vision.

"I didn't connect the dots for *years*, but I never forgot the image of this woman with an empty bottle and a bus ticket stub. She put the bottle on the bar and asked for a Gin Rickey. I hollered for the bartender and took the bottle away, throwing it in the trashcan out back—six states away from where it needed to be found. Where it would have answered questions. Where it could have stopped countless deaths. Maybe." He paused for a breath before exhaling his verdict. "Probably not."

I watched him swim in his memories, composing whatever it was he needed to tell me into something that would make sense to both of us. I waited for his focus to come back to the present. He blinked several times, his dry eyes making the tiniest little clicking sounds.

"And you don't want me to write this down?"

He shook his head, age and frailty making it look more like a tremor than an answer. "This doesn't need to be reported, just repeated. And stopped if you're up to it." His eyes cleared and he stared at me.

"It was 1938. The new labor law had passed in June, but we were still ignoring it at The Shantyman. Barely twelve years old, I was cheap child labor—and my momma depended on my pitiful under-the-table pay—so I wasn't looking to get anyone reported or fined. I did the dishes, scrubbed the bathrooms, and dealt with the vomit and piss when the drinks flowed into mouths that should have long before closed and gone home. I was young when she came in that first time. When she left the bus ticket stub with the coins for her drink, I stuck it in my pocket and kept it for years. I don't have any idea why. I guess I was fascinated with this woman who came across the whole country with nothing but an empty bottle of whiskey.

"I don't remember if she sang or just watched the open mic acts that first night. I didn't know yet to pay attention. But you can bet I remembered her clear as day when she came back thirty years later—looking exactly like she did in '38. I was bartending then, and between that and going off to Korea and back, I had seen a *lot of people* in my time. And I'd forgotten just about as many as I'd seen. But I remembered Marla. 'Course, I didn't know her name yet."

He turned and looked out at the gardens he paid someone else to keep up, his gaze wandering like a floating leaf, not settling on anything in particular, just lazily drifting along. His voice changed, becoming smoother somehow.

"*You swim, Harry?* She asked me that, as she sat on the stool and looked at the stage. I nodded and pulled up an empty glass, waiting for her to tell me what to put in it. Her knowing my name didn't even faze me, everyone in there knew my name. She wasn't looking my direction to see me nod, so I don't know if it was a peripheral response or assumption when she declared: *Everyone should know how to swim, Harry. Especially if they own a house with a pool.* She spun back toward me and looked me in the eyes. There was no expression on her face, but the swirl of mischief and madness in those eyes was familiar and I knew the drink—suddenly remembering her, remembering it, a moment before she ordered it. *You want to be a dear and drop a Gin Rickey in that glass?* She winked and pointed to the tumbler I held."

He raised his hand, fingers poised as if holding something, mimicking a long-forgotten moment. Harry closed his fingers to his palm and looked at his nails rather than me as he continued.

"Her polished nails looked so freshly done they appeared wet, and the color—the bright blood red I'd seen too much of in the war—it matched her lips, and all but jumped off in contrast to her pale skin. But those eyes. It was always those eyes I remembered. Of course, it was easier as an adult, and she seemed to come in more often for a while. And the dress helped. In 1938 San Francisco—when I was just a twelve-year-old kid scraping money for his family—a woman in a little black dress was nothing out of the ordinary. But in 1969, while the rest of the patrons' closets ranged from hippie gear to thrift store military rags as some sort of protest or pride, *she* was a bit overdressed. And she remained so the next year when she stopped by twice, and then three more times before Elvis died. Looking back, I remembered all five visits from '69 to '75. Always in the same black dress with two straps across the back. Always on open mic night. Always one Gin Rickey and then gone until the next time."

I tightened my brows without meaning to, my question appearing in my expression before it ever formed on my lips. Harry saw it. He smiled with the patience of a grandparent.

"Let me back up and break it down for you. You know who Brian Jones is—or rather, was, right?" He didn't wait for me to nod as he held up an index finger to count to one. "He's the first *official* member of what people call the 27 Club. Seems big musicians tend to die at the ripe old age of twenty-seven on a regular enough basis to make the masses twist it into superstition and urban legend, myth and a morbidly curious checklist. As if to say: you know you've made it, if you don't make it to twenty-eight."

"I've heard of this. Hendrix, Joplin, Morrison . . . "

"Sure you heard of their deaths, but what about their lives? Or rather, the moment that changed their lives . . . and secured their deaths."

"I'm not sure I follow." I was genuinely intrigued.

Having worked at The Shantyman for the past several years—as well as moonlighting as an occasional freelance reporter for the music section of the *San Francisco Focus*—music, musicians, and everything between was a big part of my everyday life.

Harry had retired from The Shantyman before I started bartending there, but he used to come in on open mic nights. He would quietly watch the bar, and the door, rather than the stage. I always thought it was strange—stranger still when he not only stopped coming in but called and asked *me* to come to *him*. I realized why as soon as he answered the door in the wheelchair. He brushed it off as an accident the previous winter and escorted me through the house to the back patio where lemonade was waiting at a small black wrought iron table.

"When Brian Jones was seventeen he got himself a guitar for a birthday present, and his love of music was cemented. He died ten years later." He watched me, my reactions.

"It was accidental though, wasn't it? An overdose or drowning or something?" I tried to remember the theories around the death of the Rolling Stones' late guitarist.

"*Something*." Harry looked at me and let the word hang out there by itself for a beat too long. "*How* he died, how *any* of them died, doesn't matter. That's just what the coroner writes down to make the fans and frenzy happy. It's the *why* rather than the *how*. Sympathy for the Devil, indeed."

I leaned forward, resting my elbows on the table and cocking my head at him. I let my obvious intrigue silently urge him to continue.

"Do you know Hendrix used to carry an old broom around school and pretend it was a guitar? I thought it was that, or maybe the ukulele he found. But I'm fairly certain it was the replacement guitar he bought at seventeen for the one *conveniently* stolen from backstage. The new one came with a higher price—one not on the tag."

He had two fingers up and tapped his opposite

index finger on the third as he raised it and continued to count.

"Joplin wasn't an instrument, just her voice. According to the rumors, she was singing on her way home one night, and that song was heard by the wrong ears. She was seventeen." He held the three fingers up for me to see.

"Do you see it? The pattern? I could keep going. They all did something, bought something, found something, or otherwise had an important musical moment at *seventeen*, and then died ten years later. Ten years. The length of the contract."

"Contract? I didn't realize Joplin had a record deal so young." I thought I knew my Janis Joplin trivia, and some bizarre tidbit could always come in handy on the next game night.

"No. No record deal. No recording label or studio in that paperwork. Nothing but the darkness and the blood inside it."

I had been reaching for my lemonade but stopped, pulling my hand back to the safety of my lap. Had Harry lost his mind? What nonsense was he prattling on about? *The darkness and its blood?*

"It's a *demon*, Gwen." He spat it out and watched me react.

I raised both brows as my eyes widened at the atrocity of his statement. "I'm too old to believe in the boogeyman, Harry. And I would have thought you were, too."

"This isn't the boogeyman. This is a demon. An actual, honest-to-goodness demon. A crossroads demon. Marla."

I opened my mouth, about to call him crazy, when

I thought of every story or television show featuring one of the fabled soul collectors. Every tall tale or conspiracy theory centered on them. "Harry . . . "

"Listen to me, Gwen. Just listen. Hear me out. Think me crazy when you leave here but hear me out." He splayed his hands on the tabletop, as if bracing reality for the tale he was about to spin.

"I didn't put it together until I had the internet. I was at the library and saw the computers. I asked the girl what it was all about and she showed me. She showed me how to search archives and find information. And when she walked away, I tried to find Marla. I'd been fascinated with her since I was a child. That black hair and white skin, red smeared across her lips and nails. She was a noir poster come to life, and only needed a cigarette in one of those old holders to finish the image.

"When I couldn't find Marla, I tried to think of the dates she'd come in, to see if I could tie her to a passing band or something. And that was when it all fell into place. The dates—every single one of them—were right after a new member joined the 27 club." He leaned forward, his wheelchair creaking as his weight shifted to the front of it. "Every. Single. One."

"Coincidence, Harry. Plus, didn't you say you saw her way back in 1938? It couldn't have been her all those times."

"You're not listening, Gwen. She's a demon. Demons don't age. Maybe crossroads demons specifically keep their youth by taking it from those who make pacts with them. Every one of those musicians had something happen when they were seventeen, and then died at twenty-seven. Each of them."

"Harry . . . "

"Ten years. That's what she gives them. Ten years to accomplish what they might. Morrison spent his senior year reading and reporting on a lot of old English books about demonology. He was seventeen. It makes me wonder just what he was looking for—the answer, or is that where he found the problem in the first place?"

"Okay, so if we believe this theory that some crossroads demon wiped out the great musicians of the 60s and 70s, then what? You said you didn't want me to report on this? You don't want this in the *Focus*?"

"No, it's not just the 60s and 70s. Jones wasn't the first. Robert Johnson knew of the crossroads."

"The old blues singer?"

Harry nodded with exuberance, as if suddenly excited I was actually part of the conversation. "He sang of them. He tried to warn us. But he couldn't hide, and no one was listening. I think he was the first. I *think*. And the latest won't be the last. Not unless you help me."

"The latest? Morrison? That was a while ago. Twenty-some years . . . "

"He wasn't the last. After him was McKernan, and then Ham, and actually quite a few since. It didn't stop when they quit burning their bras, she just targeted smaller stars."

"Wait, *help* you? What do you need me to do? An expose, or maybe a book rather than a story?"

"No no, nothing of the sort. No one listens. They just turn it into fiction and myth. I need you to *stop her*."

"Stop her?" I shook my head. "How? When? Harry . . . "

"You see the news last night? That's why I called you. Open mic night is tonight. She'll take a bus or train down from Seattle. Always seems to be public transportation with her. It'll take her twenty hours to get here. Time enough for me to get you here, to tell someone who can be there, who can stop her. I was there every open mic night for years waiting for her but never saw her. She'll be there tonight. I promise you she will."

"She? A demon? A demon who kills musicians for giggles?"

"Not for giggles, for contracts. For souls. And yes, she'll be there."

"Wait, last night . . . I didn't see the news this morning before I got your call. What happened?"

"That grunge kid, with the dirty-blond shaggy hair. I can't think of his name. She'll be down to celebrate her contract with a drink. You need to serve it to her."

"Serve what?"

"Her drink." Harry pulled out a small bottle of gin. "Use this. Think of it as saving future musicians, rather than taking out a demon if it makes you feel better."

I squinted at the little bottle as he put it on the table. I didn't believe the bottom-shelf label for even a moment.

"What's in that?"

"Holy water." He watched my face. "Holy water and nothing more. Make her a drink with this *instead* of gin. If I'm wrong, you'll have a customer complaining about weak drinks. If I'm right . . . "

"Harry, I can't do that."

He pointed to his wheelchair, "I can't. You won't. There's a difference."

"But Harry. Even if I believed you—"

"If you didn't believe me, you wouldn't have picked up the bottle."

I looked down and realized I was holding the tiny glass bottle claiming to be a single shot of cheap gin. "Holy water?"

"Holy water. Not even gin. I poured that out."

"And if I drank this myself?"

His eyes widened, "Don't do that. Please." His expression bounced through several emotions and unspoken reactions before he calmly opened his mouth and settled on his words, "It took me some doing to get that in my condition. I'd hate to waste it."

I pushed the chair back and stood, bottle still in my hand. I didn't believe him, but I wanted to believe *in* him. He'd always been a good guy, with a great reputation at the bar. There was no harm in letting him *think* I was on his side.

"Okay, Harry. Okay." I smiled weakly and dropped the bottle into my pocket. "If your demon comes in, I'll make her a drink."

"Marla. You remember her description?"

I nodded.

"Good luck, Gwen."

He was so serious when I left. So solemn. As if he'd sent me on a holy mission from which I may not return, like a general sending soldiers to battle with a salute.

I thought about our conversation when I got to work. I thought about writing up a piece for the *Focus* on my own. It was an interesting theory. And one I forgot as soon as the crowd started coming in.

The grunge star's death had people out mourning

his life through his art, and open mic night was busier than usual. The standard smattering of *true musicians*—trying to get heard by the right audience—were outnumbered by half-drunk lovers of the Seattle music scene. The tables near the stage were full, but the bar was abandoned except for the occasionally slurred drink order that then returned to their table. I heard a couple of his more popular songs a few times too many, as tone-deaf fans attempted to pay tribute. I even had to call the bouncer over to break up a fight about which Seattle band was better and who would take his place now that he was gone.

"Gin Rickey, please." The smooth female voice caused me to freeze mid-motion, as I was head down washing the rail glasses.

I looked up into the deepest, darkest eyes. Eyes devoid of emotion. Black eyes that matched the hair framing the ghostly white face. Bright red, freshly manicured fingertips pushed a ten-dollar bill and a torn bus ticket receipt across the bar at me. As she spun to watch the stage, I noticed the little black dress had two straps across the back, almost making an inverted cross. I heard myself swallow.

I wondered if she did.

I looked at the gin on the rail, but my hand went to my pocket instead. *Just holy water*, I told myself as I poured it into a glass below the ledge, out of sight of patrons and staff alike. I grabbed a half lime from the garnish bin and squeezed it into the glass. A squirt of soda and the drink was ready. I starred at the highball glass and its innocent looking drink.

She nodded her head toward the muted television at the end of the bar. Police tape at the end of the driveway outside the rock star's home provided the backdrop for a female reporter on the screen.

"You know he lived under a bridge after he was kicked out of his house at seventeen. Cold nights alone in the dark can lead to strange conversations with oneself and whoever may be listening . . . "

Seventeen. I heard the age she said. I remembered Harry's words.

I held my breath as she polished the drink off quickly, barely pausing between swallows.

Something swirled in the blackness of her eyes. Something that looked a *lot* like fear. She clutched her throat, coughed, and locked eyes with me.

I backed up, bumping into the counter and causing bottles to jostle and clank against each other.

Blood appeared at the corner of her red lips, in a dainty display of graceful macabre. She didn't bother to wipe it away as her face twisted in pain and agony. Her eyes squinted shut as her body reacted—convulsing, shuddering, flesh rippling as if something moved beneath it.

She opened her mouth and I thought she was going to scream. She slammed both hands down to the glossy varnished wood of the bar, fingers splayed, red nails like drops of blood splattered across the surface. Her eyes widened, and she looked at me, beyond me. Fear, pain, rage, and acceptance all swirled in and out of her expression.

"Tell Harry," her smooth voice had become a rough whisper, cracked and forced as she struggled to finish her sentence. "It wasn't the strychnine, Gwen. The water . . . water was enough."

I shook my head—barely, quickly, like a tapped

bobble-head—unsure what to say. Not knowing how to react.

She knew my *name*.

She *knew* Harry.

And she knew what Harry and I had done.

Her mouth still open, I saw the blackness inside and realized it matched her eyes—the depths of absolute nothing, like the infinite darkness on a starless night. And then I watched it change, as fire came from her throat.

Flames shot out of her eyes, her nose. They burst from her in a spray of heat and anger, spitting like an over-stoked campfire, sending sparks and embers to skitter along the bar rail. Just as quickly, the flames were pulled back in—not to be doused, but to burn from within as they wormed along underneath her pale skin, traveling the length of her arms and up her neck as if her veins were on fire. Her flesh reddened and blistered. Then it darkened as it burned to a blackened crisp. The tiny sounds of her death—crackling and sizzling—filled my ears, even as her own soundless scream washed across her expression. A burst of flame and fire, of pain and death, and then it was done.

Her skin and hair, her red lips and black eyes, all turned from the dark burnt color of charcoal to a spent-match gray and crumbled. She was gone. Ash, where she'd been, fell to the floor to get lost in the dust and dirt there. Nothing but a ten-dollar bill and a bus ticket stub to prove she'd ever been there.

I looked around. All the other patrons seemed to be mesmerized by the girl on stage singing a slowed-down version of *Endless, Nameless*. None of them saw anything. None of them seemed to care that a woman had just burst into flames and turned to dust.

"Hey, *Gwen*?" I turned and stared at the bouncer saying my name with a curt tone, suggesting it wasn't the first time he'd said it.

I was locked inside a terror no one shared. My heart—trying to beat free of my chest—scared me as much as the insanity of what I'd just seen. What I'd just done.

"You okay? You look like shit."

I shook my head and ran for the bathroom. How could no one have seen anything? I needed to ask Harry if any of the patrons had ever appeared to see her, to interact with her. Or was it just him. Just me.

Just the bartender she chose to show herself to?

When I stopped at Harry's in the morning I found him dead. They said natural causes, but I know better. I saw the strange burn mark on his hand.

It's been seventeen years since that night. I never wrote the article. I never told anyone what happened.

I still have the little empty bottle and bus ticket stub—tucked into the bottom of my jewelry box, hidden but not forgotten. I've thought about throwing them away on occasion, but I never seem to be able to get myself to do it. Like without the proof, it didn't happen, and if it didn't happen then I'm crazy.

I need to not be crazy.

I refilled the bottle this morning at St. Paul's down the street on my way to work. It's in my pocket. I realize now, Harry probably mixed holy water with strychnine, but Marla had screwed up by telling me I didn't *need* the strychnine. The water was enough to stop her.

At least for seventeen years.

I don't know if she'll look the same, and I worry she'll recognize me. But I have to try.

Images of the British queen of eyeliner and rehab are splattered across the television today. Poor thing never had a chance. She was talented too young. Hungry too young. And signed, sealed and delivered before she was legal.

She was found yesterday.

Tonight is open mic night.

BEAT ON THE PAST

Matt Serafini

"HEY," MOIRA SAID as they hurried across the street.

Pete didn't hear her. He was already caught up in the familiar glow of their past. A stale blot of white bulbs grew from the night to punctuate a city block of otherwise unbroken shadows. He rushed toward it, Moira's hand closed in his. She trailed behind, arm lifting like a clothesline.

"Did you sign the—"

"Talk about it later?" Pete said as he stepped to consecrated ground, looking up at the Shantyman's marquee. No mention of tonight's show. A strange omission, given the circumstances.

Moira stared straight ahead with a clenched jaw.

"Like seeing an old friend," Pete said.

"I wanted to talk about it over dinner but you—"

"We can talk about that any time," he said. "Come on."

Moira jerked her hand away and started in, leaving him to trail a few steps. "Place hasn't changed." A sigh stretched through her voice.

Pete sucked air in through his nostrils and closed

his eyes, savoring the memories of a hundred nights spent walking this corridor.

"Are we early?" Moira said.

A few solitary bodies stood scattered throughout the stage room beyond, looking like transients happy to be out of the rain.

Pete took the flyer from his windbreaker and unfolded it to confirm the date. Doors opened at 7. They were late, if anything. A little past eight now and it was tumbleweeds.

He traded the register jockey a fifty-dollar bill for two blue smiley face stamps on the backs of their hands. They passed inside.

"Same drill?" Moira said.

"Doesn't look like we've got much to worry about."

"I don't want to stand all night. I've got work tomorrow."

"So do I, you know."

She spat her breath and shrugged, heading for one of the skinny pub tables scattered around the outskirts.

Pete watched her sling her bag down and then drape her coat over the low-backed stool. The dim house lights rendered her face a dark blank beneath a clean bob of hair.

He went for drinks where the line was as sparse as the attendance. A girl with safety pins in her ears spilled Jack and Coke after swallowing two healthy sips and argued the bartender for another.

Pete's Pumas felt glued to the slab. The floor in here went sticky with the spill of a hundred tilted beverages in almost no time. And the air swirled heavy with an atmosphere of cheap draught. Tonight was the same as it ever was, only Pete wanted to know who in the hell was here to make the mess.

The girl wandered off with her refill and Pete put his elbow on the quartz slab, his forearm soaking in spilt Jack. He ordered two draughts. The bartender's hair was the color of cobwebs and she barely bothered to acknowledge him as she brought two plastic cups to tap. She handed them over. The top thirds were all foam.

She grinned dead, eyes anything but happy. Pete slapped a ten down and took the cups with a sigh. At least he wouldn't have to worry about spilling them.

"This isn't going to happen," Moira said as he neared. "Is it?"

"Sure it will." He slid a cup over and Moira took it.

"If it doesn't—"

"Hey," he said. "They're promoting it." His smile felt forced and hopeless.

"Who?"

"They printed flyers, right?" Pete said. "So, someone."

"Kids in high school."

"You're right," he said. "Should've gone on Maury Povich to get the word out."

Moira lifted an arm across her chest. Her index finger pointed to the stage at her back. "Flyers aren't doing a very good job."

The stage was empty and the crowd standing before it had the enthusiasm of a receiving line at a wake. They were a clump of the curious in frayed jeans, pushed tight against the stage so not to be usurped. Twenty bodies, maybe, all slouched shoulders and vacant conversations.

"Remember when Nick dove off there and the crowd backed away like he was boiled oil?" I asked.

"Had to drive him to the ER," she said. "Twelve stitches." A gentle laugh warmed her features and then was gone like a ghost.

He opened his mouth and drew a breath of stale beer. "I can almost taste them."

"Stitches?"

"Memories," Pete said. "Nobody tells you how fast it ends."

"Nobody tells you because the next thing is supposed to be better."

Pete took the crumpled flier from his pocket once more and placed it flat on the table. The palms of his hands smoothed the wrinkles as he eyed it for the umpteenth time. "And yet, when I said to you, *'Brainpan, one night only.'*"

"Changes nothing." Moira's eyes underwent a steely makeover.

"You've made that clear a thousand times." Pete scrutinized the paper. Its details suddenly seemed different.

"Just don't want you thinking—"

"Got it," he said. "Really. Got it."

"Doesn't seem it." Moira lifted the foamy cup to her lips, her glare hardening like cement.

He flipped the sheet of paper around so she could read it. "How's this look to you?"

Moira threw casual eyes on it and scrunched her face to remind him that minutia had never been her strong suit.

The picture was different. It had been the same since the first night he got it, standing in scrubs, holding the paper between exhausted fingers and shaking the fugue cloud from his skull after eighteen hours on his feet. His brain a blender because what was promised on the page couldn't be right. Not after all this time.

Brainpan. One night only.

The photograph that occupied much of the Xeroxed flyer's real estate was a gritty, black-and-white shot of the Shantyman's stage. Brainpan, frozen mid-set in October, 1985. Ten years ago.

The last show they'd ever played. Because as soon as the lights had gone down on their encore that night, Brainpan vanished without a trace.

Eyewitnesses cited widespread confusion right off. The money guy waited backstage to split the door, but management was nowhere to be found. The band's tour van was off the premises, and even their instruments were gone. The female groupies hand-chosen for a back room meet and greet left that night with healthy knees and empty stomachs.

Pete knew exactly what the flyer had shown. He'd spent much of the last decade wondering what that final show must've been like. A band that traded burgeoning commercial success for the sustainability of urban legend.

He and Moira would've been there if not for their October wedding and ensuing honeymoon. Deep down, he resented the priority that touristy Parisian daytrips got over the band that had brought them together. And deep down, she must've known he resented her for it, and she resented that.

"You've seen this flyer before," Pete said, unable to keep the annoyance out.

"So?"

"It's different now."

"Pete—"

"Can you look at it for more than two seconds?"

She gave exactly that, then looked up with a sneer.

"What the fuck, Mo?"

"No," she said. "I mean, I don't know."

Pete slid the paper around and smacked it with the back of his hand. "This isn't it," he said. "It's not the same picture. How is that possible?"

"Look at you, answering your own question."

He let the passive-aggressive swipe pass him by. A small piece of the corner was torn from where he'd pulled it off his windshield wiper, meaning the actual paper was the same, and only the image had somehow shifted.

Pete could see how Moira might not immediately be convinced. The image still showed Brainpan, though the band was pushed further into the background, revealing a Shantyman crowd at maximum occupancy, sardined into the space where they now sat.

His eyelids snapped open like morning blinds as he spotted two familiar bodies hovering near the front of the frame. A young couple arm-in-arm, ignoring the excitement on stage for the exchange of mutual smiles.

He didn't show Moira. The photo was too grainy, she'd say. We weren't there, you idiot, she'd say. Both of these things were true, but every detail that belonged to these young people had also been theirs. Only Mo had a side bag dangling off her hip that was decorated entirely in Minor Threat. And Pete missed his jean vest with the Circle Jerks patch that adorned the back. The longer he stared, the less he was able to reconcile it as coincidence.

"What time is it?" He asked.

Moira pretended not to hear the question. He knew she had, however, because disdain bristled through her features like ripples on a pond. Pete knew the look. Tonight it was *when are you going to get a watch?* But it was interchangeable with any one of her lingering grievances.

There was an unmanned merch table sitting against the far wall. It housed two black crates of LPs and a pile of tees. It caught Moira's eye, and she cleared her throat. "Didn't I borrow the *Spit in Sanctimony* album from Kate that one night so we could listen to it on your parent's system?"

"Borrowed," Pete said with air quotes.

"Did you ever give it back?"

"Wasn't it a gift?"

Moira started to laugh, caught herself. She might've been chewing the inside of her mouth.

"And you did more than steal it," Pete said. "Had to smuggle it out inside an old pizza box you were pretending to throw out, because she was super particular of her records."

"She hoarded them," Moira said. "Had a thousand. Maybe I should just buy her another—"

"She's on the East Coast now. Married with kids."

"Right."

"Doubt we'll ever hear from her again."

Moira stared off.

"Probably listens to grunge now anyway. That's all anyone wants to listen to. Shit's weak."

Pete glanced back toward the bar and caught the

wispy haired woman watching him. Her lying smile was wider, even less convincing. The blue lights that backlit the drink shelves behind her projected a crooked, inhuman shadow all the way across the concert floor.

The drink line was nonexistent. No chance Brainpan's fanbase had gone straight edge in a vacuum.

"It's past nine," she said, waving her watch wrist like it was on fire. "This is all a stupid joke on the suckers like us who are dumb enough to show up."

"You used to live this stuff," Pete said.

"What's the expression? *Youth is wasted on the young*?"

"You're here."

"Oh, I know that."

"These guys don't give a shit about punctuality."

Moira yawned through the corner of her mouth. "Punk rock forever, right?"

More people began to fill in. A rapid flow came pouring through the doors and broke around their table as they moved toward the stage. Footsteps everywhere. They set up station at the unclaimed pub tables. They pushed against the early arrivals up front to get as close as space would allow. They lined the walls all around the perimeter.

They moved like blurs from a faded memory. Nondescript bodies in a crowd attached to faces that resembled eraser rubs, smudges hastily scrubbed away, leaving only the basic remnants of human features.

Everybody looked like nothing. Everybody except Moira. She paid no mind. Didn't seem to notice. Her fingers hammered the table in monosyllabic boredom, staring off into the future.

Pete craned all the way left and scanned slow toward his right, blinking a few times, rubbing his eyes with the ball of his fist.

Only one other face remained in focus. The bartender's. Still watching from afar with a smile somehow wider than the edges of her face.

"What's wrong with them?" he said.

"This place seems smaller," Moira said, no indication she'd even heard Pete's question. "I was so scared the first time."

"Your dad was sure we were going to get stabbed."

"He still thinks that."

"What about their faces?"

Moira threw her head around the room and shrugged. "How much did you drink at dinner?"

"Nothing like that."

"Maybe they're spiking our drinks," she giggled.

"Do you see them or not?"

"I see an empty stage. At twenty past."

"Punk isn't customer service. It pays to keep your fanbase unhappy, so nobody gets to accuse you of selling out."

Moira thought that over and decided she didn't care. "Was no problem when I could sleep till noon. Am I supposed to be late for my 9 am tomorrow because the band I paid good money to see felt like keeping me standing around all night?"

"They'll be on soon."

Moira's chin sat in the cup of her hand. Her eyes swiveled to the tabletop.

Pete glanced at the flyer and watched the crinkled

paper. The lights in the room dimmed. A few ecstatic cheers erupted from the otherwise silent pockets of joyless spectators. His head launched toward the page to try and compensate for the flooding darkness, because in that moment he was certain the photo had shifted again.

It was anything but subtle this time. Pete and Moira on stage, faces hardened by the passage of an unknown stretch of time. They still wore patches and chains to prove to the world they lived outside its "system." They presided over a floor of close friends. Each familiar face standing just below, a union of beer bottles raised high in a celebratory toast.

A photograph of something that had never happened, yet a memory he somehow held. Pete and Moira's hands joined in the ritual of matrimony. The Shantyman had meant more to them than any church, so why not? It's how it should've been.

He crumpled the paper as his beating heart leapt up into his throat. This place knew. He hadn't told anyone about this wish and yet it knew. Knew him better than anyone.

They sat in the dark for too long. Somehow Moira's sighs were louder than everything else. Her movements became spastic. Patience frayed and ready to tear.

Silhouettes floated out across the stage. Their appearance kicked up a few rumbles of excitement as the guitar threatened a familiar three-cord shuffle. Bass hummed out in search of a linking rhythm, finding harmony with the drums that began to thump through the darkness. A figural outline posed center stage, raising its arms up and out over the crowd like a holy man about to give blessing.

"To anyone who thinks the world is getting better, here's four simple words for you . . . you're *Shit. Out. Of. Luck*!" Then it started. Driving cords, simple bass. His voice, a throat full of razor blades. The song sounded as chaotic as ever.

Brainpan thrashed through the darkness. People punched and flailed with excitement at first, stopping to consider the swindle as the set continued and the lights refused to lift. Errant cheers and then skeptical insults rose up in the seconds of silence between songs. All of it giving way to full-fledged skepticism as the show roared exclusively from inside the deepest shadows.

Pete was already contemplating the ways in which he was going to apologize to Moira. Ten years ago, they'd have thrashed around a bit, kicking and pushing bodies away. His hand would've slipped beneath the waist of her jeans to give her ass a squeeze in the dark. And she would've purred in his ear to wait for the ride home. It would've been whiskey shots in the bathroom. A joint once the show got underway.

Tonight they hadn't even come here in the same car.

Just before encore, light flooded the venue to reveal Brainpan standing before them like time unchanged. Like the decade unchanged. The crowd roared. They mashed against the stage and threw middle fingers like couples blew kisses. Moira perked for a second before remembering that time had, in fact, moved on and she needed to remain unimpressed.

Pete reached for her hand. She pulled away, bobbing her head and pretending hard at being immersed. Keeping that façade running through to the very last note, when the lights once more plunged the Shantyman into total darkness. The residual echoes of their final notes haunted the house speakers like phantoms.

Even then, Moira wouldn't look. When there were only lingering cheers mixed with static interference, she wouldn't look. And once the silhouettes glided stage left, leaving the place as vacant as they'd found it, she refused to look.

It stayed dark. They sat nearly motionless, somehow bound in place and listening to the constant shuffling of tired feet scraping past.

They were alone when the house lights finally lifted. Or nearly alone.

The bartender was still looking. Still smiling.

"It's over," Moira said. She got off the stool and started for the exit.

Pete trotted after. The floor no longer stuck to his soles. It was smooth and clean, and the place had been exorcised of the perspired body smell that lingered just seconds ago.

"Get a record on the way out," Moira said, and then hurried into the night.

Pete watched the door slam. He lifted the flyer again, desperate for what might've been. All the times he'd dreamt about that day, surrounded by people who had mattered the most at that point in their lives. People you always expected to be part of you. All of them now just memories and ghosts.

The photo was different again.

Brainpan stood clustered together, a decade of age lines etched into their faces. A comeback shot fit for Spin or Rolling Stone. Same skull make-up, green hair, and priest frocks. Only seeing them older felt wrong. Like they were never supposed to age, because all of their music was about the evils of capitalism, the corruption of banana republics, and the subversion of society. But now they looked like middle management getting a little wild at the office Halloween party. Too old to be rebelling against The Man™ without looking like a bunch of assholes.

Pete took another look around the vacant floor space and then pushed out into the cold.

TRUE STARMEN

Max Booth III

THE LINE OUTSIDE The Shantyman was way longer than Martin expected. A horde of weirdos stretched from the locked front entrance to the parking lot on the opposite side of the building. He'd nearly plowed into some Mormon-looking fucker while pulling his Craigslist-bargained Vespa into the reserved employee parking area next to the dumpsters. Hipsters usually attended the shows here. Thick neckbeards coated in Dorito dust. Semen-stained fedoras. Sarcastic T-shirts too small for the massive guts bulging out of them. But the people here this evening? Martin wasn't sure what they were. Some kind of new breed of hipster, maybe. Every single one of them wore white jeans. What kind of psychopath wore white jeans? Disgusting. Martin tried not to make eye contact with any of them as he headed to the back entrance, but the utter lack of conversation commandeered his attention. Not a single soul spoke, nor did anyone have out their cell phones. They all stood single-file, waiting silently for the doors to open at six, not even acknowledging Martin as he passed them.

"What's going on tonight again?" he asked Alice at the bar after slipping in through the back entrance. "The podcast thing, right?"

She nodded. "Yeah, the podcast thing."

"Have you gotten a load of the people waiting outside?"

"I think they're religious."

"With what religion?"

Alice shrugged. "Don't think it matters."

"Maybe they're just weirdos."

"Well, obviously."

"Just standing. Not talking. Not doing anything. All patient and content to be in a line."

"Mmm-hmm." Alice made her *told-ya-so* face. "Buncha religious weirdos. Pegged them as soon as I got here."

Martin half-grimaced, half-laughed. "Pegged them, did you?"

"Mmm-hmm." She tapped the side of her temple, emphasizing her keen sense of vision. "Pegged them right away."

"That's really rather disgusting, Alice, if you ought to know the truth."

Alice cocked her head, hand paused in mid-glass-wipe. "What are you talking about now?"

Jared, who was in the process of setting up the chairs in their proper places, shouted, "Pegged means when a woman fucks a fella in the ass. Like, with a strap-on or some such thing."

Bob, the manager, pounded his fist against the bar counter, having been interrupted from spreading out change for the register. "Jared! Don't say things like that."

"Don't say things like *what*?" Jared straightened his spine and stared at Bob with genuine curiosity.

"Things like 'when a woman fucks a fella in the ass' or 'with a strap-on or some such thing.'"

"But that's what pegging means, Bob. I'm just telling Alice the facts."

Bob shook his head and waved his finger at him. "You can't say 'when a woman fucks a fella in the ass' or 'with a strap-on or some such thing' to Alice. She's a grandmother."

Alice scoffed and slammed down a freshly cleaned glass. "Oh, nonsense, I'm barely a grandmother."

Jared raised his hand, like he was back in school and desperately had to pee. "How can someone be *barely* a grandmother? They either are, or they aren't, right?"

Alice started to explain but Martin cut her off. "I think what she means is, some grandmothers are proper grandmothers. Like, they're old and have fake teeth. But Alice isn't very old. She's only middle-aged. And her teeth are probably real, too." He turned back to Alice. "You don't have fake teeth, do you?"

Alice grinned wide, revealing a big set of nicotine-stained chompers. "That proof enough?"

Martin studied the smile for a while then shrugged. "Well, yes, that definitely proves it, all right." In all honesty, he had no qualifications to make such determinations, but he doubted anybody here was going to call him out about it. Not like they could do any better. Nobody working at the goddamn Shantyman had much going for them, which was sort of nice, in a way. It gave them all a shared quality of degeneration. Sometimes it was nice to have something to bond over, even if that something was a total lack of a desirable life.

Bob spit a wad of chewing tobacco into a glass Alice just finished cleaning and said, “Which one of you millennials plans on explaining what the hell a podcast is, anyway?”

Alice cursed under her breath and rewashed the glass.

“It’s . . . like radio.” Martin threw up his hands as if that might put things in a better perspective. “But different.”

“It’s like *Serial*,” Jared said.

“Season one or season two?” Bob asked.

“Uh. Either?”

“Ah.” He left the bar and headed toward the back corridor without another word.

Martin joined Alice behind the bar and helped prepare for the evening. “What *is* this podcast, anyway? Something like . . . Stargazers United, right?”

Jared imitated a game show buzzer going off. “Wrong! It’s *Shoegazers* United.”

“Shoegazers?”

“Mmm-hmm.”

“It is not a podcast about shoegaze.”

“Why would I lie about this?”

Alice cleared her throat. “Maybe I’m more than barely a grandmother, after all. What the hell is *shoegaze?*”

Martin started to answer but Jared interrupted. “You know. It’s like My Bloody Valentine.”

“My *what?*”

“Dinosaur Jr.? Flying Saucer Attack? A Place to Bury Strangers?”

"Jared, I—"

He started counting off the names with his fingers. "Kitchens of Destruction? The Jesus and Mary Chain? A Sunny Day in Glasgow? Alison's Halo? The Away Days? The Boo Radleys? The Brian Jonestown Massacre? Kill Hannah, for God's sake?"

"Who's *Hannah?* Who's *killing* her?"

"Ringo Deathstarr? Pale Saints? Pity Sex? *Cigarettes After Sex?* Any of this ringing a bell, Alice?"

"I have no idea what you're saying right now."

Martin sighed. "He's naming bands. Shoegaze is a music genre."

"Oh." She contemplated the thought, then shook her head. "No, the folks performing tonight, they aren't a band."

Jared straighten a crooked line of chairs and said, "Maybe they just talk about famous shoegaze bands."

Martin refused to believe this. "The podcast is not called Shoegazers United."

"Then what is it called, smart guy?"

An idea occurred to him. He looked up at the banner above the stage. "Starmen Unified."

"Haha. Now who's making shit up?"

"No, seriously." Martin pointed at the banner. "Starmen Unified."

Jared followed the direction of Martin's finger and laughed again. "Well, I'll be pegged by Alice. You're right."

Alice gasped. "I'll be doing no such thing to you."

He turned and winked at her. "Oh, the night is young, dear Alice. The night is young!"

The trouble started almost as soon as Martin stepped outside. Holding a stamp pad, he shouted for everybody to have their IDs out and ready to be checked, and literally the *first goddamn guy* in line protested.

"You don't need my identification. You don't need any of our identification." He crossed his arms over his chest like an actual child.

This wasn't the first time some idiot gave him shit at the front door. "Nobody under eighteen is getting in here. Get your license out or go home. I honestly don't care, either way." He didn't have to be nice to these weirdos. The Shantyman did not offer refunds on tickets. The only person they might possibly complain to would be Bob, and he was a way bigger asshole than Martin could ever aspire to become.

Martin and the guy at the front of the line held a staring contest for a while, then he sighed and started digging around for his wallet. Martin grinned. He always won this game.

He squinted at his driver's license and wondered if the guy had actually traveled all the way from Baltimore to see a live podcast performance in San Francisco. Judging by his peculiar clothing, it wasn't entirely out of the question. He shrugged and returned the license.

"Let me see your hand." He lifted the stamp, desperate to move on to the next person in line.

The guy shook his head. "Absolutely not."

"If you plan on drinking alcohol, I gotta stamp your hand."

He grimaced. "I would never subject myself to such poisons."

"Whatever, dude." He had already wasted enough time on him. Martin moved on to the next guy in line, who took one look at the stamp and also shook his head.

"Bylines state we are not to alter our flesh in any shape or form."

"Uh. What?"

He pointed at the stamp. "Ink is considered an illegal amendment of the body. I must refuse."

"It's only temporary. It . . . it washes off."

"Every sin is permanent, no matter how long its visibility lasts."

"You won't be able to drink without the stamp."

"True Starmen refuse all temptations of intoxication."

"Right."

Martin stepped away and shouted, "Okay, show of hands. Who here actually plans on purchasing alcohol tonight?"

Everybody's arms stayed down.

"That's what I thought."

Martin unhooked a walkie-talkie from his side-holster and thumbed it on. "Hey, uh, Bob? Nobody here will let me stamp their hands."

Static feedback on the other end. "Uh, why not?"

"Says it's a sin."

"A sin?"

"Yeah." Martin glared at the line of people, all of them watching him with intensity. "They're a bunch of weirdos."

"Well, they won't be able to drink if they don't got the stamp."

"That's what I told them."

"And?"

"They don't drink, either."

"They don't *drink?*"

"That's what they said."

"Jesus fucking Christ. We're ruined."

"Should I make them all go home?"

Long pause on the other end, like Bob was seriously considering the idea. "Nah. Let them come in, I guess."

Martin thought about continuing to check IDs but decided he didn't really give a shit if someone under eighteen slipped in tonight. The less he had to talk to these assholes, the better. The whole point of checking IDs wasn't to make sure kids didn't get in, anyway. It had more to do with being able to stamp someone's hand. If someone's hand was stamped, then they were much more likely to purchase an alcoholic beverage, having figured there would be no point in letting a perfectly good hand-stamp go to waste.

He lit up a cigarette and gestured at the front door. "Well. Go on inside then, I guess. Someone to the left will scan your tickets as you walk in."

Every single one of them cast a murderous glare at the cigarette in his mouth.

Evidently True Starmen also didn't condone nicotine addiction.

Like he could give a shit.

"Hello, San Francisco! How in the heck are you fellas tonight? Oh yes. That's what I like to hear! As you almost undoubtedly already know, I am your host, Daniel Ray Burnside, and these are my *faithful* co-hosts, Lee Anderson and Paul Gauge, and we are the True Starmen! Yes, yes, thank you so much, thank you for coming out here to this great city, to this wonderful establishment. We've had tonight planned for . . . well, since the very first episode of our show, haven't we? It's hard to believe, isn't it? All those years ago, and the time has finally arrived. I hope you are ready, my fellow Starmen. I hope you're ready to embrace your destinies. Because tonight? Tonight is going to change all of our lives. Tonight is going to change *everything*."

"I was just reading about these starfish fellas," Bob said, urging Martin to close the door behind him. He'd urgently radioed him up to his office on the second floor about a half hour ago, just as the podcasters walked out on stage. Not a single person in the crowd applauded their arrival. They had all just sort of . . . nodded approvingly, to which the podcasters nodded in return. Weirdos, the whole lot of them. Martin had taken his sweet time going up to the office, figuring he'd linger downstairs awhile and check out what was so great about the podcast. Thirty minutes later, he still had no idea what the fuck they were talking about.

Martin sat across from Bob. "Starmen. Not starfish."

Bob brushed the correction aside. "Po-tay-to, po-tah-to."

"I really need to get back down there."

"Did someone decide to buy a drink?"

"No."

"Then I don't see how you can be useful."

"Gee. Thanks, Bob."

"I was reading about them. About these . . . these *Starmen*."

"You googled them?"

"I googled them."

Martin waited for more but was offered nothing further. "Okay. *And?*"

"And . . . " he gestured at his computer monitor, which faced the opposite direction of Martin, " . . . these are some weird individuals."

"That's what I've been saying. Isn't that what I've been saying?"

"Yeah." Bob couldn't argue with facts. "That's what you've been saying."

"Well, what did you find out, then?"

"Huh?"

Martin slapped the back of Bob's monitor. "On the computer. What did you find out?"

"I didn't call you up so you could slap my computer, Martin."

"I barely slapped it."

"I just sat and watched you do it. Full contact. Palm, fingers, everything. It even made a slapping sound."

"What is a slapping *sound?*"

Bob clapped his hands together. "Kind of like that."

"It was barely a slap." Martin sighed, looking at where he'd left a dent on the back of the monitor. "How much did this heap of junk cost you, anyway? Twenty bucks?"

"Try three hundred, mister."

"When did this cost you three hundred?" He laughed and wiped spit from his mouth. "Surely not recently."

"Just last month! What are you trying to say? I got a heck of a deal."

"Are we talking just the monitor or was the computer included too?"

"What do you mean?"

"This." He slapped the monitor again and smiled at how quickly Bob winced. "This is the monitor. And the tall skinny thing below your desk, that's the computer."

"Oh. No. Just the monitor." He folded his hands in his lap and admired the brightly lit contraption. "Heck of a deal, I'm telling you. You wouldn't believe what I talked him down from. Originally, I mean."

Martin rolled his eyes and checked his wristwatch. He did not actually own a watch, so he just glanced at his bare wrist for a couple of seconds. Same thing, basically. "Bob. I should really get back down there."

"Do you know what an incel is?"

Martin nearly spat out his drink, then remembered he wasn't drinking anything. "Uh. Kind of."

"It means someone who is *involuntary celibate*."

"I don't . . . I don't know if this is an appropriate workplace conversation, Bob."

Bob pointed at the floor. "These podcasters, that's what they identify as. Incels. And their fans—them, too. What do you know about these kinds of people?"

Martin shrugged. "They're kind of a joke, right?"

"A joke?"

"Yeah. Like. They go on Reddit and talk trash about women. Blame them for all of their troubles. Claim they can't get laid because girls hate *nice guys*. That kind of dumb shit."

"Are they dangerous?"

“I seriously doubt it.”

“The reason I ask is,” he pointed at the monitor again, still not realizing Martin couldn’t see it from across the desk, “I found a couple articles about this podcast. The Starmen people. And a few of them—of the articles—they talk about these Starmen being involved in some kind of a cult.”

“A cult?”

“Mmm-hmm. Like those Scientologists and Waco whackjobs.”

“What are you talking about?”

Bob strained his brow. “There were reports I read. People leaving their families, moving in together at . . . what do you call them? Communes. Like with hippies and whatnot. A few women also complained about receiving disturbing packages in the mail, too. All from followers of this podcast. Lots of harassment lawsuits, stuff like that.”

“Have they hurt anyone?”

“I didn’t see anything about people getting hurt. But I did see one article speculating that they might . . . uh, you know, eventually lead into hurting someone. That they’re building some kind of . . . incel army.”

“A horde of neckbeards, wielding fedoras and Vampire Weekend vinyls.”

“I don’t know what that means.”

“What do you want me to do about any of this, Bob?”

“Well, nothing. We can’t kick everybody out because they’re a cult. Wait. Can we?”

“At this point, they’re almost finished.”

“Mmm.” Bob nodded and leaned back in his chair. “I hope they don’t give us some reputation as a bar that welcomes cults. Just my luck, every single week, another cult at The Shantyman."

Martin cracked his neck and stood. "I feel like people exaggerate when it comes to cults, anyway. Like, what's so bad about them? Isn't everybody these days in *some kind* of cult?"

Bob paused, seriously contemplating the question, then shook his head. "No. That sounds like bullshit to me."

Martin nodded. "Yeah. It sounded like bullshit as the words were leaving my mouth, but it was too late."

"Sometimes, maybe think before talking, Martin. Haven't I told you that before?"

"No."

"Oh. Well, I meant to."

Martin turned to leave but Bob called his name again. "Yeah?"

Bob opened his mouth to say something, then closed it. Repeated the action a couple more times. Trying to figure out his wording. "Do you think it's silly for me to be worried?"

"About who? The Starmen?"

Bob nodded.

"Nah."

"It's just that. I see the word cult, and I think of those Jonestown fellas. You know. The Kool Aid drinkers and such."

"They all killed themselves, right?"

Bob nodded. "A mass suicide."

"And you think something like that might happen at The Shantyman?"

"I just think we should be cautious with fellas like this. Cult fellas."

Martin laughed. “I think we’re going to be just fine, Bob.”

Then the office door swung open and Jared stumbled inside, drenched head to toe in blood. “Holy shit,” he said, gasping for breath, “you will not believe what just happened.”

JUST TO BE SEEN

Somer Canon

"ALL RIGHT, PRETTY LADY. You're gonna have yourself a swell time here at The Shantyman," the young man said. He fussed over jumping out of his car and running to her side to let her out. He offered her his hand and helped her to her feet.

She surveyed the dark but bustling parking lot like a queen taking account of her lands. The fool from whom she had accepted the offer of a date was practically hopping, so pleased was he to be seen with the likes of her. He didn't know that she simply needed a ride to The Shantyman that night so that she could see the leader of the band, Will Fontaine.

She pulled her cheap coat closer about herself, and she smiled remembering the balmy summer evening just a mere three months earlier. The night Will Fontaine had held her hand after his band had played for an outdoor crowd. The night he kissed her.

She glanced at the young man who offered her his arm. He seemed nice enough, but he was no Will Fontaine. Will was tall and blond and talented. In short, everything that her heart had ever wanted.

She looked around disinterestedly as her date

purchased tickets. She drank in the looks of those around her as the young man slipped the coat off of her shoulders in the coat room, knowing that she looked simply delicious in her two-tone silk gown. Her newly bleached hair, á la Jean Harlow, was in perfect waves around her face. Most others were in less formal attire. People came to The Shantyman to dance, and of course, drink. Even before Prohibition was thrown out, San Francisco wasn't a dry town.

She smiled sweetly at her young man and asked for a champagne. She wouldn't dare be seen drinking anything else that night. Not by Will Fontaine.

She leaned back onto the bar, extending her arms and making herself look like a fixture of the place. Around the perimeters were small tables and chairs, but in the middle were people scorching the floor boards, dancing away to the music of the band. Will was front and center, playing his horn, intensity making his fair features smolder at her across the room. She stared at him, willing him to look at her.

It didn't happen. Annoyed, she threw her champagne back in one gulp and turned to the bartender.

"I'll have another, please. He'll pay," she said, jerking her head toward her young man.

Both men scrambled to fulfill her wishes and when she had a fresh glass of bubbly in her hand, she strode through the dancers, knowing no one would dare to bump her and cause her to spill on her silken glory. She made it to the front, to just before the stage, and waited. Her heart stopped when Will's eyes found her. His sensual lips puckered as he played his horn.

But before she could wave, or even smile at Will,

his eyes left her and swept the herd of dancing people at her back. Furious, she stomped back toward the bar and went into the ladies' room. It was only a small water closet, room only for one woman at a time, so she could glare at her reflection in the mirror in peace.

"You stupid, ugly fool," she hissed. "You changed your looks so much that he doesn't recognize you!"

That summer night, Will had kissed a slightly chubby girl with mousy brown hair. She stood there now, blond and trim, doing her best to look like a misplaced Hollywood glamor girl. Her dress looked like one that she had seen Joan Crawford wear in a magazine and her mother's missing bottle of Clorox bleach told the tale of her knew platinum locks.

She took a deep breath and smiled sweetly at her reflection. She stood up straight and admired her figure in the alluring gown.

"Yes, you're gorgeous. There's no way he'll ignore you tonight." She said before heading back to the bar for another champagne.

There was a tall woman at the bar, her dark hair worn unfashionably in long curls. She was about two decades out of style, her shoes and dress hopelessly old and not belonging in such a swinging club. The woman was drinking something out of a tall glass, sucking on a straw lazily and swinging in time with the music. She looked at the young glamor girl and smiled.

"You look like you're here to make a scene, honey," the woman said.

"Simply having a nice night out is all," she answered. "I'm here with a fella."

"That young fool over there searching the room for you?" The woman pointed to one of the tables and there was the young man looking alone and miserable, scanning the throng of dancers for his fancy date. She lifted her arm and caught his eye. She smiled sweetly and gestured him over. He tripped and fell, but still made it to her in one piece.

"Hey honey, I need another drink," she said in her soft, childish voice.

"Another champagne for the lady," the young man automatically demanded.

When her drink was in her hand, she patted the young man on the cheek and turned away from him, leaning back on the bar and watching Will Fontaine make musical love to the room, not just to her. She grit her teeth.

"That fella playing the trumpet is a dish, ain't he?" The dark haired woman asked.

Giving up on pretense, the young girl nodded dreamily.

"I came here to be with him again," she said. "Will and I have history together."

"History, huh? Well, history is important, you know. This place here, it has history. Lots of it. Stood here for decades even before the big earthquake. Lots of interesting people been through here. That bugle blower up there? Honey, he ain't that interesting. If you're wanting attention from a fella, I suggest you stick with the man plying you with drink, hoping only to be seen with your pretty self. That fella up on stage is a love 'em and leave 'em kind and they're far from rare."

"You don't know what you're talking about! Will is wonderful and when he realizes who I am, we'll run away together, and I'll tour with him and we'll be happy."

"You're young and allowed to be stupid," the woman said, looking down into her dwindling drink. "But that youth fades, honey, and guys like that remain only as bad memories."

"Well you're old and stupid and mad that there aren't any men looking at you!" She hissed. She bared her teeth at the woman. "I won't sit here and listen to you. Just because you got used up and tossed aside doesn't mean Will is like that! You're just a bitter old hag!"

The woman grabbed her, a hand so cold that it hurt clamped down on her forearm and the glamor girl couldn't move.

"Don't make my mistakes, little girl. I've got all kinds of neat ideas on how to really make a splash!"

The chill left her, and the girl lurched away from the woman. When she regained her balance, she turned to scream at the crazy hag, but there was nobody there. The tall glass was empty, the chewed up straw was perched inside and there was no out-of-style woman with rag curls anywhere to be seen.

The young woman found herself suddenly unbothered as a rush of purpose flooded her. In that strange moment, she knew how to get Will Fontaine to see her. The bartender was busy shaking a drink at the opposite end of the bar. She lifted herself so that she could see over the bar into his workspace. There was a paring knife sitting next to several slices of lemon. She swiped the knife, taking a moment to look around to make sure that her theft wasn't witnessed.

Again she walked through the dancing bodies, the music and their interest in each other acted as a cloak for her. At the right of the stage was a door that read

STAFF ONLY. She went through. She was in a corridor that showed a flight of upward stairs to her right. Slightly to her left was a door that read STAGE ACCESS. She went through and found herself momentarily blinded by the lights at the front of the stage. When her eyes adjusted, she saw that some of the dancers were stopping their movements and looking at her curiously. The band, noticing the diverted attention of their audience slowly stopped, one instrument at a time. Will was the last to turn and look at her.

"Will," she said to him, the feeling of his eyes fully on her draping her in ecstasy. "I came to see you tonight. I'm here to see you, Will."

She clutched her left hand to her heart and walked slowly to the object of her desires. Will frowned at her and took a step back. Tears filled her eyes.

"I just wanted you to notice me," she said softly. "I just wanted you to see me!" She screamed. She struck out with the paring knife. His arm came up defensively and the blade sank into his hand. He screamed. She screamed. She stabbed again, this time making purchase in his neck. She stabbed again, blood arcing out of him and all around her like a wet and gleaming fireworks display. She was vaguely aware of screams. There were many hands on her, several arms wound about her. Will had gone pale and still, his grip on his neck was going limp. She screamed and twisted in many grips, too many to hold her, and she stood at the front of the stage and put the blade on the left side of her neck.

"For you, Will!" She said before stabbing the tip into the delicate flesh and ripping toward the center of her throat. More screams as she fell to the floor. Everyone was running away, leaving The Shantyman to get away.

A table fell over, and the two chairs sitting on top of it crashed to the floor, a tangle of legs and wooden tops made a hellish clamor.

Everett Lincoln jumped and pulled one of his earbuds out, the voices from the podcast he'd been listening to while he swept the floors sounding soft and distant. He was alone in the room. There was no reason for the table and chairs to fall. He sighed and walked heavily to the front and set everything back to rights. He looked around again to be certain that he was alone and continued his sweeping.

"This place gives me the damn creeps, man," he said to nobody at all.

PARODY

Jeff Strand

THERE HADN'T BEEN a good song since 1989. Chester didn't know what the last good song was, but it was in the '80s for sure. Everything since then was pure garbage recorded by talent-free "musicians" who were recruited by tone-deaf executives in fancy suits. It was all about money these days. Not in the '80s. The '80s were about the music, and the music videos, not the almighty dollar.

Chester didn't even recognize any of the songs "Weird Al" Yankovic was parodying anymore. They were still brilliant, but they might as well have been original compositions. "I Think I'm A Clone Now" instead of "I Think We're Alone Now" was genius. "Word Crimes" instead of "Blurred Lines" might have been clever but he had no frickin' idea what the "Blurred Lines" song was all about or who sang it and he had zero desire to find out.

That's why "Zany Chester" only parodied songs from the '80s.

"Material Girl"? How about "Material Squirrel," bitches? "Born To Run"? Try "Born To Pun." "99 Red

Balloons"? "100 Red Balloons." And that was barely *half* of his oeuvre.

He couldn't believe that The Shantyman wouldn't let him play there.

Oh, they had plenty of excuses. Their biggest one was that he didn't play any instruments . . . and he didn't have a band. Instead, he played the original song on his iPhone and sang over that. The manager had suggested that, while it wouldn't change their decision about booking him, he should at least try singing to a karaoke track with the vocals removed.

Screw that. Anybody could sing to a karaoke track. When you had to *compete against the original artist* . . . well, that was a true parody. Weird Al was a god, but he'd never been onstage at the same time as Michael Jackson, performing "Eat It" while Michael was performing "Beat It." The manager of The Shantyman just didn't get him. Chester knew this was true because the manager had told him point blank: "I don't get you."

Chester offered to perform for free. The manager said he'd never even entertained the idea of paying him. Chester offered to pay a nominal fee for the stage time, which he would recoup through new pledges on his Kickstarter campaign. The manager said that he couldn't afford to lose the customers. Chester suggested that he could shove the entirety of The Shantyman up his ass. The manager asked him to leave.

That is why Chester was standing in the audience, listening to the awful, awful, awful opening act, whose lyrics didn't even make any sense (he was no racist, but you shouldn't have to look up every third word on

Urban Dictionary to know what a band was singing about), and preparing to rush the stage between acts and get in one song.

He knew how it would go. He'd leap up on stage with his iPhone. The audience would be momentarily confused. The manager would narrow his eyes, not quite sure where he remembered Chester from. Chester would pick up the microphone, which the opening act had left in place, and he'd say, "Ladies and gentlemen, I'm Zany Chester! Thanks for coming out tonight! Does anyone remember George Michael?"

It wouldn't matter if the audience cheered, shook their heads and shrugged, or failed to answer the question altogether. Chester would press play and the opening notes of "Faith" would fill the club. Everybody would immediately become fifteen to twenty percent happier; George Michael's music did that. But the crowd would never suspect how much the threshold of their happiness could rise until he began to sing "Wraith."

As he and George Michael sang the first few words in perfect harmony the manager would realize who Chester was. His face would redden with fury, a red so bright that Chester could see it even in the dark club with stage lights shining in his eyes. The manager would frantically gesture to the bouncers. They would nod, and move forward, one headed toward each side of the stage. There'd be nowhere to run. Chester wouldn't have much time. Ten seconds at the most, and he'd have to make every single one of those seconds count.

Maybe he'd wink at the manager. Maybe he wouldn't. He hadn't decided yet.

" . . . *if I could touch your birdie*," he'd sing.

The club-goers, expecting him to say "body," would be taken aback. They'd thought this was a simple George Michael/Zany Chester duet, but no, it was something so much more. They were getting new lyrics. Witty lyrics. They were hearing one of the catchiest songs of all time but in a hilarious new way. "Weird Al" Yankovic, talented as he was, had never done a George Michael parody ("I Want Your Socks" was often incorrectly attributed to him), and his omission was what would catapult Chester to stardom.

With less than four seconds before the bouncers dragged him off the stage, Chester would know that he had to give it his all. This was the musical performance that would make or break his career. This was the moment that he would recall fondly, with a light chuckle, in each of the documentaries made about his life.

"I was wrong, obviously," the manager would tell the camera. "How could I have known? How could any of us have known?"

Those four seconds would be astounding. The audience, expecting to hear "*And I've got to think twice*," would laugh and gasp with delight when the lyric became, "*And I've got head lice*."

That's when the bouncers would clamp their hands on his shoulders.

He'd try to sing the next line, but they'd pull him away from the microphone. Though he had a powerful voice, the acoustics at The Shantyman weren't good enough to compete with the laughs and gasps of the audience.

They'd boo as the bouncers dragged him away.

The manager would realize that they were booing the bouncers, not Zany Chester.

The manager would realize that he'd made a mistake.

A terrible mistake.

Somebody up front would shout, "Let him play!" Others would join in. Soon the entire audience would be chanting "Let him play! Let him play! Let him play!"

The manager, flustered, would fire the bouncers on the spot. Then he'd walk up to the microphone, tug at his collar, and say, "Ladies and gentlemen, I'm proud to present . . . Zany Chester!"

The crowd would go berserk with joy. Chester would tap his iPhone screen to start the song from the beginning. When he finished performing "Wraith," the audience would demand another song, but he wouldn't do it. Another band was waiting to go on. Cutting into their stage time would be tacky.

The manager would apologize to him. "I guess even I can still learn new things about this business," he'd say. "I'd like you to be my next headliner."

No, that was going too far.

"I'd like you to be my next opening act."

Chester would accept his offer without a trace of bitterness. Because, yeah, people messed up. Numerous studios had turned down the chance to make *E.T. The Extraterrestrial.* Hell, M&Ms had turned down the product placement offer, leaving Reese's Pieces to swoop in and get the glory. Sometimes people simply made bad decisions. The job of the creative artist was to make them realize that they were wrong.

Boy, did this opening act suck.

Chester wasn't nervous at all. He'd thought that he would be, but there was really only one way this could go. Adoration. And why should he be nervous about receiving adoration?

"Thanks for letting us party with you tonight," said the front man of the opening act, after they finished a song about the number 420, the significance of which was baffling to Chester. April 20th, maybe? You shouldn't have to be a calendar expert to enjoy a song.

Were they done?

"We've just got one more for you . . . "

Dammit.

The opening act (Chester couldn't remember their name, and they couldn't be bothered to put a band logo on their drums; he certainly wasn't going to wander over to their merch table to find out) went into their final song. He hoped it was short.

The lyrical part of their song was short, but the self-indulgent bass solo went on forever. Were bass players even supposed to do solos? Admittedly, Chester wasn't completely sure which was the guitar and which was the bass, so it may have been a guitar solo. Still too long and self-indulgent.

However, the song did eventually come to an end. "Thank you," said the front man. "We're Eleven Mile Walk. Stick around for Replacement Kindle." The band members waved to the audience and walked off the stage as the lights came up.

Then they walked back onto the stage. What the hell were they doing? An encore?

No. They were breaking down their equipment. Chester didn't have a roadie either, so he didn't judge another performing artist for having to do their own manual labor. But the audience was already losing focus, and though he hadn't envisioned doing this with other people on the stage (except for the bouncers) he needed to move now.

He ran up onto the stage and stood in front of the microphone. "Hello, ladies and gentlemen, my name's—"

The microphone was off. Why had they turned it off? What if somebody needed to make an important announcement? He tapped on it a few times, then glanced back at the Eleven Mile Walk front man. "Do you know how to turn this back on?" he asked.

"They probably shut it off from the sound board."

"Could you ask them to turn it on?"

"And you are . . . ?"

"I'm the middle act."

"Nobody told me there was a middle act. If you want them to turn on the mic, that's all on you."

Jerk. Chester would totally have used his connections to get the mic turned back on if things were the other way around. He frantically waved to the guy working the soundboard and mimed that he wanted to speak into the microphone. The guy looked confused.

Fine, Chester would just have to do his concert without a microphone.

No, wait, the audience was already being way too loud. They wouldn't hear a word of his hilarity. He needed a goddamn microphone.

He kept gesturing to the mic. Finally, the guy shrugged and flipped a switch.

"Hello, Shantyman!" said Chester, as Eleven Mile Walk continued to tidy up after their set. "You are in for a treat! My name is Zany Chester, and I'm going to rock you like a baby!"

The audience seemed disinterested. He hoped to God they didn't think he meant anything dirty by that. His lyrics could be risqué, but of course making love to babies was entirely off-limits, even at his most edgy.

He hadn't plugged in his iPhone. He wasn't even sure *where* to plug in his iPhone. Even with the volume turned all the way up, nobody but the members of Eleven Mile Walk were going to hear the music. He couldn't sing without the background track. Even Weird Al didn't sing without accompaniment.

He was losing his audience! He was losing his audience! He was losing his audience!

This was a disaster! He wouldn't get to perform his George Michael parody! He'd grown all this stubble for nothing!

"Please," he said to the guys on the stage. "I have to plug this in. You've gotta help."

"Give it here," said the drummer, extending his hand. Chester hesitated for a moment, thinking the drummer might intend to steal his phone, but, no, that was ridiculous, and he'd have to take the risk. He handed over the phone, and the drummer plugged it in to an amp.

Saved!

"I'm going to rock you like a baby" hadn't gone over well (and, in retrospect, it was a terrible line to get an audience psyched about a musical performance—he was surprised he didn't catch that during the hundreds of times he'd mentally rehearsed saying it). A do-over was in order.

"Hello, Shantyman!" he said. "You are in for a

treat!" Too egotistical? Too late now. "My name is Zany Chester, and I'm going to take you back to the '80s. The 1980's, that is! Here's my take on that George Michael classic, 'Faith,' but I think you'll find that my version isn't quite what you remember!"

He winked at the audience.

Nobody winked back. In fact, they looked at him as if he was kind of creepy.

Oh well. Weird Al could be creepy, too. No shame in that.

The drummer was still holding on to his iPhone. Chester took it from him, pressed "play," and then set it on the amp because the cord wasn't long enough for him to carry the phone around with him while he performed.

The opening notes to "Faith" began to play. Most of the people in the crowd were looking at him, so he was off to a good start. The manager was nowhere to be seen, and the bouncer (just one, which was nice) remained at the door. This was going to work.

"*Oh, I guess it would be nice*," he and George sang, "*if I could touch your body . . .*"

No! It was supposed to be "birdie!" He'd accidentally sang the original version! It was like when Don McLean accidentally sang part of Weird Al's parody of "American Pie" except in reverse!

He could fix this. Nobody would notice.

But the next line didn't make sense without "birdie" in the previous line! He'd have to stick with George Michael's original lyrics for that line, too, and then cross over into his parody immediately after that.

The audience did not seem to be enjoying his musical performance. Chester refused to panic. The "head lice" lyric would win them over. It was irresistible.

"*And I've got head lice . . .* " he sang.

Nobody laughed. Nobody even chuckled. Nobody even smiled. Nobody even stopped frowning.

He kept going. He'd gotten off to a shaky start with the whole microphone thing and the audience just needed time to catch up.

Somebody booed.

"You suck!" somebody shouted.

"Get off the stage!" shouted somebody else.

Chester stopped singing. He hurried over to the amp and shut off the music. Screw these people if they didn't appreciate his effort to bring a bit of joy into the nihilistic pit of black despair that was their lives.

"Leave the parodies to Weird Al!" shouted the same guy who'd told him that he sucked.

"Weird Al never parodied George Michael!" Chester shouted back at him.

"Yes, he did!"

"He did not! 'I Want Your Socks' wasn't him, dipshit!"

"No, he parodied him in the 'UHF' video!"

"That doesn't count!"

"It was a parody of the frickin' 'Faith' video!"

"But it was just a visual parody! It wasn't a spoof of the song itself! It's not the same thing at all!"

"We'll just have to agree to disagree!"

"Fine. Whatever. Do you all want me to leave? Will that make you happy? Will you at least get a chuckle out of watching me slink away in shame?"

"Yes!" shouted multiple people.

"Quit disrespecting his memory!" shouted a man in green.

Chester didn't think he'd heard that right.

"What did you say?" he asked, pointing to the man.

"I said, quit disrespecting his memory! George Michael is rolling over in his grave!"

"What do you mean?"

"I mean just what I said!"

"George Michael's not dead."

"Ummmm . . . yes, he is. Has been for a while."

Chester looked around the audience. Most of them were nodding.

No.

It couldn't be.

Holy shit.

He wasn't going to cry . . . he wasn't going to cry . . . he wasn't going to cry . . .

"But when?" he asked. "How did it happen? Why didn't it make the news?"

"It was all over the news!" shouted a woman from the back. "Where have you been?"

Chester could feel his entire world collapsing. He knew he'd never again be Zany Chester. Not just the stage name—he knew he'd never again be in a zany mood. His fantasies of a standing ovation were over, and not simply because it was a standing room only venue. This was to be his first and only performance.

He wished he had a few moments to himself so he could mourn George Michael properly, but that wasn't an option. He had to act now if he was going to ensure his immortality in the history of musical performances. Though he'd hoped that it would be because of the stellar reaction to his song, he'd come in with a backup plan.

Chester took out a pocketknife.

He snapped out the blade. He had to stab somebody quickly, before anybody realized what was about to happen. The drummer was closest, so Chester slammed the knife into his chest, pulled it out, and then stabbed him again.

The audience didn't do anything. They just kind of stared at the stage, as if thinking, "*Maybe this is all part of the show. His song was terrible on purpose, and we were supposed to think that we were seeing a disastrous musical performance, but it was all misdirection for the moment when he pretended to stab a dude.*"

The drummer, of course, knew it wasn't fake. He touched the bloody wound and gaped at Chester in horror.

"I . . . plugged in your phone for you . . . " he said, before collapsing onto the stage.

It was true. The one guy in the entire club who hadn't been a complete dick to him was the one he stabbed. Chester felt bad about that.

The other members of Eleven Mile Hike (Eleven Mile Walk? Which was it? And why was Chester squandering his final thoughts on trying to remember the band's name?) also knew it wasn't a simulated stabbing, but they apparently weren't inclined to rush at a guy holding a knife.

"Security!" the bass or guitar player shouted.

Chester knelt down and stabbed the drummer a few more times. For his piece of resistance, or whatever the French version of that phrase was, it was important that the bouncers think of him as a serious threat and not be gentle with him.

A woman screamed.

He wanted the crowd to panic but not panic so much that they missed what he was doing. A lot of cell phones were recording him. He begged God not to let him mess this up, although God had probably bailed on the whole endeavor after Chester stabbed the drummer.

A bouncer rushed onto the stage.

Chester dropped the knife.

His timing had to be perfect.

The bouncer ran at him, then did the exact move Chester had hoped for: he yanked Chester's arm behind his back.

"Hey, everybody, look at me!" said Chester. "I'm *break*dancing!"

Chester did a violent twist. Though he couldn't hear the bone break over the horrified noises the audience was making, he could definitely feel it. He'd known it was going to hurt, obviously, but not *that* bad! He should've tested it out beforehand. Well, no, that would have been impractical.

"Did you hear me?" he asked. "*Break*dancing!"

Did the audience realize he'd just broken his arm? Shit, they didn't, did they? His joke didn't make any goddamn sense if they didn't know his arm was broken. He'd expected the bone to protrude, but it remained completely contained within his skin.

Also, his expectation had been that he'd be able to wiggle free of the bouncer and do an actual breakdance, at least as well as he could with a broken arm flopping around. But he remained firmly in the bouncer's grip. This could not be going more poorly.

What if he broke his arm even more?

Chester twisted again, and—oh, yeah, that did it. The bouncer shoved him down and stepped away, as if Chester's insanity might be contagious. The audience let out a really loud frickin' gasp. Protruding bone for sure.

He picked up the knife. The timing on the breakdancing joke was completely fouled up, but he had a Plan C. It involved a less famous, though equally classic, dance from the '80s: the Sprinkler. Yes, the dance where you pretended to be a lawn sprinkler. Anybody who said they didn't enjoy the Sprinkler was a damned liar.

Chester was starting to feel a bit dizzy. Didn't matter. The show was almost over. "Hey, everybody!" he shouted. "I'm doing the Sprinkler!"

He jammed the knife deep into his neck. Blood poured down over his hand, which was exactly what he needed. Finally, something was working out perfectly.

He did the Sprinkler, sprinkling blood into the audience as he did so.

Success! It would be, he was confident, the most legendary performance of the Sprinkler in the history of dance. What performance would even come close?

Nobody was laughing. That was okay. Maybe somebody would smile thinking back upon this night, or get a chuckle watching the video on YouTube. That's really all he wanted.

Chester collapsed. Then he died, feeling zany.

ASCENDING

Robert Ford

LOVE HAPPENED SLOWLY *and then all at once.*

I don't remember who described love that way, but it was exactly that with Layla and me. It started as a prank. My best friend Josh stole my phone, downloaded the CupidsArrow app and set up a fake account for me under the name "PikachuLUVR." After I found out, I fixed the profile details he'd put in (I *don't* find farm animals erotic, nor have I *ever* collected Pokémon). Swipe down to ignore and swipe up if you thought they were an *angel of love.*

Corny, I know. A few days in, I saw LaylaGirl's profile.

LaylaGirl
Age: 23
Zodiac: Don't Care
Interests: Reading/Writing, Music, Life
Seeking: Idk. Let's find out together. ;)
Turn ons/offs: Ask

She seemed interesting so in a rare moment of bravery, I sent her a message. My friend Josh will walk up to any girl in the room—even if she's a Victoria's Secret model—and chat her up as if they've known each other forever. Make her laugh. Get her number. It's like *breathing* to him. I do *not* have that ability.

A single online message turned into conversations and soon I found myself checking in with her first thing in the morning and last thing at night. It was exciting, getting to know each other.

LaylaGirl: So . . . do you give your phone number out a lot?

PikachuLUVR: Idk . . . 5, maybe 6 times this week.

LaylaGirl: Oh.

PikachuLUVR: To Human Resource departments as I'm applying for jobs. =)

LaylaGirl: LOL! Ahhh ok. :) NOW I feel special! Hahaha

PikachuLUVR: Good! I like making you feel special.

LaylaGirl: You do, Naz. You're very sweet. I like talking with you. A lot. =D

When my parents got to America, they thankfully left the old ways behind. Arranged marriages and caste systems. Instead, they embraced their new country—especially rock and roll. My mother was always quoting lyrics or things musicians said. They became her wise men.

Instead of *Red Fish, Blue Fish*, my mother read the

poems of the Lizard King himself, Jim Morrison. I missed out on *Clifford the Big Red Dog*, but I got a master's degree in Bob Dylan, Jimi Hendrix, and Cream.

For my tenth birthday, my parents bought me The Beatles *White Album* and a brand new Team Murray bicycle. The bike had metallic red foam pads and freestyle wheels and looked magical. I was invincible on this stallion.

I couldn't have been more wrong.

I rode into the woods along the dirt trails of the construction crew building a neighboring development. One day, I got the idea to ride an uprooted tree and jump off the jagged stump at the end of it. There I was, hauling ass to acid-fueled Hendrix blasting in my ears. I rode onto the tree trunk, made it to the end, and for half a second, I was flying. Major Tom leaving the confines of Earth itself.

Except Ground Control had a serious problem. The spokes of my rear wheel caught in the tree roots and I slammed into the pile of rocks beneath.

I broke my right arm, my collarbone, and two ribs. Hobbling back home, crying and bloody, it was the first time I ever heard my mother speak her native tongue, as she came wailing to my rescue.

That injury changed the course of my life.

I recuperated in bed and my father let me use his laptop to pass the time. He also bought me a copy of *The Hobbit*.

I hate to admit it, but the book went untouched. The laptop however . . .

I started reading about programming. On the third day, something clicked. Maybe it was Janis Joplin screaming in my ears or Pete Townshend blasting away, but it all just made sense. In less than two weeks, I learned C+ code. I moved on to JavaScript, then html, which, by that time, seemed juvenile.

In every other way, I am *admittedly* unremarkable. I have *one* friend—Josh. I've never had a girlfriend though I've been on a few dates—all set up as doubles by Josh—and one time a girl kissed me. I've never gotten drunk or stoned. I've never even been to a concert. Was never voted school president or class clown. Always the last one picked for teams in gym class.

But I can code *like a beast.*

I wear headphones when I code, typing to the rhythm and pace of the music. It somehow all meshes together and makes sense. In many ways, it's the only thing that ever really has.

That, and when Layla and I fell in love.

PikachuLUVR: My being Indian isn't a problem for you is it?

LaylaGirl: I don't think so, not really. I mean . . . are you Indian or are you INDIAN?

PikachuLUVR: I don't worship a cow in the backyard if that's what you're asking. :)

LaylaGirl: No arranged marriages or payment in farm animals and jewels?

PikachuLUVR: No, no. My parents left all of that behind when they left India. Fell in love with America and its fast-food, MTV society with open arms. Besides, when we get married, payment will be in expensive bourbon and rounds of golf at private clubs. Lol

LaylaGirl: Oh? We're getting married now?! =D

PikachuLUVR: Whoaaaaaa slow down! You American girls are SO fast! I didn't say NOW . . . Let's wait at least a week or so. :)

LaylaGirl: HAHAHAHA! Ok. Got a deal, babe. ;)

I had given her my phone number about a week after first messaging her, but she hadn't used it yet—every conversation had been on CupidsArrow. Layla worked in public relations at Stapleton and Baker, an advertising agency in downtown San Francisco. She didn't talk much about it, but there were a lot of late nights and it really seemed to stress her out.

One day, out of the blue, I got a text message.

LAYLA: I want to see your face when we talk. So does Chaos. Hahaha! Videochat later?

Sounds stupid, but it was like moving to the next level, you know? Maybe you don't. Maybe it's strange and weird and messed up, but it was a big deal. Phone calls and video chats became the norm. We talked about our pasts and she introduced me to Chaos, her cat, and everything seemed like it was going great. Then her messages started getting brief. She kept saying she was just tired. It had been two months since we'd started talking and I wondered if she was getting bored with a *virtual* relationship.

I didn't tell my parents *or* Layla, but I stopped applying for jobs on the east coast and turned my attention to San Francisco. Near *her*.

Two weeks ago, I got an email from BayTech, an up and coming blockchain technology company. Cutting-edge projects with people scrambling to work for them. They loved my résumé and after a twenty-minute phone interview, I got an email saying they wanted to fly me out to meet in person.

I took several deep breaths as I read the email. It felt like launching off the tree trunk as a kid, soaring into pure blue sky. Except *this* time, I was going to make the landing.

"Are you for real?"

I smiled at Layla's question and leaned back on my bed. "The way they made it sound, the interview is a formality at this point and I'll be the lead programmer on a new project *sooo* . . . "

Layla was silent on the other end and I could hear Chaos meowing in the background.

"Naz, I . . . "

"Look, don't freak out. I'm not asking to move in or anything. I'll get my own place. We haven't really met in person but so what? I . . . " I took a deep breath and let it out slow. "I'm in love with you, Layla. I've never felt this way about anyone and I—"

"There's things about me you don't know, Naz."

"And there's things about me *you* don't know. But

I want to find out. I want to be with you. I thought you'd be happy about this."

"I am, it's just . . . you're too good for me."

"Yeah, since being on the phone, the butler's interrupted me twice and I had to yell at the maid because she dropped the good silver. What do you mean, *too good* for you?"

The phone was silent again. "I'm afraid once you . . . you say you love me but what if we meet and you end up hating me? It's . . . there's things going on you don't know about."

I could tell she was crying.

I felt sick. Tears blurred my eyes and I sat up on the edge of my bed. "If you're going to break up with me, just do it and get it over with. But I need you to answer one question for me, honestly. Are you in love with me?"

The quiet stretched out like an endless ribbon, and softly, *so* softly, she replied. "Yes."

I let out a breath I didn't realize I had been holding. "Then there's *nothing* you could say or do to make me hate you."

"You don't understand."

"My flight comes in at 5:23 Friday evening and I'll see you face to face. I'll understand *anything* you want to tell me and more importantly, *you'll* understand. Two days."

She sniffled on the other end of the line. "Okay honey."

"I love you. Baby, please get some rest. I think you're just working too hard lately."

"I'll try. I love you, too." Her voice was still tender, but I could tell as she said those words, she was smiling.

I ended the call, tossed the phone on my bed and leaned back.

My phone dinged.

Layla: Naz, are you for real?

Me: For REAL, for real. I mean everything I said. I PROMISE!

Me: Two days, honey. 5:23 San Fran time.

Four hours later, long after I'd gone to sleep, another text from her.

Layla: Please be for real.

I got an email confirmation on the flight out of Newark. I texted a screenshot to Layla and got two kissy face emojis in response.

My parents drove me to the airport. My mother wrapped her arms around me tightly and had tears in her eyes.

"Y' know . . . David Bowie said I don't know where I'm going from here, but I promise it won't be boring."

"Nice one. And Bob Dylan said there is nothing so stable as change." She smiled proudly, and I hugged her tightly. She smelled of lavender. "I love you, Mom."

My father smiled at me, put his hand out and I shook it. Still holding my hand, he gave me a half hug and put his free hand on the back of my head, pulling me closer. "Let us know when you land, ok?"

"I will, Dad. I love you."

I texted Layla a selfie with the plane waiting on the

tarmac outside the terminal window and got no reply. I figured she was still busy at work. It seemed they had *really* been keeping her hustling lately.

I boarded the plane, buckled up, and leaned my head back against the seat.

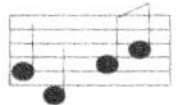

In contrast to Newark Airport's strange *alien-nest-in-a-dirty-gutter* vibe, San Francisco Airport was clean and light. Vaulted ceilings with enormous glass openings, allowing light to flow into the building. It felt exciting and fresh, full of hope.

I waited at the luggage carousel and pulled out my phone.

Me: Landed!! Waiting for my luggage and will be right out!!

Outside, I scanned the faces for Layla but didn't see her as I watched cabs come and go.

For over an hour at the airport, I waited and watched people come and go. Happy families. Businessmen. Even a limo with a suited and capped driver standing outside with a sign: WAGNER. I watched a longhaired guy with dark sunglasses pull his luggage to the curb and step inside the luxury escort. The driver packed the bags in the trunk and they drove off to do whatever rock stars do.

I checked my phone once more, wheeled my luggage to the curb, and waved a cab.

Layla's building. Tan stucco exterior. Side-by-side apartments. Nice landscaping. The sight of it made my heart beat faster. In my mind, I had imagined all sorts of scenarios—her opening the door and the expression on her face as she pulled me into her open arms. Maybe she would cry a little.

Yeah, I know. *I know*. Reality *very* rarely mimics fantasy.

I knocked and the vertical blinds at the window near her front door rippled and I saw a black cat hop onto the window ledge, rubbing back and forth against the glass. I could hear a muffled meow and I put a hand against the window. "Hi there, Chaos."

I knocked again. "Hello?"

I called Layla's cell and it went directly to voicemail. "Layla, hey, it's Naz. I um . . . not sure if you're putting out fires at work or something, but I'm here. Did you forget about the time or maybe I wasn't clear or something? Just . . . call me back."

I patted the window. "See you soon, buddy. I'll give you a good back scratch in person."

There was a black plastic garbage can at the side of the front porch and I pulled the cap off. Empty and surprisingly clean inside. I tilted it down and lifted my luggage into the can and popped the lid back on.

"Okay, San Fran. Show me what you got." The Golden Gate Bridge and stretch of Bay water welcomed me but I shook the idea off. It was important Layla and I were together the first time I saw the waters. Maybe it was the idea of her showing me around, taking me to all the spots she thought were amazing. I didn't want to spoil anything, I guess.

I headed in the opposite direction, hands in my pockets, phone on full volume in case Layla called, and breathed in a new city with a smile on my face.

As I passed people on the sidewalk, they smiled

and nodded at me. *That* was different. Most people in Jersey had a *what-tha-fuck-you-lookin-at* scowl on their face as they made eye contact.

I stopped at a crosswalk, undecided on which direction to go. A light pole in front of me had a flyer pasted to it:

ASCENSION NIGHT
AT THE SHANTYMAN
Bands • Drink Specials • Open Mic • Good Times
Two blocks East on Howard St.

I walked a few steps and stopped. *I was moving out here, not only for Layla, but for a new life. New things. New experiences.* I turned to look at the flyer again. I smiled to myself and headed in the direction the flyer pointed.

The outside of the Shantyman lived up to its name—weathered siding that hadn't been painted in a few decades and a flat black marquee above the entrance. A short blonde in a halter-top walked inside the building.

Inside, the bar was dimly lit and the ceiling was a flat black sheet of barn roof tin. A few people sat at tables. I took a seat at the bar and a short man with spiked gray hair gave me a nod as he racked pint glasses.

"Don't get many techies in here." The bartender grinned.

"Techy?"

"Programmers. Computer geeks. *No offense.* They're usually downtown at the trendy spots sippin' hundred dollar bourbon or some shit."

"I'm not from here."

"No shit?" His grin grew wider. "No one's from here, pal."

The bartender stuck his hand out and I shook it automatically. "Name's Gigs. So you're out here for an interview but something else has got you twisted up. Lemme guess . . . a woman?"

"How . . . "

"Spend enough time behind here and people's expressions are an open book."

He reached beneath the bar, withdrew two shot glasses, and started pouring Jack Daniels into each one. "On the house, along with my advice. You'll do fine on the interview." He set the bottle down and swung a dishtowel over his shoulder.

"Don't get all worked up about the girl. If women didn't smell nice and look pretty, we'd be hunting them from horseback. I once dated a girl who told me I was making my sandwich wrong. Bitch, *I'm* the one who's eating it. How am I making my *own* sandwich wrong? Whatever. I hear she's blowin' guys from Microsoft for meth down in the Tenderloin district. Life's a funny thing but it works out how it's supposed to."

I pulled one of the shots closer and sniffed the liquor. "God's master plan and all that?"

Gigs put his hands flat on the bar top. "Fuck no, kid. God's a blind man with Alzheimer's. Sometimes you have to take a leap of faith all on your own."

I put the liquor against my lips and sipped. It burned against my tongue and tasted of charcoal and oak.

"*Jeeeezus Chriiiist.* You pack your tampons on the flight? *Do the shot!*"

I laughed, then tilted the glass and swallowed the rest, feeling the fire flow down my throat and into my stomach.

"My man." He nodded his approval. "Enjoy the show tonight. There's an opening band called Cutthroat followed by Balls Deep in Hell. Then it's open fucking mic for the rest. Music's loud enough to make your ears bleed but the crowd will be fun. Loosen up. It'll all work out."

"Thanks, Gigs."

He went off to the other side of the bar to some customers. Stagehands were setting up equipment and checking lights. *My first shot.* I could already feel it working, the mild buzz taking hold. I waited until Gigs wasn't paying attention and took a sip from the second glass.

I checked the messages I'd sent to Layla. *Still unread.* I turned my stool away from the bar and dialed the main number of her office.

"Stapleton and Baker."

"I'm trying to reach Layla Zimmerman."

There was a pause on the line. "May I ask who's calling?"

"I'm Nazir Bahl."

"*Frommm?*" The receptionist drew the word out as she said it.

"I'm . . . Layla's boyfriend."

"Oh, I . . . " Another pause. "Hold please."

Classic rock kicked in on waiting and Don Henley's voice filled my ears.

"Hello, this is Ann Wildasin. I'm head of human resources. May I help you?"

"Um, yeah. I'm not sure why uh . . . I'm trying to reach Layla Zimmerman."

"Layla Zimmerman hasn't been an employee of Stapleton and Baker for . . . two months at least. Is this a job reference or for health insurance?"

"Health insurance?"

"In her condition . . . " I heard the sound of papers being pushed around on a desk. "I'm sorry, they didn't tell me your name. I assumed this was a query for health insurance. I'll put the paperwork through myself to extend it for her if she needs it. Unethical to talk about, but screw it, this place is closing the doors next week anyway. They did that poor girl wrong. Wasn't her fault that predator son of a bitch boss of hers–"

I hung up the call. *What the hell was going on?*

I drank the rest of the shot straight down and pulled a twenty from my pocket, setting it on the bar. I caught Gigs' attention, pointed to the shot glasses and nodded.

The place was starting to get crowded. A couple of girls wearing black corsets and leather mini-skirts flirted with a guy near the stage. Waitresses catered to groups sitting at tables ordering drinks. A man in a sleeveless T-shirt did sound checks on the stage.

I could feel the warm glow of alcohol in my stomach and the looseness of my body. It made me smile and nod to myself. Even with Layla's silence, I had to admit, I was feeling pretty all right.

Among the crowd, I could hear snips of conversation.

"What did it feel like for you?"

"I couldn't take it back."

"It really was the best thing for everyone."

A couple shouldered up to the bar beside me. "It

was finally over, you know? I didn't have to deal with what he was doing to me ever, *ever* again." The girl was speaking to a guy in his mid-twenties, wearing a saggy sweater and a beanie.

"I know, right? Like all this weight was gone." The guy waved at Gigs.

"Good evening and welcome to Ascension Night at The Shantyman!"

A man's voice boomed over the speakers and the crowd yelled and raised their glasses in response.

"We've got a lot of good music lined up, and let's give a warm welcome to Cutthroat!"

The crowd went nuts as heavy bass and electronic music cut through the noise. The stage was still dark but a spotlight flared on and I watched someone descend from the ceiling on a cable, upside down, wrapped in yellow crime scene tape.

That set people into a frenzy and as the hard-hitting industrial music filled the place, the crowd moved and swarmed as one. *Yes, indeed, not in Jersey anymore.*

Gigs had filled my glasses and left change without me even noticing. I drank one quickly, shaking my head at the burn. All my life I'd stood against the wall, watching *other* people live life. I suddenly wanted to be a part of all this.

Grabbing my drink, I left the bar stool and moved into the throng of people, swaying and bouncing in sync with them. Leather corsets and lace neck collars were everywhere. People smiling and laughing. A bearded man wearing a suit and a pained expression on his face bobbed his head to the beat. A girl with purple dreadlocks danced beside him. As I maneuvered, I saw him turn to her and blatantly stare at her breasts and speak loudly over the music.

"Incredible cleavage, but in the right bra, they would be *amaaaaaazing!*"

The girl threw her head back and laughed, grabbing his hands and putting them on her chest, pressing her tits together. His hands left a wet angel-wing impression on the shirt as he pulled away. They laughed and the man turned to look at me as I stepped around them. His gaze looked raw and red and bloodshot. I gave one last glance behind me and the two of them were staring, odd amused smiles on their faces.

The first song came to an end and the lead singer tore free of the crime scene tape and stood to face the crowd and their roar of appreciation. Dry ice machines began to spit out fog from corners of the stage and the band started their next song.

A waitress glided through the crowd holding a tray of empty plastic shot cups. She was dressed in all black and had some sort of dark green lei draped around her neck. She smiled and winked as if she knew me, moved closer, and gave me a soft kiss on the cheek before she vanished into the group of people.

A pair of men, both dressed in suits swayed to the music. The older man gave the younger one a fatherly clap on the shoulder and they clinked beer mugs. Beside them, a thin rail of a man wore a leather jacket and had a safety pin pierced through his right eyebrow. Everyone seemed to *belong*. It was a bar full of diversity and I melted right in. I felt like I was *part* of something.

I arrived at the edge of the stage. The bass was so

deep and loud, I could feel the fabric of my jeans vibrating against my skin. I drank the rest of my shot and set the glass on the stage. The crowd became one, surging and moving like a school of fish in deep waters.

"*Thank youuuuu,* Shantyman!" The music ended and the lead singer upended a bottle of water over his head, shaking his hair side to side and spraying the crowd. "We're gonna take a short break so grab another drink and tip the staff, dammit! They're working hard to get you fuckers drunk. Balls Deep in Hell is gonna rock the stage next!"

The lights in the bar rose to a dull glow. Like a tide, the crowd turned for fresh drinks. I leaned back against the wooden platform, feeling the dry ice fog curling over the sweat on my skin. I closed my eyes and leaned my head back, catching my breath and smiled to myself.

And I felt her.

It had happened before, that feeling. I'd know right before Layla was going to text or call me. I'd reach for my phone and it would go off in my hands, making me smile. I'd just . . . *know.*

I put my hand in my pocket, then froze as I gazed at the crowd.

A split-second view of a girl's face and I saw Layla. People moved and she disappeared behind them, but it was her. Leather jackets and black T-shirts hid her like a stage curtain and when they moved again, there she was, a soft smile on her face. She wore jeans and a faded Nirvana shirt. Her hair and the shoulders of the shirt looked damp and she was holding a bundle of wet cloth close to her chest.

There it was—the Hollywood love story moment. I

took a step toward her, then walked faster as she moved from the group of people toward me.

"Layla, it doesn't matter what happened. I'll—"

She lifted a finger and put it against my lips and a tear fell down one cheek. She slid a cool hand around the back of my neck and pulled me to meet her lips.

For the briefest of moments, I wondered if the weather outside had changed and turned to cold rain, as her lips and face were chilled and I could feel moisture on her skin. But then I was lost in the sensation of her lips against mine. She tasted of salt and something earthy. I ran my hands into her hair and felt the wet silkiness of it in my fingers.

"I love you more than I knew I could love." She whispered. "Thank you for that."

I leaned my forehead against hers and watched more tears spill down her cheeks.

"Everything will be okay. I love you, too."

She opened her eyes and they looked filmy, like sea glass. I pulled back and realized the bar crowd had grown quiet. They were watching us, and though I didn't care, they all appeared somewhat bashful, as if they had been expecting this moment, yet reluctant to see such an intimate thing.

Layla moved away slightly and reached for the bundle of material she held, parting the folds of cloth with her hand so I could see.

The gentle face of a baby was nestled in the bundle. Its skin was pale in the light of the room. Layla brushed a fingertip against the baby's bottom lip and it pursed them together and opened its eyes, swiveling the milky orbs to focus on me. It gave a light cough and foam bubbled at the corner of its lips. I watched a sand crab pull itself free from the tender, moist mouth before it skittered away among the folds of cloth.

I staggered backward.

"Isn't he beautiful?"

The bearded man in a suit stepped forward and ran his hand over the baby's head. He turned and his face had changed in the light. Chunks of flesh were chewed away, and his gray lips were frayed off, exposing his gums. Silver dollar circles of ruined skin pockmarked his face and when he smiled, his teeth shone brightly.

The crowd stood in a semi-circle behind Layla, smiling with approval. They were all so pale. Puddles of sandy water gathered at their feet on the wooden floor and I saw the waitress pull a rope of wet seaweed from around her neck. She let it fall to the floor with a sloppy smack and grinned. An eel glistened and wriggled around her high-heeled feet, splashing in the water as its circular mouth pulsed.

The piss ran down my leg before I registered the warmth, but it was enough to break me from the moment. I bolted toward the exit, ignoring the murmurs of the crowd and Layla's hurt expression.

"You promised!" The baby sputtered and began to cry.

Layla's screams were behind me as I slammed the metal release on the door and tripped onto the sidewalk. Pain bloomed like red tulips on my elbows and knees as I skidded on the pavement.

I stumbled to my feet and didn't stop running until I reached the bridge, then finally slowed enough to kneel and throw up in the weeds. The whiskey and vomit filled my mouth. Both knees of my jeans were bloody and I could feel the cloth sticking to the flesh.

From here, the breeze of the bay flowed over me. The stink of the water. In the darkness, the lights of the Golden Gate shimmered on the dark water below.

The metal railing felt hard and unforgiving beneath my hands and I peered over, seeing a long steel-mesh net bolted to the underside of the bridge. I stepped higher, felt the railing press against my waist, the cold seeping through the damp fabric of my jeans. The water below swirled like black mercury, beckoning. Standing there, I lifted my hands skyward, letting the air wash over me. For a moment, it felt like I was flying.

Jim Morrison once said love cannot save you from your own fate.

Off in the distance, I heard a baby cry.

THE SOUTHERN THING

Adam Cesare

I FEEL LIKE a phony.

Not because I am one.

No. It's not like I'm here after hearing one or two songs on Spotify and impulse-bought a ticket for tonight's show.

I'm a *fan*. A hardcore fan. Have been for years. Have been for, let's see now, at least ten years. I found the band right after *Decoration Day,* which was—what?—2003? Actually, now that I do the math, that's way more than ten years. God, time flies.

Well. Maybe phony is too strong a word. But I do always feel *inauthentic* when I see my favorite band play.

You see, the Truckers hail from Athens, Georgia and the co-founders grew up in Alabama.

They are a southern band. A southern American rock band.

And I am a Yankee.

I can't change that and wouldn't want to learn how to talk in the accent even if I could.

I grew up outside of New York City and went to school in Boston. I am not a good old boy. A Good Ol' Boy.

But neither are the musicians, really. They write and sing about the South with pride, but not *that* kind of pride. The Lynyrd Skynyrd tailgate crowd kind. No, the Truckers are progressive, like me. They voice their frustrations with backwards thinking, push against stereotypes of what southern men and women are like.

But, still, the Truckers are authentic in a way that I will never be able to claim.

And even with my insecurities, I make it worse. Because what's less authentic than my current situation?

I'm standing in a near empty San Francisco bar, sipping at the cheapest beer they sell, and trying to look busy on my phone. I've arrived way too early. I often do this when I'm seeing the Truckers. I can't seem to help it. I get excited early in the day and then show up at the venue at doors, even though I know the warm-up band won't be on for another hour after that.

I've never been to this place before, never even heard of it. The Shantyman?

Well, I guess that's not that odd. I've only been in town for six months now. I barely have the hang of public transit. I use Lyft to get everywhere even though it's twice as expensive as any city I've ever lived.

But that's to be expected, I guess. Everything here is expensive. Even the "cheapest" beer I'm nursing turned out to be six bucks.

At least I'm paid commensurate with the raise in prices. But don't tell that to my neighbors. They hate that I'm here. Well, I shouldn't take it so personally: they hate that the tech industry is here. Twitter, Facebook, my employer. Doesn't matter that I write ad copy for a living, couldn't produce a single line of code and don't understand much of the conversation I overhear in our sweet cafeteria. No, the hippies of San Francisco would like to see me dead.

I don't think of myself as yuppie scum, but I guess I'm not the salt of the earth blue collar guy I'm trying to project with my band t-shirt and dirt flecked jeans, either.

I take a big swig of overpriced PBR to calm my nerves against what could become a spin back down to *You're a Phony* territory.

Hmmm. I shake the can. Getting low. If I don't switch to liquor, I'm going to have to pee several times during this show. But if I do switch to liquor and have to be in early tomorrow . . .

I shake my head. This is supposed to be fun, an escape. Don't think of work with its open-office layout and its free on-site laundromat.

It's hard to get a read on the Shantyman's clientele. Are they hipsters or authentic residue of the Haight-Ashbury days? It's still early, but the warmup is onstage tuning his guitar, so there's been some fill-in since I first got here.

I work my way back to the bar. If this were Philly I'd be able to get a citywide special, a shot and a beer, for five bucks, but there's no use pining for the East Coast. This is where I am now. This is where I'm successful and don't have to hack it out with freelance tutoring jobs and writing fiction that earned me even less money than it did readers. This job is respectable, even if the people of San Fran don't respect it or me.

The bartender is definitely my type, tattoos and midriff, but I'm guessing I'm not hers. I arch my eyebrows and lay my wallet against the rail, but it's hard to get her attention even when I'm one of only three people at the bar.

"It's supposed to be fun, fella."

"Huh?" I say. Some asshole has sidled up next to me.

"I said it's supposed to be fun. You look like your dog died." He says, smiling broadly to show he meant no offense. I must have that apprehensive New Yorker look I put on whenever a stranger tries to talk to me.

His voice is . . . is that a put on or does he really talk like that?

"Oh, I love the Truckers, just looking to get a drink and I'll cheer up." I put some warmth into my response, but also some finality. I don't need a buddy. Or a date. I just need a drink.

"I'm just messing with you. I know how it is, on a work night. This fuckin' job, right?"

"This fuckin' job," I say. He's a fan too, I guess.

The bartender comes over and asks me what I want. Maybe talking to another patron makes it seem less likely I'll hit on her, if that's what she was worried about. I can't blame her, must happen all the time.

The warmup has started. Singer-songwriter stuff sounds good. I'll buy his CD if he's selling them. Some artists don't anymore. I work in tech but I swear to fuck if he's just got a postcard with a QR code on it, I'll never listen to his music.

A few songs go by as I nurse my drink, then turn to grab the bartender for another.

"I like this guy," my new drinking buddy says. He hikes a thumb back toward the stage. He said 'like' as 'lie-ka' and I have to ask.

"Where you from, dude?"

"Muscle Shoals."

"No shit?"

"Yeah, it's in Alabama."

Oh, I'm aware. I take a step back from the bar, they've brought down the houselights in here but it's still not as crowded or dark as it'll be in a few minutes.

I take it back, this guy's not an asshole: he's fucking cool.

His clothes are similar to mine but there's a layer of—what?—grit to them that mine don't have. Even with wearing these jeans through the weekend, I haven't accrued the worn crust on them that he has. His t-shirt's paper thin, carbon dating would probably place it alongside vintage-era Allman Brothers.

But what really impresses, beyond the outfit and the city of origin, is his skin. It's worn, sun-beaten and wrinkled, though I'm betting he's not too much older than I am. Is it too much sunlight or does he smoke? I should pick up smoking.

He's wearing boots.

"Name's Chuck," he says, using cowboy cool to break my stare-down with his work boots.

I shake his hand and, like the crow's feet at the corners of his eyes, his palm feels like worked leather, not rough but *tough*.

I tell him mine and then turn the conversation back to him. "What are you doing out here, if you don't mind me asking? Are you with the band?"

"Ha! I wish. No, I've got business outside of town and heard they were playing. Wasn't going to miss an opportunity."

"Business outside of town" is probably a regional marketing conference for plumbing equipment, but the way he says it sounds so cool that I don't ask him to elaborate. Better to print the legend. Besides, there's no time to ask.

The band is taking the stage.

Usually, I would push up front so I can be right by Cooley's feet and watch his fret work, but why move? I've got access to the bar, a clear line of sight to the men's room so I can head over to pee when it's not crowded, and a new buddy who's increasing my southern rock social capital by his proximity.

They open with one from the new album. The Shantyman has filled in substantially and the crowd is a mix. Old and young, hip and un-, loosened ties and snatches of henna tattoos: there was an even spread. Not that I was paying too much attention. I watched the show.

The crowd is polite for the new stuff, clap and hoot and chant "D!B!T!" in small pockets, but of course it's the third song that gets them really revved.

"One of my favorites," Chuck says, clinking the bottom of his beer to the top of mine. We smile at each other and drink.

I find myself mouthing the words, pointing out the chorus with a crooked finger, but then stop when I see that Chuck is more sedate in his reaction, a head nod and a toe tap. I mirror him.

The Truckers play long shows. They're good like that.

Usually I've visited the bathroom at least once by this point in their set. I've got a pea-sized bladder and take in a lot of liquids. I don't want to lose my prime positioning, but better to go during a song I've heard them do recently than possibly miss one they don't play much.

At the risk of losing my spot, I turn and put my can in my place, nod to Chuck, then cut through the bobbing and vibing crowd to the bathroom.

Hopefully Chuck will be my southern-fried guardian angel and protect my spot. But maybe we're not there in our relationship.

The bathroom is clean and shakes with the reverb of the band. Even still, there's the familiar whoosh in my ears that comes from giving your eardrums a break from a rock show.

I take the urinal in the corner, hoping against hope that no other patron needs to go and use the one next to me. I get pee shy. Not proud of it, but it's par for the course on my neuroses.

"Great show," a familiar voice says.

Chuck has followed me into the bathroom.

"They're always good," I say, but fuck I'm not going to be able to go if I have to carry on a conversation.

He takes the urinal next to me. He probably thinks nothing of it. I hear the tinkle start.

"How many times you seen'em?" he asks. There's no competition in the statement. If he wanted to turn it into a pissing contest, he'd win. Quite literally.

But then the thought comes, unbidden. Unbidden and—let me assure you—*unprecedented.*

This guy wants me.

I tuck myself back in. No use even trying at this point, even though I really need to go, am almost swimming in it

I flush the urinal, even though there's no need. I can hear Chuck slowing down.

And he doesn't struggle as I grab him by the back of the neck and pull him into the stall.

"Hey man I'm not."

Just stop talking, I will him. I know an invitation when I hear one. But the protestation fits with his whole aesthetic. Who ever heard of a southern boy who's going to invite you inside?

But that's what I'm looking for, what I crave.

Authenticity.

It takes me three songs to remove all of Chuck's skin and slip inside.

Like I said, his hide is tough. But damn is it fine.

Nobody bats an eye as I work my way back to my spot through the crowd.

Chuck's shirt sticks to the part of my lower back that Chuck's lower back doesn't cover.

The bartender mouths a scream as I introduce myself. "I'm Chuck, what's your name?" The drip between my eyebrows is cooling.

She screams again as I get a leg up over the bar.

Nobody stops me.

Nobody seems to hear her over the noise.

Their attention is on the rock show.

I feel real.

RUNNING FREE

Brian Keene

THERE WAS THIS news story I remember from about twenty years ago. This guy in Pennsylvania was dying of cancer. He had no health insurance. No life insurance either. Hell, he didn't have much of anything, except a wife and a kid and a mountain of debt. And cancer. This guy, dying and desperate, decides to rob a bank to provide for his family. What happens if the cops arrest him and he goes to trial? Life in prison? What does he care? He's terminal. So, he did it, and he got caught. Never even made it out of the bank. His family were left with shit, other than that mountain of debt, and he died in prison not long after his trial.

Normally, a bank robbery in Pennsylvania doesn't make the news all the way out here in California, but this one did because some people got killed during that botched heist, and because many suspected the robbery was a real-life inspiration for the *Breaking Bad* television series—except instead of robbing a bank, the dying guy become a meth cook.

Both of those cases—the real-life and the fictional—dealt with regular guys . . . good guys . . . forced to go bad because of cancer. I always found that fascinating, the idea that all it takes is one bad day for your average upstanding citizen to become a guy like me.

Me? I was always bad. So, when the doctors told me I was dying of cancer, I didn't turn to robbing a bank or becoming a methamphetamine kingpin. I didn't do any of that shit.

I took up long-distance running.

See, unlike that schmuck in Pennsylvania, I had health insurance. Had life insurance, too. I know that in the movies, they depict guys like me as living off the radar—not having Social Security numbers so we don't have to pay taxes, and shit like that. Don't believe it. Not paying your taxes is some world class stupidity. That's how they got Capone, you know? No, what you do is you live your normal life—wife, kids, mortgage payment, credit cards. Get yourself a W-2 or a 1099. Definitely get yourself a 401K. Make everything legit, and then, the money you make from your real job? You can launder that shit yourself on stuff like groceries, gas for the cars, and toys for your kids. You can pay for stuff like that in cash without setting off any alarm bells. And Christ, have you seen the cost of living in San Francisco lately? You can spend a lot of cash here just on daily expenses.

When I got sick, I went for three opinions. The first doctor gave me six months. Said if they had caught it earlier, they might have been able to cure me. The second doctor agreed and said six months to a year. The third doctor concurred with them. So, six months minimum. A year maximum. I didn't tell my wife or kids. Didn't tell anyone. I sat on that shit, mulling it over. They say there's stages to dying and grief, but I don't think I went through those. I didn't get angry. Didn't get sad, at least, not sad for me. I grieved for my family and felt guilty about the pain they'd have to go through when I was gone. The sadness they'd feel. My youngest is only ten and on the spectrum. He dotes on his father. Losing me will crush him. So, yeah, I felt terrible about that. Worrying about my family was what kept me awake at night. But the cancer? The dying?

I made my peace with that early on.

Guys in my line of work . . . and girls, too, I guess . . . Listen, we've got diversity and intersectionality movements in organized crime, same as any other workplace. So, let's just say people in my line of work. That better? People in my line of work—there's always a chance you could die. We carry that shit around with us. We live with dying every day. You learn not to dwell on it, or else you end up with an ulcer or anxiety or an addict or worse.

My day job was a mid-list crime fiction writer, except that there isn't a mid-list anymore. And in truth, my real job? There isn't much of that anymore, either. So, no, dying wasn't the problem.

Money was the problem, just like that asshole in Pennsylvania.

Now, how can that be? Well, it's not like I can leave a big wad of cash in a plastic grocery bag for my wife. And even if she knew how to spend it wisely, so as to not arouse suspicion, plastic grocery bags full of cash are fewer and farther between these days, thanks to the Russians and the cartels from south of the border and goddamn Chinese cybercrime. Their cuts keep getting bigger and bigger, and we get squeezed out. But there's still the life insurance policy, right? And it's one hell of a payout. My family will be set when I'm gone. They'll make more off putting me in the ground than I ever made for them on the side, and certainly more than I ever earned from those fucking paperbacks.

The problem is the life insurance policy itself.

See, when I first bought that life insurance, they sent me to a doctor for a physical and I had to fill out this questionnaire and all this other shit. And I lied. The part where it asks if you smoke, and if so, for how long? I said no. In reality, it had been one—sometimes two—packs per day, since I was eighteen. I quit when I was fifty. I'm fifty-one now. So, if I died of cancer that was attributable to smoking, my life insurance policy was null and fucking void.

But if I died from a heart attack while exercising?

Payday . . .

My heart was up to the challenge. For years, my wife and the doctor had been on me to change my diet and exercise more. My old man died of a heart attack. His old man, too.

Die of cancer? My family doesn't get dick. Die of a heart attack? They get a payout.

So, what I did was go to the store and buy a fancy pair of running shoes, and some jogging clothes, and all that other shit—everything except a fitness tracker. Last thing I need, even at this stage, is the Feds being able to track me. Same reason I carry one of those pay-as-you-go burner flip phones, rather than a smart phone. Same reason I keep telling my family no when they ask if we can have one of those creepy artificial intelligence things Amazon sells that turn on your lights and play music for you. Same reason I'm not on Facebook or Twitter or any of that other crap.

Anyway, I bought all that running shit and brought it home, and my wife was . . . surprised. I've never been one for exercising. In the past, anytime somebody preached the gospel of running to me, I'd remind them that Jim Fixx—the asshole fitness guru who wrote *The Complete Book of Running*—died of a heart attack while running. Now, here I was, trying to do the same. My wife didn't know that, of course. She just knew that I'd suddenly developed the urge to get in shape. After her initial shock wore off, she was happy and supportive. Hell, I hadn't seen her that happy in a long time. You'd think I'd brought home a diamond necklace or two tickets to an all-expenses-paid vacation in Tuscany by the way she reacted.

That made me feel guilty, too.

Guilt . . . you try not to dwell on that, same way you do with death and dying. I know that some of the things I've done were wrong. I know that I'm not a good person. I've stolen from people. I've hurt people who couldn't pay up—broke bones and noses, sent them to the emergency room. And yeah, I've killed people, too. Four times, in fact, over the last thirty years. Like I said before, I'm a bad person. But I didn't struggle over the things in my past. The only time I felt guilty was when I hurt or disappointed my family in some way. Lying to my wife always brought on a bad case of remorse, and this time was no different, especially seeing how happy she was.

But, I was locked in now, so fuck it.

I started running.

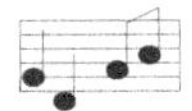

I do a lot of my business at this bar called The Shantyman. It's in the Tenderloin district, so that's where I did my run every day. I'd switch up my route, same as with everything else in my life. That's because you never want to get too predictable. Worse thing a guy like me can do is become a creature of habit—become predictable. That shit will get you killed. Going home the same way every day or eating at the same goddamned restaurant you eat at every Friday night makes things easy for those wishing to do you harm.

There are other bars and clubs in the Tenderloin. Big live music venues like the Warfield and the Great American Music Hall. Alternative theaters like Piano Fight, the EXIT Theatre, the New Conservatory, Counter Pulse, the Phoenix, and dozens of others. Used to be a lot of strip clubs there, too, although most of those have been closed down now. The Mitchell Brothers O'Farrell Theatre is still there, but it's a shadow of its former self—kind of like it got cancer, too, and survived, but wasted down to nothing in the process.

The guys who showed me the ropes when I was a young man, coming up? They used to operate out of the O'Farrell, and some of the other strip joints, as well. Hell, this entire district has always lent itself to our profession, going all the way back to the days of Prohibition. Merchant seaman used to come rolling in, flush with cash, and our guys—I'm talking the guys who were doing this when I was just a kid—would alleviate them of every last dollar.

Not so much these days.

Everything is different now. Even The Shantyman. I guess the place was always a dive, but it used to have historical significance, you know? Janis Joplin and Jefferson Airplane played there back in the day, when they were first starting out. Years later, so did Metallica, back when they were still underground up-and-comers. These days? You can still hear live music there, but that's at night. I'm too old for that shit. In the afternoon, the only music you hear is from the jukebox.

Anyway, I ran a different route through the Tenderloin every day, and always ended up at The Shantyman. Now, I know what I just said about not being a creature of habit, but I also said I do a lot of my business there. As a result, The Shantyman is a place where I felt relatively safe—at least, as safe as somebody in my line of work can ever feel. But, if I'm being honest here? I felt safe from the cancer at The Shantyman. I knew the regulars. I had my usual booth, facing the door. I knew my bourbon of choice would always be in stock. The place was always a nice transition from my criminal activities to my home life. Spend the day loaning money and taking bets and all the other crap, you don't want to go home with that shit still in your head. You don't want to go home if the Raiders or the 49ers didn't beat the spread. You don't want to go home if there's still blood on your knuckles from the deadbeat whose lips you had to pulp. No, you never take that shit home with you. So, what I'd do is have a few drinks at The Shantyman before I went home to my family. It was my refuge. And once I got the cancer and started running, it provided another sort of refuge.

A refuge from the disappointment of not keeling over on the sidewalk somewhere in the Tenderloin.

Because I ran every day, but that heart attack eluded me. I ran through squalor and splendor. I ran over garbage and cracked concrete and used needles and people shitting in the streets. I ran around hipsters and twinks, techies and the homeless. I ran past trendy coffee shops and artisanal cupcake stands and Chinese, Japanese, Greek, Thai, and Italian restaurants. I ran by cars blaring hip-hop and house and techno and metal and political talk and that terrible shit that passes for pop music these days. I pushed myself until my feet hurt, and my lungs and chest burned, and my vision narrowed to pinpricks. I forced myself onward when my ears rang, and I got dizzy and my skin felt flushed. I gritted my teeth in expectation when my chest tightened, and my pulse jackhammered in my throat. But still . . . nothing. I got winded. I coughed up blood. I got blisters on my heels and toes. I ran, and I ran and I ran, but still no heart attack.

And so, at the end of my run, I'd sit in my booth at The Shantyman—dripping with sweat and breathing heavy—and have a few beers until I had the courage to go home.

That shit went on for a month.

"If there's something going on, I need you to tell me."

I picked up the remote and paused the television. I was on the end of the couch, legs propped up on the coffee table. My wife had her head on a pillow in my lap. I'd been stroking her hair absentmindedly while we binge-watched a show that neither of us were really paying attention to She'd been playing on her phone, and I'd been thinking about dying.

"What do you mean?" I asked.

She sat up and stared at me. "You've been acting different. I see it, and Vinnie sees it, too. He asked me yesterday if Daddy was mad about something."

I frowned, trying to remember if I'd been short with my son. "There's nothing going on. Why did he think I was mad?"

"Because you're distracted. He's ten, and notices that. I notice more."

"Like what?"

"You're losing weight. You're paler. You don't eat like you used to."

"It's the running," I lied. "You're always after me to lose weight. I've cut down on the macaroni and gravy, is all."

"That's not all, and you know it. Is this a work thing . . . ?"

"Twenty-two years together, baby. Don't make me make you an accessory after the fact. There's no statute of limitations like in the movies."

She shook her head. "Not that. I know better than to ask about that. I meant the writing. You haven't done that in weeks."

I seized on her assumption. "Yeah, it's the writing. I've just been lost in my head, I guess. Publisher offered me a twenty-five hundred advance, but I'm stuck for an idea. I've been mulling that over."

"Two-thousand five hundred dollars?" She shook her head. "I remember when they used to pay you five thousand for an advance."

"The world has moved on, babe. Desperate times call for desperate measures."

She reached down, took my hand, and squeezed it. "Well, just try to be more open with Vinnie, okay?"

I nodded. "I will."

I turned the television back on, and she turned her attention to her phone once more, and I was glad for that, because it meant she didn't see the tears welling up in my eyes.

A week into the second month, I figured the cancer was spreading to my brain. I'd been pushing myself even harder—running farther and longer and faster, and it was definitely taking a toll on me, but still no heart attack. The closest I came was one day when, in front of a bakery, I started coughing and hacking and couldn't breathe. Suddenly, it felt like somebody had grabbed my heart in their fist and was giving it a squeeze. My arm tingled, like it was asleep, and my ears rang. When everything started to spin, I remember thinking that this was it, this was what I'd been working toward. I was gonna have a heart attack, right there on the street, and even if they did an autopsy on me, and figured out I had cancer, the cause of death was still going to be heart attack, and my family would get the payout. I dropped down to my knees, and then it passed. A few people gathered around me in concern. Most just walked on by, though, obvious in their efforts to ignore it and not get involved. Of the small handful who stopped, half of them just pulled out their phones, ready to record my death and then put it on YouTube.

Only one person asked if I was okay.

And when I looked up at him—if I'd had the breath to do it, I would have screamed.

First guy I ever killed was this Mexican. Now look.

It ain't like what you see in the movies. Somebody owes you money, the last fucking thing you want to do is kill them. A dead person can't pay you. But this Mexican, he was into us large. And he was running his mouth on the street about how he'd gotten away with it, and fuck us, and we weren't shit. So, we had no choice. I shot him twice—once in the throat and one in the head. Last time I saw him was when his body was slipping beneath the surface out in the bay.

But now I was looking at him again.

The guy looked at me in concern. Then he reached out and tentatively patted my shoulder.

"You okay?" he asked again. "You want us to call an ambulance?"

I stared at him, eyes wide. "How are you . . . I saw . . . "

The ringing in my ears vanished, and the vertigo passed. Worse, my pulse returned to normal and the tingling in my arm went away. Once again, the heart attack had disappointed me. As my vision cleared, I realized that the guy crouched down next to me wasn't the Mexican after all. He bore a resemblance, sure, but it wasn't him.

Shaking my head, I waved him away and tottered to my feet, still wheezing and hacking. My palm was slick with blood and phlegm. When the onlookers noticed that, they backed the fuck up, which I was glad for.

"I'm okay," I insisted. "Thanks."

That time, I didn't run, but walked.

If it had just been the Mexican guy on the street, I'd have just thought it was a case of mistaken identity. A brain fart. But then I started seeing the shadows, and that was when I became positive the cancer had spread to my brain.

I noticed the first one the next day. I was running again, still intent on killing myself, although by that point I'd started to think of other ways I could commit suicide without making it look like that. I jogged by this homeless woman camped out on the sidewalk. She'd tied a piece of string around the tail of a dead rat, and she was swinging it at anybody who got within range. Every time she did this, she threw her head back and cackled, revealing gray teeth and bleeding gums. But what caught my attention was the little black cloud over her shoulder. It was about the size of a baseball, and it looked exactly like what I just described it as—a tiny storm cloud, like a baby version of the big black thunderheads that come roiling into the city off the bay. If you tried to focus your eyes on it, the whole thing turned blurry. It seemed to . . . vibrate. I don't know if that's the right word, exactly. The thing looked like it was there, but maybe elsewhere, too. Like it was occupying two spaces at the same time or some shit. But I saw it, for real, floating there right beside her head. The crazy bitch didn't seem to be aware of it, and neither did anybody else. I blinked my eyes, trying to clear them, but the shadow remained.

I started running again, wondering what the fuck that had been. Something wrong with my vision? A hallucination? I'd Googled the shit out of cancer when I first got diagnosed. When it spread to the brain, hallucinations happened—phantom smells and sounds and seeing things that weren't really there.

I figured that's what it had been.

Then I started seeing them everywhere. It was like people's shadows had a shadow of their own—miniscule smoke-like blobs, always hovering just over their shoulders, right next to their heads. I saw them on my runs, and when I was working. I'd go around the Tenderloin, making my pick-ups, and the poor saps who were into me for various amounts had them floating next to them. Not every person in the city had one, but the amount who did was still staggering. I saw them with the hipsters and twinks, techies and the homeless. I saw them as I ran past the trendy coffee shops and the artisanal cupcake stands and the Chinese, Japanese, Greek, Thai, and Italian restaurants. They were especially thick outside of bars and nightclubs, abortion clinics and needle exchanges, doctor and psychiatrist offices, and other places where desperation and depression hung thick.

I decided it was one of two things. Either I was suddenly seeing auras, and despite what the New Age holistic pagan bullshit artists tell us, all auras are black . . . or the cancer had spread to my brain.

I figured the latter was a pretty safe bet.

I ran harder. Punished myself more. Coughed up an obscene amount of blood and phlegm. Thought my lungs might explode. Dropped more weight.

But was still alive, despite my best efforts.

I'd just finished a run, and was kicking back in my booth at The Shantyman, nursing an IPA and mopping the sweat off my brow when Tony Genova walked in.

Tony's with an East Coast crew, the Marano Family, although I don't think they qualify as a family or even a crew anymore. Old man Marano died two years back, after a long battle with Alzheimer's. The Feds never got him, but I guess that fucking disease did. And in the years leading up to his death—I'm talking about long before they ever diagnosed the old guy—he was up to some crazy, heinous shit. Like I said before, I know I'm not a good person. None of us are. But the shit that Marano had his people doing? That was fucking evil. Tony and his buddy Vince got caught in the middle of that firestorm, but they came out okay. I know for a fact they both cut corners where they could—not necessarily refusing orders, but not doing as commanded, either. Rumor had it that Tony and Vince might have been the ones who took out Marano, rather than the Alzheimer's, but far as I know, it was just that—rumor.

Used to be Tony came out here four times a year for business, and I was always his point of contact. These days, the Marano organization was in chaos, with different factions vying for control, and even more of them getting arrested or working as informants. From what I'd heard, Tony had sort of retired—well, as much as anyone in our line of work can ever actually retire—and was freelancing now. So, I was surprised to see him when he walked in, grinning that fucking shit-eating smirk of his.

He also had a little shadow cloud hovering over his shoulder.

I smiled as he sauntered over, then stood up and gave him a hug. This was my first opportunity to try to touch one of those tiny clouds. It's not like I could walk up to some stranger on the street and do it, and my family didn't have them. So, while he was squeezing my ribs, I gave his back a hearty couple of slaps and then his shoulder. My hand went right through the thing, as if it were smoke. The blob congealed again as soon as my fingers had passed through it. There was no smell, no tactile sensation . . . other than a second of coldness.

"Tony fucking Genova." I kept my tone light. "What the hell are you doing in San Francisco?"

I sat back down and gestured at the empty seat on the other side of the booth. He slid into it, still grinning. The jukebox switched from Guns n' Roses to Soundgarden.

"Believe it or not, I'm out here on vacation."

"Vacation? Get the fuck out of here."

He held up his right hand, palm out. "Swear to Christ, Mikey. All the times Vince and I come out here on business, I never got to really see the place, unless you count warehouses and strip joints" he glanced around the interior of The Shantyman "and this fucking dump."

"Hey, watch it now. I like this dump. It's got tons of history."

He shrugged, still smirking. "Mea culpa, buddy."

"How is Vince, anyway? He come with you?"

It wasn't until then that Tony's smile vanished. When he spoke, I had to lean forward to hear him.

"Vince passed about six months ago."

"Oh, Tony . . . I'm sorry to hear it. Was he . . . ?"

I didn't finish the sentence. I didn't need to. He knew what I was implying.

"No, it was fried potato skins. Remember how he used to love those fucking things?"

I did. I'd watched Vince eat them right here in this booth, plate after plate of baked potato skins piled high with sour cream and bacon and chives.

"Heart attack?"

"Yeah," Tony said. "Facedown in a plate of potato skins at this club in Baltimore."

"Jesus . . . "

I didn't know what else to say. And the irony wasn't lost on me, either. There I was, running my ass off, actively engaged in attempting to give myself a heart attack, and that fat fucking Vince had one without even trying.

That time of day, The Shantyman had a skeleton crew. Milos behind the bar and Anna floating between the tables. She saved my ass that day, Anna—came sidling up to the table while that uncomfortable silence hung there in the air between me and Tony, and asked him if he wanted anything. He ordered a Basil Hayden's on the rocks. I looked at my nearly empty IPA and decided to do the same.

"Make that two, hon," I asked. "And see if Milos can make us an order of potato skins?"

Anna snapped her gum. "You got it, Mike."

Tony watched her ass as she walked away. Then he turned back to me. His smirk had returned.

"Fucking potato skins? Really, Mikey?

I grinned. "We'll toast the fucker."

Tony leaned back in the booth and laughed.

Over on the jukebox, Soundgarden gave way to Johnny Cash, singing—pleading—for somebody to save him from a darkness.

I called my wife and told her I'd be home late. She didn't ask where I was. All these years together, she just assumes it's "business"—and not the writing kind.

Tony and I got shitfaced. We talked about old

times, and he told me about the things he wanted to see while he was in town. All the touristy shit that us who live here just take for granted. Eventually, he asked how I was doing. Commented that I'd lost weight. But his tone was one of concern—not the kind of voice you use when you're congratulating somebody. I didn't tell him about the cancer, because I still didn't know if he really was out here on vacation, or if there was some ulterior motive. If somebody somewhere had designs on our crew, then I didn't need word getting out that I was sick. That could start all kinds of trouble, and the people I worked for didn't need that shit, and I certainly didn't either.

But Tony's always been good at seeing through bullshit, and I could tell he knew something was up. So, while I didn't come out and tell him the truth, I didn't exactly lie to him, either.

"I've been seeing things."

He stared at me, his expression even. I signaled Anna, ordering us a twelfth round of bourbon. The empty plate of potato skins sat between us. The Shantyman had filled up by then. I wasn't usually there that late, so I wasn't used to seeing it that crowded. The evening staff had come in—bar-backs and waitresses and two more bartenders. The jukebox had been switched off and a band was setting up on the weathered stage—some young female country singer out of Nacogdoches. Seemed like a weird fit for The Shantyman, but then again, most of what passes for country these days sounds pretty much like 1970s southern rock.

"Seeing what?" Tony pointed at the collection of empty whiskey glasses between us. "Pink elephants?"

I chuckled. "In this town, you can see pink elephants all goddamned day long. No, I'm talking about something else."

Just then, Anna hustled over with two more drinks.

"Damn," Tony said turning his grin on her. "You always that fast, darlin'?"

She returned the smile. "My wife says I am."

Tony waited until Anna had cleared the empty plate and glasses off the table. Then, after she'd gone, he leaned forward.

"So, what then?"

I took a deep breath, puffed my cheeks out, and then exhaled. "Ah, you wouldn't believe me."

"Try me."

"Okay." I hesitated, and took a deep drink, felt the burn slide down my sore throat, which was raw from coughing. Then I described the little black clouds I'd seen floating around some people. Tony didn't smirk. Thank Christ for that. I like the guy, but I think I might have hit him if he had. No, he sat there and listened intently, his expression attentive but as unreadable as the best poker player in Vegas. When I was finished, he simply nodded.

"So, let's hear it," I groaned.

"Hear what?"

"You breaking my balls. Telling me I'm going crazy."

"I don't think you're crazy, Mikey."

I frowned, waiting for him to burst into laughter. He must have sensed my skepticism.

"I don't," he insisted. "Maybe they're psychopomps or something."

"Psychopaths?"

"Psychopomps," he corrected me. "It's a Greek word. Means spirit guide. But they exist in just about all of the major religions."

"I don't know," I replied. "It's been a long time since I've been in church. I guess last time was when Vinnie got baptized. But I don't remember anything about psychopomps."

"Azrael, the angel of death, is a psychopomp in Christian, Jewish, and Muslim faiths."

"These don't look like no angels, Tony. They're little blurry blobs of black smoke."

As I said it, I eyed the one floating next to him, and thought about mentioning it.

"Well, maybe they're demons, then."

I decided to keep my mouth shut. Instead, I said, "Demons?"

He shrugged. "Sure. Why not?"

"You never struck me as the kind of guy who believes in that shit."

Tony took a sip of his drink before responding. "I've seen things that would give you nightmares."

"No thanks." I shook my head. "I have enough of those."

"Oh, me too. Anybody lives the life we lead, they're gonna have nightmares. I have my own, and not just about the things I've done or people I've killed. I've always dreamed weird shit. Giant crab monsters and getting lost in this endless maze with people I don't know and zombie Santa Claus."

I suppressed a chuckle, because it was clear from his expression that Tony didn't think it was funny.

"But I ain't talking about dreams," he continued. "I've seen shit in real life that I can't explain. Nobody can explain it. And once you see something like that, it makes you a believer. Like, take flying saucers for instance. I never believed in those. Then, about eleven years back, Vince and I saw one. We were driving this little backroad in Maryland, well after dark. Saw it clear as day, just hovering there, lighting up the whole sky. It wasn't a fucking weather balloon or any of those other bullshit excuses. It was some kind of unidentifiable aircraft."

"Yeah, but that's different, Tony. Something like that, it could have been the Department of Defense testing out some top secret new weapon, like they did with the stealth bomber and Area 51. There weren't aliens there. It was just them testing the B-2, before the public knew about it."

"Maybe. But I've seen other shit, too."

"You really believe in demons? In Hell and Heaven and . . . what did you call them?"

"Psychopomps."

"Yeah, those."

"I don't know," he admitted. "The older I get, the more I think about it. But I don't know. And I don't think these preachers and priests know either."

We were both quiet for a moment. We sipped our whiskey. Then Tony's trademark smirk returned, slowly creeping across his face.

"I figure we'll find out when we're dead."

At that moment, the band started up, and it got too loud to hear each other. It was hot in The Shantyman, but despite that, I shivered.

I kept running. Kept seeing those little blobs. Kept losing weight. Kept coughing up blood.

Kept living, despite my best efforts.

Kept ending my run at the Shantyman.

One day it was foggy and raining, so I cut my run short. Dying or not, I didn't want to be out jogging in that shit. The Tenderloin gets a particular rank smell when it rains—a musky, heavy stench. The bar, by contrast, smelt like Heaven—stale beer and cheap perfume and vape smoke (because they'd outlawed smoking cigarettes in bars and restaurants years before).

Anna was on duty, and I'd just ordered a drink from her, and was staring at my phone when the tingling started in my arm. It crept up slowly, and I wondered if this was it. Like before, that day out on the sidewalk, that giant fist returned and started squeezing my heart.

This is it, I thought. *Here we go . . .*

I suddenly felt very hot, but also started shivering. It made me recall that night with Tony, when we'd stayed here drinking. What was it he had said?

The pain in my chest grew stronger, and I found it hard to breathe. My ears started ringing. I glanced over to the bar, but Anna was talking to Milos, and neither of them noticed.

I thought about my wife and kids. I fumbled for my phone, intent on texting them.

Then the pain stopped. It didn't subside. It didn't fade. It just abruptly fucking stopped.

"Son of a bitch," I groaned. "What the hell do I have to do to make this happen?"

I glanced up again to see if anyone had heard my

little outburst, but Milos and Anna were gone. So were the few scattered patrons that had been in the bar a moment before. Instead, there were three people I'd never seen before. The first one was obviously religious, given the Bible he was carrying. The second guy was some sort of Weird Al Yankovic-looking motherfucker. The third was a young guy who was dressed weird, like he'd just come from some kind of nineteenth century historical reenactment or something. The three of them were seated along the bar, huddled together over drinks. The Weird Al clone raised his glass to me and nodded. I frowned. Then I noticed that the lighting in The Shantyman was different—in that there were no lights. No jukebox playing, either.

Power went out, I thought. *But where the fuck is everybody?*

It occurred to me that none of the three strangers had smoke blobs floating over their shoulders.

I picked up my phone, intent on checking the news. I also still felt the urge to text my family. Granted, the heart attack seemed to have passed, but it still felt very important to me that I should reach out to them, especially if the power outage was city-wide. When I thumbed the button to unlock my phone, it didn't work. The phone was dead, too.

"Shit."

"They don't work here."

I looked up and saw the three patrons approaching my booth.

"How's that?" I asked.

"Your phone," the Weird Al guy said. "It won't work here."

"Why not?"

He shrugged, and then stuck out his hand. "I'm Chester."

"How ya doing, Chester? They call you Chester the Molester?"

Ignoring my jab, he motioned to the priest. "This is Harvey Matthews. He shot himself here in the green room. I broke my neck while on stage over there."

I slid out of the booth and got to my feet. "And who's the cosplayer over there?"

"That's Matthew. He got clubbed over the head by the original owner of this place and shanghaied. You'll have to excuse him if he doesn't say much. While at sea, cannibals cut out his tongue."

"Oh, I see." I stared at each of them in turn. "You guys are fucking crazy."

Chester smiled sadly. "I'm afraid not. We're here to help you, Michael."

"How the fuck do you know my name? Who sent you? Is this some kind of prank? Somebody busting my balls?"

"It's not a joke," Matthews replied. "We're here to show you something."

"I don't want to see what you have. What, you gonna pull out your cock like you do to the altar boys?"

I shoved past them and headed for the door, doing my best to look imposing, even though I was wearing running shoes and a track suit. They didn't try to stop me, but Chester called out as I reached the exit.

"Michael, you don't want to go out there."

"Oh, yeah? Why not?"

"Because you won't be able to get back in."

I sneered. "Listen, shitbag. I been coming here for years. I'm a regular. I can come and go any time I like."

Then I pushed the door open and stepped outside. The sun was a muted, silver shadow of itself, and the parking lot and surrounding streets were covered in thick fog. The city was quiet—scarily so. I'd never heard it like this. There were no cars, and no people.

But there were hundreds of the smoke things. They were clustered around The Shantyman, as if waiting for me. They bobbed up and down in the air, drifting closer. I took a step back as they began to shimmer and grow larger. Then they slowly changed shape, coalescing into humanoid figures, devoid of any facial features or other characteristics. Soon, I found myself surrounded by tall, black figures.

As they reached for me, I stumbled backward, fumbling behind me for the door. When I couldn't find it, I risked a terrified glance over my shoulder. The Shantyman was gone. I turned back, and the city had vanished, as well. It was just me, and the fog, and the shadow creatures.

They crowded around me, arms outstretched. Screaming, I did the only thing I could.

I started running again.

WE SANG IN DARKNESS

Mary SanGiovanni

"Children cried out
For lullabies
As wind and fire
Tore open the skies
The old remembered
When the world was ours
A world of electric
and metal towers
Our tongues were cut out
Ears made deaf and dead
But we sang in the darkness
'Til our throats bled"
—"Revolution" by Apocophilia from The Masters are Calling
released March 2035, Eldritch Records

THE WEIRD CAGE we'd found on the stage of The Shantyman night club had obviously been constructed for the purpose of containing the thing inside it. Bluish metal poles formed the floor and framework of a rectangular object about eight feet high by five feet wide and deep, paneled with something that was not quite glass and not quite liquid, but somewhere in between. The cage hummed when any of us got too close to it and shimmered with vague rainbows, like an oil slick on water.

The thing that sat on the floor inside the cage appeared to be trapped. I half expected it to growl or scream or call for help when it saw us, but it didn't. It didn't pace angrily or rattle the metal bars. It just watched us with those large, obsidian eyes. I watched back. I wanted to be able to read something in them, some inkling of thought or emotion, something relatable, something of human feeling.

It wasn't human, though, and if it carried any emotion at all, it wasn't in the eyes.

We had also found a dead body lying outside the cage, just in front of it. Roger thought it was a government guy, a scientist, maybe. The dead man had on a white jumper that did look a bit like a hazmat suit, but it had no identifying logo on the back. He—the dead guy, not Roger—lay face-down, though from what I could see, there wasn't much left of a face. The flesh near his temples and ear was singed. The rest looked . . . dissolved. Erased. I'm not sure how else to describe it. Roger had suggested that maybe the man had gotten too close to the water-glass stuff; that had been enough to keep the rest of us off the stage and on the far side of the room, away from the body and away from those dark, empty eyes.

I can't say we were scared just then. We probably should have been, but like the rest of the world, we'd all been following what was going on for the last three years. News on the Internet and TV gave people cherry-picked pieces of information; we got far more accurate and complete news from the conspiracy theory podcasts. Of course, you had to pick the information out from all the crowing about the conspiracy folks being right—about experiments in sound and vibrations, about the effect of those vibrations on the electromagnetic fields of the human body, how the right tones at the right vibrations worked like a sonic key of sorts, opening up holes in the sky, in the universe, and letting other universes fall in.

Remember that first interdimensional flux, when we lost all those breeds of cattle and horses? I was a kid, then, maybe five or six but I remember my ma telling us we couldn't go to Red Robin anymore, because the price of hamburgers had gone up so much. I was in middle school during the second flux, the one that destroyed enough of the bees to negatively impact agriculture and so many bats that the mosquito population, particularly those carrying the Red River Virus, soared. I remember all the trees at the park whose trunks took on weird bulges and twists because of alien vines. At least, they looked like vines, but they hummed and smoked a little and smelled like the inside of old trash cans. Once, I'd seen them squeeze a dog to death just because it got too close.

I was in high school when that outpouring of strange alien beasts brought their spit and teeth, their blood, their claws, and the mites on their skin through the sky hole in Atherton. Sure, maybe those illnesses they spread weren't deadly because their biology is so different from ours, but I remember all those classes cancelled or quarantined when some student was sent terrified to the nurse because he or she suddenly sprouted long growths or glowed green, or dripped those foul-smelling brackish fluids from ears, nose, and the corners of the mouth. I remember the evacuation drills, because creatures would wander onto school property or crash through windows sometimes, drawn to the noise of school bells and chatter and movement.

We'd learned to live with those shifts in society; every day, we coped with the alien and unusual in our streets, our homes, our social media. Food and drink changed. Medicine changed. Homes and schools changed. Politics changed. Art changed. Jobs changed.

Music, of course, changed the most drastically. This coming April would have marked six years that I had been working at The Shantyman. When Congress enacted the federal music ban eight months ago, it didn't just break my heart, but it put me out of a job. I suppose the government's fears were not unfounded; the sounds and vibrations *could* have continued opening portals to other worlds. It was possible, now that the tech was out there. Nonetheless, it was the one thing none of us adapted very well to. There were no more bar bands, no more music promoters or record labels, no concert venues or opera houses. Spotify, Google Play, and iTunes pulled their music and focused their business on audiobooks and podcast talk shows. Music, as primal to the human soul as storytelling, was now a crime, and suddenly, the rock gods that had made churning one's way through adolescence remotely bearable were criminals and murderers. They fought it—we all did—but it only made things worse. The flora and fauna of that other world followed the sound. They thrived on it and multiplied. They fed on it and grew stronger, and their grip on our world grew tighter.

We could have music, or we could protect ourselves and our loved ones. So the elimination of everything from commercial jingles to the national anthem to lullabies became part of the new normal, whose creeping stranglehold was so very much like those alien vines.

And we accepted it, like we'd come to accept wars no one was ever really going to win and laws taking away fundamental rights in the name of safety or technological progress and everything else the conspiracy folks warned us about. We accepted being silenced.

And when folks took martial law in stride a few months ago, they told themselves the scientists and the soldiers had needed to commandeer homes and businesses to set up containment units. They told themselves those scientists and soldiers would bring back the old normal again. That's a funny thing about humans in these situations; they hold onto hope, no matter how crazy or absurd that hope might be. They adapt to radically new lives and all the while hold onto the idea somewhere in the backs of their minds that these universally life-changing events are temporary, and that Someone In Charge Somewhere is going to make it all right again.

It didn't work like that; it never could have, even if the ones like that thing in the cage hadn't come through.

We weren't as afraid as we should have been at finding one of those creatures, even if it was in a cage. If anything, we were more annoyed that the new normal was intruding on our one last trip down memory lane. We were angry that a representative master of that invading, choking otherworld was intruding on one of the last standing monuments to an art form that defined us and the most important eras of our lives. Angry doesn't even adequately describe the feeling, to tell the truth. It was more like a feral kind of loathing, part anger and part fear, which fed the ignition of another primal force—bloodlust. I wanted to kill the thing, and I admit, if I'd had a means to do so then and there, I would've. It wasn't a fugitive or a prisoner in that cage; it wasn't something yanked away from everything familiar and safe and thrust into an alien world; it wasn't another sentient, feeling being. Not in those first moments, it wasn't—not to us. When we walked into that club, it was a monster, a thing whose very existence had ruined all our lives, and instinctively, I wanted it dead.

And then Joey noticed the door locks.

Some time while we were gawking and glaring at and cursing the creature and its attendant dead body, those vines I told you about snaked out from beneath the cage. They moved fast and silent in the gloom of the club's interior, and it's kind of a wonder they didn't wrap around our legs; I'd heard they could squeeze a calf muscle so hard that they could rupture it. They didn't come near us, though, not just then. Instead, they'd tangled around the legs of chairs and tables, then around doorknobs and through keyholes. The acid-stuff inside them had fused into useless, immobile lumps of metal in the door handles and locks of all four exits accessible from the stage room, as well as the women's room and the inner doors to the cloak room and both corridors leading out. Maybe we pissed the thing in the cage off, or our voices agitated the vines, or we somehow aroused in both a mutual, murderous kind of hate. Maybe it was some kind of otherworld lockdown, or maybe the vines just did what alien vines do. I don't know how it happened, but it did, and we found ourselves confined to one bathroom, the bar, the backstage green room . . . and the main stage, with that . . . thing. We were trapped.

Proximity to the cage or maybe the creature inside it fried our cell phones; we discovered that right away. The damn things wouldn't even turn on, let alone let us text or call anyone or even take a picture of the thing. Not that it really made too much of a difference, anyway—I mean, who could we have called? 911? The police? The military? And what would we have said, that we had snuck into my old boss's club without permission, specifically to play music in secret and to reminisce about old times, and had instead gotten ourselves locked in with one of the government's little pet projects? It wasn't exactly the kind of situation we wanted to post on the band's Facebook or Instagram. Some of us already had police records and others were on probation; none of us wanted to see the inside of a prison, especially the way they are now. And I had seen too many conspiracy documentaries about people knowing more than they should and ending up with mysterious incurable illnesses or in unexplained fatal accidents.

We were on our own. For the time being, we had to sit and wait.

I took the first watch, the shift from midnight until four. My brother Joey would take over after that. Just then, he and the guys were crashed out backstage on the flimsy, stained, lime-colored velvet couches and on the sticky floor, their leather jackets folded like pillows beneath them or draped like blankets over their bony bodies. They didn't care. They were exhausted. We all were.

Another funny thing is how even in the face of the terrifying and unbelievable, little quirks that make people human force their way through. An interdimensional being capable of melting faces clear off a human head was right in front of me, not even four feet away from where I sat on the edge of the stage, and I was debating whether I could get away with sneaking off to take a piss. I didn't, though; beneath the uneasy peace I'd made with the situation, I couldn't quite turn my back on the creature, even in a cage, or leave it unattended.

I found myself thinking about the cage, too, after a time. *Was* it really? I couldn't help wondering if it was keeping that thing in or keeping the rest of *us* out . . . and that seemed like an important distinction, if we were going to get out of there.

As I sat there fiddling with a *Shantyman* matchbook I'd found in my jacket pocket, I wondered what my old boss, Ferguson, would have thought of all this. He'd taken his time closing up shop, pushing the government grace period right up to the limit. Then everything happened pretty fast. Gigs were cancelled, papers signed, and we were doing rounds of shots to celebrate the closing of the club. He told us the government had paid him off, and that he was happy to unload the club on them; it was *their* problem now, and he was off to early retirement. Ferguson was probably fine—probably retired someplace tropical where the women wore next to nothing and the sun and surf would keep the arthritis from kicking off in his bum knee. He probably wasn't thinking about this place anymore. That's how we came to normalize his disappearance. He was off to some island and the club was now the government's albatross and he was better off being free of it. He'd never even asked me for the key back.

Of course, I knew better, deep down; Ferguson had left the club and cut us loose because he'd had to. Someone had insisted he make a clean break, and a fast one. He didn't believe a single word he'd said during that last day of work, and certainly not during that final gathering. He'd been a good boss and a good man, and Jack and Emory and I had liked working for him. He knew we counted on our pay and he always looked out for us, sometimes fronting us smokes or advances on our checks or even money from his own pocket to make sure we were fed or had coats in the winter. And he'd cut us some pretty damn generous bonuses when he'd let us go, "courtesy of the government dicks taking over this place." He'd tried to laugh when he told us, "We're finally out of here, thank the metal gods," and we tried not to notice the wistful look in his eyes when he said it.

See, Ferguson lived for music. He loved discovering new bands and giving them a stage to play on. He could bitch all he wanted about San Francisco rent and taxes and paperwork and the pain in the ass that was The Shantyman, but music was in his soul, and without it . . . well, the government wouldn't need goons orchestrating some disappearance or accident to kill Ferguson.

I glanced at the clock above one of the fused-shut, vine-encrusted doors. It was six-thirty. We hadn't brought anything other than the clothes on our backs, our wallets, car keys, a few joints, and Eddie's guitar. We hadn't expected to be there long enough to need anything else. We'd assumed from the cage that The Shantyman was still an active containment or research facility, and that employees would probably be back by Monday morning. We thought a day, day and a half was little more than an inconvenience, really. When Monday morning came and went, we chalked it up to some holiday none of us could recall just then. By the end of Tuesday, the panic set in. Even if it took some time to find a way in around those fused locks, we thought we should have seen or heard someone from the outside world. When most of Wednesday came and went, and even the painted windows stopped changing colors with the rising and fading sunlight, we knew something was very wrong.

I didn't say it to the guys, but every shift I took sitting across from that thing in the cage, the surer I was that either the outside world was gone, or we were somehow gone from the outside world. I think I knew it because the thing in the cage wanted me to know. At first, I thought it just wanted us to feel as isolated and alone as it did, and I almost felt sorry for it. Then it started getting into my head, making me think crazy things about every groan and creak of the old building.

Its withering silence never broke, but every time I got within feet of the cage, I'd feel cold all over, and while I stood there shaking, it would show me things—pictures in my head of faceless, disjointed things lurking in the shadowed, long-untouched corners of the club and hordes descending from the ceiling like amorphous, eyeless spiders. It showed me swirling galaxies of blue-black stars, strange nebulae, and exploding suns just outside the club. It showed me the vines bursting through every crack in the club walls and slithering under the ruined doors until the building began to crumble all around me, and I was hurtling through alien space on a chunk of concrete floor, my frozen body imploding, eyeballs floating away into endless nothingness . . . .

I shook my head. I was sitting inches from that liquid glass, though I would have sworn I'd never moved so much as an inch from the edge of the stage. I jerked away from the cage, my vision still blurry. My head hurt and my arms and legs ached and my heart thumped silently in my chest.

I was also ravenously hungry.

My attention drifted to the bar. Nothing had been done to change the place yet; it still looked pretty much like it had when I worked there, with the exception of the cage a few feet away and a few immaculately empty desks out on what used to be the dance floor. I assumed the acoustics of the place assisted them in researching the effects of sound on the portals they'd opened, so maybe modifications weren't needed. The bar was still intact and the shelves remained fully stocked with bottles, but we were running out of stuff to eat. The Shantyman didn't serve food, but Ferguson used to set out pretzels and chips in small bowls on the bar. We'd nearly run through all the bags he'd left in the cabinets behind the bar. Joey smoked the last of the weed that morning, and had been particularly hungry all day.

There was plenty of booze, yeah, but I didn't drink anymore. I had the one-year chip from AA on a chain around my neck and I was proud of that. I'd been a mess of a drunk, the violent and reckless kind that even other metal-heads came to avoid. No one picked you up out of your own puke or even bothered to turn you on your side when you were a drunk like me. Even the worst speed freaks and dope fiends half-hoped you'd get to the overdose part sooner rather than later, because no one could keep going like that and it was painful to watch, and there was really no other direction your life was going to go anyway.

I shocked the lot of them when I quit drinking, and blew their minds when I stuck to sobriety for a year. I spent it learning the bass guitar and got pretty good at it. My whole recollection of that blurred and tumultuous time was of throwing myself into learning that bass—even the changes in the world around me took a back seat to that simple hard scrabble for my life. I played when I got the shakes and I played when every part of my body was screaming to get stupid knock-down drunk. I'd never cared about learning to play anything before, but for that year, it was all I had. It was a kind of hope, I guess—a faith in the possibility of something existing that makes getting up in the morning worthwhile. A therapist once told me I was perpetually driven by the journey, not the destination. Maybe that was true. Probably it was. Maybe finding a reason to live would never be as satisfying or illuminating to me as the search for that reason. I guess that's why I'd never picked up how to play any one specific song all the way through. It was the learning, not the knowing.

Regardless, it kept me sober. I didn't want to drink; the thought of it made me feel a little sick, to tell the truth. I felt a distinct aversion to the glittering rows of glass even then, with the monster on the stage and the mismatched shadows growing longer and more distorted and somehow noisier, even though the windows had stopped letting in light.

I clenched and unclenched my fingers. I wanted to play so badly, first little breezes of melody, then whirlwinds whipping around the room, drowning out all the things that I used to think alcohol could wash away.

I told myself the bass was a crutch, and I didn't need it to not drink. I actually mumbled the words out loud until the panic from looking at those bottles subsided. We were okay. We might be stuck at the moment, but it wasn't like the thing in the cage was shooting laser beams at us from its eyes or anything. We were alive and in one piece. We could hang out there for a few days more if we had to, no problem. We'd be okay. It would all be okay . . . .

Someone might notice we were missing and come looking for us—my girlfriend or Joey's or Roger's. It was more likely they wouldn't. Shara was used to going long stretches without hearing from Roger, and both Kelly and Dana had their kids this weekend. Most likely, no one would miss us until Monday or even Tuesday. We were looking at a few days, at least, without anything but water . . . and booze.

I tried to ignore the gnawings of hunger in my stomach and returned my attention to the thing in the cage. It might have been sleeping, but it was hard to tell. Its eyes looked half closed and it was sitting so still that it could have been a statue, some gargoyle concert prop or something.

It didn't look at all like those little grey men you see on t-shirts and *Aliens Unsealed and Exposed* shows. For one thing, it was kind of a gun-metal color, and was probably about seven feet tall. It had gotten up only once since we'd been there, and I saw that it stood on two legs whose knee joints bent backward like a bird's. They were no scrawny bird legs, though. They were sinewy, muscular, like the rest of it. Its hands and feet were large and taloned, and its head was crescent-shaped, like a moon or a grin with its corners pulled back over its shoulders. Its jaws were large and I thought I'd caught a glimpse of tiny, pointed teeth behind those thin, black lips.

And it had those big, black unfeeling eyes, just glassy enough to reflect my face back at me when I looked too closely into them. I didn't like looking the thing in the eyes.

"W-why did you lock us in here?"

I didn't intend to say the words out loud, but they hung there in the air between us, my voice hollow and small in the shadows.

If the creature understood me, it didn't let on. It watched me, silent and unmoving.

"Aren't you hungry?"

No response. I shifted my weight. I was getting stiff sitting there on the stage floor, and the silence was starting to get to me.

"Is anyone coming for you?"

The creature tilted its head. It was the first genuine movement it had made in hours.

"Do you fucking understand anything I'm saying?"

I held my breath, waiting. I wanted it to answer me. If it was anything more than an animal in a cage, then I could maybe let go of some of the anger. It was the anger, I told myself, that was making me restless—that desire to bash its head in with Eddie's guitar.

When it remained unmoving and utterly quiet, I let go of that held breath in a hostile rush of air and turned away. The silence was almost palpable, a weight on my shoulders, a thickness coating the insides of my nose and throat. I began drumming on the edge of the stage by my knee.

I hadn't realized I was humming until a voice behind me joined in. For a few seconds, the voices were the only thing that existed in the gloom. Then I caught on and I shut up. My head snapped up and the stage lurched in my vision. My gut clenched. I turned slowly back to the creature in the cage.

The last note—the alien voice—trailed off. The creature tilted its head at me and slowly repeated the same bars from The Rolling Stones' "Paint It Black" that I had just hummed. I scooted closer to the cage and softly, I sang that same segment with the lyrics. The space between its eyes crinkled as if it was thinking.

Then it sang the words back to me in perfect English and intonations . . . in my voice.

My mouth hung open.

"You understand me?" I asked shakily.

It looked at me a moment, its expression placid

and, I assumed, uncomprehending, then turned away from me.

"Hey! Hey you," I said a little louder. "How—how did you . . . do you understand? The song, do you know that song?" I supposed it was possible that the creature had heard it on some scientist's radio—maybe the dead guy had been a fan back when he'd had a face—or maybe it had picked up the song through whatever sound transmissions had brought it to this dimension.

I tried another one, softly singing a few bars of Ozzy's "Killer of Giants." I wasn't a terrifically great singer, but I wasn't terrible, either. I could certainly carry a tune, especially if I knew it well, and the creature in the cage . . . well, it matched me note for note. Excited as I was, I forgot that singing out loud was forbidden by law and common sense, and as I sang Metallica's "Sanitarium" to it and it sang back, I actually laughed out loud. It didn't understand one goddamned spoken word I said, but it was communicating, alright. It could hear the sadness in ballads, the adrenaline and anger of thrash metal songs, the good-natured fun of party songs. I saw emotion reflected in those shining eyes; I saw sentience. I'd say I saw humanity there, but who's to say that thoughts and feelings are the exclusive domain of human beings?

I think my struggling attempts on Eddie's guitar were what woke up the guys. They came flying out of the back room as if I'd set in on fire.

"What the hell you doin'?" Joey asked.

"It talks!" I replied.

"What?" Eddie, still bleary-eyed, stumbled toward me, looked down at his guitar, and frowned.

"Well, it doesn't talk, exactly, but it knows music. Listen."

I gave up trying to play the guitar and sang a few bars of the band's first hit, "Revolution." The creature in the cage sang along with me, this time in Joey's voice. Joey sank to his knees, his mouth hanging open.

"Ga-daaamn . . . it fucking sounds like me," he whispered.

"Yeah, it can do that, imitate voices. I don't know how it knows, but it does."

"Does it understand the words?" Charlie asked. He was the band's drummer didn't talk much, but when he did, he usually came right to the point. "Can we talk to it, ask it to let us go?"

The guys all looked at me.

"I don't know," I replied.

"What do you mean, you don't know?" Joey threw his hands up angrily.

"I mean, I don't fucking know. How would I? I only just found out it could sing like, ten minutes ago."

Eddie took the guitar out of my hand and strummed it. "Hey, fucker, let us goooo-ooo-ooo," he sang. "We don't wanna starve in this place no mooo-ooo-ooo . . . ."

The thing tilted its head and regarded Eddie with what I think was a quizzical stare.

Then it began to sing to us.

My vision blurred until I couldn't see more than the hazy, transfixed silhouettes of my brother and his band. I reached out to the nearest figure but my hand wavered in and out of the world. It didn't hurt, and I wasn't scared. On the contrary, my skin all over felt like a living thing, every part of it rippling across my body in vaguely pleasant little waves. Nothing mattered just then but the music of the creature in the cage. It filled the core of my being, lifting me up. It was orchestral, choral, a thousand voices across aeons of time and space coming together, tapping into the heartbeat and breathing of the universe, and my own heart and lungs joined in. It soothed every old hurt, dispelled every old fear, and opened up vistas in my mind's eye of other worlds hurtling through alien space, of stars which were more than stars twinkling between moons named for alien gods. I had no form, no limitations; I was a traveler through the dreams and memories of a collective of otherworld souls, moving like the wind, like the voices, like my own universe and the universe of others . . .

Then I woke up.

I guess maybe I floated in and out of consciousness for a while, maybe unwilling to let go of the music. I remember snippets of visions which came to replace the gorgeous, impossible landscapes of the music. I remember blood—a lot of it—and partially dissolved limbs. I remember screaming, and disjointed lights, and rough hands. I remember the clinking of empty bottles.

Then darkness, all-encompassing.

Then the hospital, its stink of bleach and too bright lights, and the government men with all the questions.

They said I went crazy, locked away so long in that club. Eleven days, they said, with little water and no food . . . until I began eating the others. The booze, they told me, must have dulled my senses—my common sense or sense of humanity or decency, their looks said—enough to do what I'd done. They'd found my passed out in a fairy ring of empty booze bottles, pale and skinny and stinking of sweat and rotting meat.

I'd only eaten some of them, they told me. Their faces, their fingers, their bones, their vocal chords. I'd left a lot of meat behind, the impractical cannibal.

When I asked about the thing in the cage, they pretended not to know what I meant. They'd found nothing in the abandoned old club except me, the bottles, and the bodies. I described the thing. I described its cage and the dead scientist—*that* had been the only dead and rotting body, I swore it. They gave each other odd looks and scribbled in their notepads, but when I pressed the issue, they told me I had hallucinated it. Of course they did; the government wasn't going to cop to anything so careless and dangerous as leaving one of their pets behind for an unsuspecting public to stumble on.

When I insisted that the thing had done all that killing, had dissolved the others with its voice, when I bolted up in the hospital bed and pulled against the wrist restraints and insisted that the creature had used music to drug and kill my brother and friends, they called a doctor. I screamed at them to find it, to find the creature in the cage so they could see and understand but really, I wanted the music. I needed it.

So, I sang instead. I tried to mimic what I remembered of the creature's song, but it wasn't the same, not even close. There was a pinch in my arm and my sight grew dim, but I kept singing. I sang in the darkness until I swallowed blood and before that darkness swallowed me, the silence swept my voice away.

ABOUT THE AUTHORS

ADAM CESARE is a New Yorker who lives in Philadelphia. His books include *Mercy House, Video Night, The Summer Job,* and *Tribesmen*. His work has been praised by Fangoria, Rue Morgue, Publishers Weekly, Bloody Disgusting, and more. His titles have appeared on "Year's Best" lists from outlets like Complex and FearNet. He writes a monthly column for Cemetery Dance Online. He also has a YouTube review show called Project: Black T-Shirt where he discusses horror films and pairs them with reading suggestions. www.adamcesare.com

ALAN M. CLARK has produced illustrations for hundreds of books of fiction, some non-fiction, a few textbooks, and several young adult fiction and children's books. His awards include the World Fantasy Award and four Chesley Awards. He is the author of twelve novels and four collections. His Jack the Ripper Victims Series—thriller novels about the lives of the murderer's victims—has now been completed with *The Prostitute's Price*, the story of Mary Jane Kelly. The novel is scheduled for released by IFD Publishing in the second half of 2018. He comes from Nashville, Tennessee, was educated in San Francisco, California, and currently lives in Eugene, Oregon. www.alanmclark.com

BRIAN KEENE is the author of over forty books, mostly in the horror, crime, and dark fantasy genres. His 2003 novel, *The Rising*, is often credited (along with Robert Kirkman's *The Walking Dead* comic and Danny Boyle's *28 Days Later* film) with inspiring pop culture's current interest in zombies. Keene's novels have been translated into German, Spanish, Polish, Italian, French, Taiwanese, and many more. In addition to his own original work, Keene has written for media properties such as *Doctor Who, The X-Files, Hellboy, Masters of the Universe*, and *Superman*.

Several of Keene's novels have been developed for film, including *Ghoul*, *The Ties That Bind*, and *Fast Zombies Suck*. Several more are in-development or under option.

Keene's work has been praised in such diverse places as The New York Times, The History Channel, The Howard Stern Show, CNN.com, Publisher's Weekly, Media Bistro, Fangoria Magazine, and Rue Morgue Magazine. He has won numerous awards and honors, including a World Horror Grand Master award, two Bram Stoker awards, and a recognition from Whiteman A.F.B. (home of the B-2 Stealth Bomber) for his outreach to U.S. troops serving both overseas and abroad. A prolific public speaker, Keene has delivered talks at conventions, college campuses, theaters, and inside Central Intelligence Agency headquarters in Langley, VA.

DOUG MURANO lives somewhere between Mount Rushmore and the mighty Missouri River. He is the Bram Stoker Award-winning editor of *Behold! Oddities, Curiosities and Undefinable Wonders* and the co-editor of Bram Stoker Award-nominated *Gutted: Beautiful Horror Stories*. Doug is an Active

Member of the Horror Writers Association and was the organization's promotions and social media coordinator from 2013-15. In 2014, he served on the World Horror Convention's steering committee as its social media director. He is a recipient of the HWA's Richard Laymon President's Award for Service.

Follow him on Twitter: @doug_murano. Visit his official web presence: www.dougmurano.com.

BRYAN SMITH is the author of more than thirty horror and crime novels and novellas, including *68 Kill*, the cult classic *Depraved* and its sequels, *The Killing Kind, Slowly We Rot, The Freakshow,* and many more. Bestselling horror author Brian Keene has called *Slowly We Rot*, "The best zombie novel I've ever read." *68 Kill* was adapted into a motion picture directed by Trent Haaga and starring Matthew Gray Gubler of the long-running CBS series Criminal Minds. 68 Kill won the Midnighters Award at the SXSW film festival in 2017 and was released to wide acclaim, including positive reviews in The New York Times and Bloody Disgusting, among others. Bryan has also co-scripted an original Harley Quinn story for the *House of Horrors* anthology from DC Comics.

Bryan's first several novels were released in mass market paperback by Leisure Books. His more recent releases have come from his own imprint, Bitter Ale Press. Numerous new projects are forthcoming.

GLENN ROLFE is an author from the haunted woods of New England. He has studied Creative Writing at Southern New Hampshire University, and continues his education in the world of horror by devouring the novels of Stephen King, Ronald Malfi, Jack Ketchum, and many others. He and his wife,

Meghan, have three children, Ruby, Ramona, and Axl. He is grateful to be loved despite his weirdness.

JEFF STRAND is the four-time Bram Stoker Award-nominated author of 40+ books, including *Blister, A Bad Day For Voodoo,* and *Wolf Hunt*. Cemetery Dance magazine said "No author working today comes close to Jeff Strand's perfect mixture of comedy and terror." He lives in Atlanta, Georgia.

JOHN SKIPP is a New York Times bestselling author, editor, film director, zombie godfather, compulsive collaborator, musical pornographer, black-humored optimist and all-around Renaissance mutant. His early novels from the 1980s and 90s pioneered the graphic, subversive, high-energy form known as splatterpunk. His anthology *Book of the Dead* was the beginning of modern post-Romero zombie literature. His work ranges from hardcore horror to whacked-out Bizarro to scathing social satire, all brought together with his trademark cinematic pace and intimate, unflinching, unmistakable voice. From young agitator to hilarious elder statesman, Skipp remains one of genre fiction's most colorful characters.

JONATHAN JANZ is the author of more than a dozen novels and numerous short stories. His work has been championed by authors like Joe R. Lansdale, Brian Keene, and Jack Ketchum; he has also been lauded by Publishers Weekly, the Library Journal, and the School Library Journal. His novel Children of the Dark was chosen by Booklist as a Top Ten Horror Book of the Year. Jonathan's main interests are his wonderful wife and his three amazing children. You can sign up for his newsletter, and you can follow him on Twitter, Instagram, Facebook, Amazon, and Goodreads.

Born and raised in Wisconsin, **KELLI OWEN** now lives in Destination, Pennsylvania. She's attended countless writing conventions, participated on dozens of panels, and has spoken at the CIA Headquarters in Langley, VA regarding both her writing and the field in general. Her works include the novels *Teeth, Floaters,* and *Six Days*, novellas *Waiting Out Winter, Wilted Lilies*, and *Forgotten*, more of both and the collection *Black Bubbles.* Visit her website at kelliowen.com for more information.

MATT HAYWARD is a Bram Stoker Award-nominated author and musician from Ireland. His books include *Brain Dead Blues, What Do Monsters Fear?, Practitioners* (with Patrick Lacey), and the upcoming *The Faithful.* He curated the anthology *Welcome to The Show*, and is currently writing a novel with Bryan Smith. Matt wrote the comic book *This Is How It Ends* with the rock band Walking Papers, and received a nomination for Irish short story of the year from Penguin Books in 2017. His work has appeared in *Clickers Forever, Tales from The Lake Vol. 3, Lost Highways, Dark Moon Digest* and many more.

Hailed as "one of the best new voices in horror fiction" by Brian Keene, **MATT SERAFINI**'s books include *Feral, Devil's Row, Island Red,* and *Under the Blade*, which FilmThrills called "one of the best slasher films you'll ever read."

He co-authored a collection of short stories with Adam Cesare called *All-Night Terror* and his short fiction has appeared in numerous anthology collections, including *Dead Bait 4*, and *Clickers Forever: A Tribute to J.F. Gonzalez.*

He has written extensively on the subjects of film and literature for numerous websites including Dread Central and Shock Till You Drop. His nonfiction has also appeared in the pages of Fangoria and HorrorHound.

Matt lives in Massachusetts with his wife and children.

MARY SANGIOVANNI is the author of the *The Hollower* trilogy (the first of which was nominated for the Bram Stoker Award), *Thrall, Chaos, Chills*, and the forthcoming *Savage Woods*, and the novellas For *Emmy, Possessing Amy, The Fading Place*, and *No Songs For The Stars* and the forthcoming *A Quiet Place At World's End*, as well as the collections *Under Cover Of Night, A Darkling Plain, Night Moves*, the forthcoming *A Weirdish Wild Space,* and numerous short stories. She has been writing fiction for over a decade, has a Masters in Writing Popular Fiction from Seton Hill University, and is a member of The Authors Guild and Penn Writers.

MAX BOOTH III is the Editor-in-Chief of Perpetual Motion Machine, the Managing Editor of *Dark Moon Digest*, and the co-host of Castle Rock Radio, a Stephen King podcast. He's the author of many novels and frequently contributes columns to both LitReactor and Gamut. Follow him on Twitter @GiveMeYourTeeth or visit him at www.TalesFromTheBooth.com. He lives in Texas.

PATRICK LACEY was born and raised in a haunted house. He lives in Massachusetts with his fiancee, his Pomeranian, his over-sized cat, and his muse, who is likely trying to kill him. Follow him on Twitter

(@patlacey), find him on Facebook, or visit his website at https://patrickclacey.wordpress.com/

RACHEL AUTUMN DEERING is an Eisner and Harvey Award-nominated writer, editor, and book designer from the hills of Appalachia. Her debut prose novella, *Husk*, was published in 2016 and drew praise from many critics and fellow writers. Her upcoming novel, *Wytchwood Hollow*, is set for publication in 2018. She has also written, edited, lettered, designed, and published comics and short prose for DC/Vertigo Comics, Blizzard Entertainment, Dark Horse Comics, IDW, Cartoon Network, and more. Deering is a rock 'n' roll witch with a heart of slime. She lives with a bunch of monster masks in rural Ohio.

ROBERT FORD fills his days handling marketing and branding projects. He has run his own ad agency, done a lot of freelance, baled a lot of hay, forked a lot of horse manure, and once had to deal with a very overripe iguana.

He has written the novels *The Compound,* and *No Lipstick in Avalon*, the novellas *Ring of Fire, The Last Firefly of Summer*, and *Samson and Denial*, and the short story collection *The God Beneath my Garden*. In addition, he has several screenplays floating around in the ether of Hollywood. He can confirm the grass actually is greener on the other side, but it's only because of the bodies buried there.

SOMER CANON lives in Eastern PA with her husband, two sons, and five cats. Her preferred escape has always been reading and writing and horror has always been the hook that catches her attention best. Feel free to find her on social media and never fear, she's only scary when she's hungry!

THE END?

Not quite . . .

Dive into more Tales from the Darkest Depths:

Novels:

House of Sighs (with sequel novella) by Aaron Dries
Beyond Night by Eric S. Brown and Steven L. Shrewsbury
The Third Twin: A Dark Psychological Thriller by Darren Speegle
Aletheia: A Supernatural Thriller by J.S. Breukelaar
Beatrice Beecham's Cryptic Crypt: A Supernatural Adventure/Mystery Novel by Dave Jeffery
Where the Dead Go to Die by Mark Allan Gunnells and Aaron Dries
Sarah Killian: Serial Killer (For Hire!) by Mark Sheldon
The Final Cut by Jasper Bark
Blackwater Val by William Gorman
Pretty Little Dead Girls: A Novel of Murder and Whimsy by Mercedes M. Yardley
Nameless: The Darkness Comes by Mercedes M. Yardley

Novellas:

Quiet Places: A Novella of Cosmic Folk Horror by Jasper Bark
The Final Reconciliation by Todd Keisling
Run to Ground by Jasper Bark
Devourer of Souls by Kevin Lucia

Apocalyptic Montessa and Nuclear Lulu: A Tale of Atomic Love by Mercedes M. Yardley
Wind Chill by Patrick Rutigliano
Little Dead Red by Mercedes M. Yardley
Sleeper(s) by Paul Kane
Stuck On You by Jasper Bark

Anthologies:
C.H.U.D. Lives!—A Tribute Anthology
Tales from The Lake Vol.4: The Horror Anthology, edited by Ben Eads
Behold! Oddities, Curiosities and Undefinable Wonders, edited by Doug Murano
Twice Upon an Apocalypse: Lovecraftian Fairy Tales, edited by Rachel Kenley and Scott T Goudsward
Tales from The Lake Vol.3, edited by Monique Snyman
Gutted: Beautiful Horror Stories, edited by Doug Murano and D. Alexander Ward
Tales from The Lake Vol.2, edited by Joe Mynhardt, Emma Audsley, and RJ Cavender
Children of the Grave
The Outsiders
Tales from The Lake Vol.1, edited by Joe Mynhardt
Fear the Reaper, edited by Joe Mynhardt
For the Night is Dark, edited by Ross Warren

Short story collections:
Frozen Shadows and Other Chilling Stories by Gene O'Neill
Varying Distances by Darren Speegle
The Ghost Club: Newly Found Tales of Victorian Terror by William Meikle
Ugly Little Things: Collected Horrors by Todd

Keisling
Whispered Echoes by Paul F. Olson
Embers: A Collection of Dark Fiction by Kenneth W. Cain
Visions of the Mutant Rain Forest, by Bruce Boston and Robert Frazier
Tribulations by Richard Thomas
Eidolon Avenue: The First Feast by Jonathan Winn
Flowers in a Dumpster by Mark Allan Gunnells
The Dark at the End of the Tunnel by Taylor Grant
Through a Mirror, Darkly by Kevin Lucia
Things Slip Through by Kevin Lucia
Where You Live by Gary McMahon
Tricks, Mischief and Mayhem by Daniel I. Russell
Samurai and Other Stories by William Meikle
Stuck On You and Other Prime Cuts by Jasper Bark

Poetry collections:
WAR by Alessandro Manzetti and Marge Simon
Brief Encounters with My Third Eye by Bruce Boston
No Mercy: Dark Poems by Alessandro Manzetti
Eden Underground: Poetry of Darkness by Alessandro Manzetti

If you've ever thought of becoming an author, we'd also like to recommend these non-fiction titles:

Where Nightmares Come From: The Art of Storytelling in the Horror Genre, edited by Joe Mynhardt and Eugene Johnson
Horror 101: The Way Forward, edited by Joe Mynhardt and Emma Audsley

Horror 201: The Silver Scream Vol.1 and *Vol.2*, edited by Joe Mynhardt and Emma Audsley
Modern Mythmakers: 35 interviews with Horror and Science Fiction Writers and Filmmakers by Michael McCarty
Writers On Writing: An Author's Guide Volumes 1,2,3, and 4, edited by Joe Mynhardt. Now also available in a Kindle and paperback omnibus.

Or check out other Crystal Lake Publishing books (http://www.crystallakepub.com/book-table/) for more Tales from the Darkest Depths. You can also subscribe to Crystal Lake Classics (http://eepurl.com/dn-1Q9) where you'll receive fortnightly info on all our books, starting all the way back at the beginning, with personal notes on every release. Or follow us on Patreon (https://www.patreon.com/CLP) for behind the scenes access.

Hi, readers. It makes our day to know you reached the end of our book. Thank you so much. This is why we do what we do every single day.

Whether you found the book good or great, we'd love to hear what you thought. Please take a moment to leave a review on Amazon, Goodreads, or anywhere else readers visit. Reviews go a long way to helping a book sell, and will help us to continue publishing quality books. You can also share a photo of yourself holding this book with the hashtag #IGotMyCLPBook!

Thank you again for taking the time to journey with Crystal Lake Publishing.

We are also on . . .

Website:
www.crystallakepub.com

Be sure to sign up for our newsletter and receive two free eBooks: http://eepurl.com/xfuKP

Books:
http://www.crystallakepub.com/book-table/

Twitter:
https://twitter.com/crystallakepub

Facebook:
https://www.facebook.com/Crystallakepublishing/
https://www.facebook.com/Talesfromthelake/
https://www.facebook.com/WritersOnWritingSeries/

Pinterest:
https://za.pinterest.com/crystallakepub/

Instagram:
https://www.instagram.com/crystal_lake_publishing/

Patreon:
https://www.patreon.com/CLP

YouTube:
https://www.youtube.com/c/CrystalLakePublishing

We'd love to hear from you.

Or check out other Crystal Lake Publishing books for your Dark Fiction, Horror, Suspense, and Thriller needs.

With unmatched success since 2012, Crystal Lake Publishing has quickly become one of the world's leading indie publishers of Mystery, Thriller, and Suspense books with a Dark Fiction edge.

Crystal Lake Publishing puts integrity, honor and respect at the forefront of our operations.

We strive for each book and outreach program that's launched to not only entertain and touch or comment on issues that affect our readers, but also to strengthen and support the Dark Fiction field and its authors.

Not only do we publish authors who are legends in the field and as hardworking as us, but we look for men and women who care about their readers and fellow human beings. We only publish the very best Dark Fiction, and look forward to launching many new careers.

We strive to know each and every one of our readers, while building personal relationships with our authors, reviewers, bloggers, pod-casters, bookstores and libraries.

Crystal Lake Publishing is and will always be a beacon of what passion and dedication, combined with overwhelming teamwork and respect, can accomplish: Unique fiction you can't find anywhere else.

We do not just publish books, we present you worlds within your world, doors within your mind, from talented authors who sacrifice so much for a moment of your time.

This is what we believe in. What we stand for. This will be our legacy.

Welcome to Crystal Lake Publishing—Tales from the Darkest Depths

CPSIA information can be obtained
at www.ICGtesting.com
Printed in the USA
BVHW04s1157150818
524602BV00010B/96/P

9 781643 704715